THE INNOCENT BYSTANDERS

Department K didn't tell John Craig why Kaplan was important. That wasn't his business. His business was to get Kaplan out of Turkey despite the very hostile attentions of competing intelligence services, including his own! Very quickly Craig realises that there is no-one he can trust on this violence-strewn journey except himself; and that there are probably no innocent bystanders.

THE INNOCENT BYSTANDERS

THE INNOCENT BYSTANDERS

by

James Mitchell
writing as James Munro

Magna Large Print Books
Long Preston, North Yorkshire,
BD23 4ND, England.

British Library Cataloguing in Publication Data.

Mitchell, James (writing as Munro, James)
        The innocent bystanders.

        A catalogue record of this book is
        available from the British Library

        ISBN   978-0-7505-4134-3

First published in Great Britain in 1969
Ostara Publishing Edition 2014

Copyright © James Mitchell 1969

Cover illustration by arrangement with Ostara Publishing

The moral right of the author has been asserted

Published in Large Print 2015 by arrangement with
Ostara Publishing

Magna Large Print is an imprint of Library Magna Books Ltd.

Printed and bound in Great Britain by
T.J. (International) Ltd., Cornwall, PL28 8RW

Chapter One

It was time to go, and two by two the men embraced, looking in wonder into each other's faces, trying to read there what they felt: tension, fear, and an overwhelming joy. Zhelkov went first, in his hand the little packet of poison that Goldfarb and Kaplan had prepared. His task was dangerous, because when he fed the dogs a guard watched him, careful to see that he stole none of their food. But Zhelkov was dexterous, and the poison found its way into both food and water. He was very gentle with the dogs that night, fondling them, calling them by name, till the guard ordered him out and slouched off to his hut, and Zhelkov sat by himself and watched the dogs slump down and sleep. They always did, after their meal, but this time they did not finish their food.

Klein, Goldfarb, and Kaplan came next. They had the wire cutters Zimma had made, and the skill to use them. Over and over they had practised on baling wire tougher than the obstacle in front of them. They sat by the wire and waited as the sky darkened. Then Moskowitz and Avramov brought out their mattresses and began to beat them. This was a common enough sight in the camp, where fleas and bedbugs abounded, but this time there was a special reason. The mattresses would protect them against the wire. Next it was Daniel, followed by Asimov and Gabrilovich. They were the rear guard, and in their pockets were the knives Zimma had made for them. Daniel had picked the other two because they were the fittest and hardest of the ten, and he had trained them well. They left the hut and moved, past the powerhouse and the guardroom toward their huts. The sky was dark now, and as they passed the stables the light came on, ponies stamped, and there was the chink of harness. In another five minutes the signal would sound for them to go inside their huts, and a guard would go to release the dogs. Daniel stepped out quicker. When the lights went each man had to be as near a guard as he could, without causing suspicion. Without the guards' carbines they would have no chance at all, and this work mustn't be wasted, he thought. *Must not.* And yet I feel it. Something is wrong. Where is Zimma?

Zimma had prayed once more, alone, and God had heard him and clearly answered. When Zimma had heard all that God had to say, he rose, picked up the axe that was in the tool shed, and limped toward the powerhouse. As he did so, Moskowitz and Avramov rolled up their mattresses and walked toward the wire, hanging on the outskirts of the crowd that was already moving toward the huts. Zimma kept on walking, a man who had been sent to chop wood and was returning his axe, and nobody noticed or cared. When he reached the guard, Zimma went straight up to him, mumbling a question. The guard motioned him forward impatiently, and Zimma advanced two more steps, then swung the axe, and the blade bit deep into his head, severing the back of the skull. Zimma picked up the guard's carbine and turned. After a moment of incredulous quiet, prisoners were running, yelling, to their huts, away from the powerhouse to which the guards were racing. Zimma shot the first two guards and stepped into the powerhouse, a prayer on his lips. He was very happy. Quickly he found what he wanted, and limped forward. Hear ye, Israel, he said aloud, and swung the axe for the last time.

The darkness when it came was total, but already the men with the wire cutters had moved into position, the men with the mattresses close behind. The pandemonium around them was so complete that men had eyes only for their own huts, thought only of the terrible revenge that would be taken for the powerhouse sentry. When Zimma fired, Daniel attacked his guard, who was trying to push his way through a crowd of prisoners to reach the source of the shots. Asimov and Gabrilovich followed his lead. Zimma had given them a wonderful opportunity, and they took it. Daniel's hands snapped the life from the guard as if it were thread. Gabrilovich and Asimov used their knives. All three men killed quickly, but without pity. The one Asimov killed had been his lover.

They took the carbines and ammunition pouches and grouped together. No one stopped them; every face they saw was filled with incredulous horror. Then the lights died and they raced to the wire, the mattresses went down and they were through, running, Daniel in the lead, feeling his way along the track that he had memorized, eyes closed, for the last three weeks. They fought the clearing in the forest and lay panting as Daniel called out their names. Asimov, Avramov, Daniel, Gabrilovich, Goldfarb, Klein, Moskowitz, Zhelkov. Of Kaplan there was no sign.

Goldfarb said at last, 'I think he knew he had no chance. He did this to help us.'

Daniel heaved up the great stone that covered their hoarded food.

'I hope so,' he said, 'but there is something wrong. I know it.'

Quickly he gave each man his share of the food, then put into each hand a nugget of gold.

'We split up now?' Moskowitz asked.

Daniel said, 'In a moment. First let me

have the weapons.'

He distributed them carefully. The best shot in each team got a carbine, the rest had knives. Gabrilovich led a team, and so did Klein. Daniel's team of four was reduced to two: Zimma dead, Kaplan missing.

'Go now,' said Daniel. 'Asimov and I will be the rear guard.'

They said no word, and it was dark still, but their silence was filled with meaning. Then Gabrilovich and Klein left, and the others followed.

'What do we do?' Asimov asked.

'We move north,' said Daniel.

'North? But that's the wrong way.'

Daniel said nothing for a moment, then: 'We'll draw off the pursuit,' he said and smiled.

'You're a good man,' Asimov said.

Daniel remembered the jingle of harness in the stable.

The ponies had been saddled and ready even before the breakout. No point in going into all that with Asimov; not now. The boy admired him too much.

A squadron of guards, mounted on ponies, overtook Gabrilovich's team before dawn and killed them all at a loss of a man and two ponies. It took them longer to find Klein's team, because they had lost their route, and when they did, Klein's team fought hard. The guards wanted one prisoner at least, but in the end only Zhelkov was left alive, and he died of wounds on the way back. The guards lost two more men. Shortly afterwards the Uzbek commandant was shot by firing squad, and his second-in-command, who had led the pursuit, was promoted in his place. For six months Kaplan, Daniel, and Asimov were posted missing: after that they were presumed dead.

To die in Volochanka is not perhaps such a terrible thing; to survive is infinitely worse. Volochanka is special. It is designed, as Hell was, for the fallen angels, and like Hell's its final torture is despair. The achievement of the ten was that they faced despair and did not let it defeat them. Gabrilovich began it, with the kind of accident that only later they learned to recognize as the hand of God. Gabrilovich had been a mining engineer, and worked in the coal mine. It was part of his rehabilitation; learning how the miners themselves lived and worked and suffered, so that if society again found him acceptable, he, the intellectual, would know what workers must endure as a result of his decisions. His rehabilitation consisted of hauling a truck loaded with coal for fourteen hours a day from the face to the shaft. Zimma helped him. Zimma had been a doctor, specializing in survival techniques. For three years he had worked on the training of astronauts. They had hauled the trucks together for days, collapsed like exhausted animals in their rest periods, wolfed their appalling food at noonday, and talked hardly at all. Talk was dangerous, it led to nostalgia, and nostalgia only increased the just-bearable weight of suffering that each man bore. Then one night Gabrilovich had a dream: it re-created vividly the new suit his father had bought him for his barmitzvah, and the smells of the food his mother had cooked, the delicate dry flavour of Crimean wine. Gabrilovich wanted very much to share the weight of that dream. It was too much to carry alone. He had looked at Zimma that noon, gulping his lukewarm soup, dividing up his bread – Zimma always saved some of his bread, and Gabrilovich hated him for it – then he had spoken the words.

'Zimma, forgive my asking, but are you Jewish?'

Zimma stared at him, incredulous. He was transported back immediately to an Embassy party in Stockholm. He had worn a suit he had bought that morning, he remembered, a dark rich blue that exactly matched the pattern on his tie. A silk tie made in Italy. There was a young Swede at the party who had been to Washington and told American stories in English. One of them had been about the millionaire who had lost all his money in the depression. His wife had left him, his children disowned him, his house and cars were taken away, and he had nothing. One day he stood in the bread line waiting for a handout. It was a bitter day in February and he had no overcoat, so to keep himself warm he, who had had millions, wrapped himself in old newspapers, picked up at random from trash cans, and one of them was the *Jewish Chronicle*. As he stood waiting, in line, a Cadillac drew up by the curb and its chauffeur opened the door to a Jewish lady, snug in chinchilla, secure in diamonds, who walked down the line and gave each man a quarter. When she got to the former millionaire she saw the *Jewish Chronicle* wrapped across his chest.

'Forgive me for asking,' she said, 'but are you Jewish?'

'Jesus,' the former millionaire said. 'That's all I needed.'

And Zimma had remembered, totally, completely, the party, his suit, his tie, the young Swede and his story, and he had laughed. It was the first time anybody had laughed in that coal mine, except a guard. It was a beginning.

At first it had been enough that there were two of them. They had begun by exchanging biographies, but from the start the nostalgia was carefully rationed. They had concentrated more on the fact of their Jewishness, and how much it had contributed to their being in the camp, even after the terrifying old madman had died in Moscow, convinced till the last that Jewish doctors were poisoning him. Then Avramov began to eat with them, and he too began to talk. Avramov had lectured on political science in Riga. It had been Zimma who brought in Moskowitz, and then Avramov reported that Daniel, who had lived in his hut, would like to join, but Daniel worked in the forest. He could not come and talk in the mine. Daniel was also the camp's millionaire. He had been a soldier and had risen to the rank of major. He was strong and ruthless and had somehow stored away a little hoard of gold. One day Avramov brought word that Daniel would donate some of his gold to hiring a meeting place. Moskowitz, a former lawyer, sought an interview with the commandant of his sector of the camp. The commandant had first beaten Moskowitz, who expected it. The commandant, an Uzbek, always beat prisoners who asked for interviews. But in the end he agreed. They could meet for an hour once a week. The place they were given was a toolshed, the entirely unofficial rent a hundred roubles a month. The limit of their membership was to be ten, a number Moskowitz accepted at once, it was the number of the minyan. But they said nothing of religion. Not then.

Daniel brought a young poet with him, and

the poet, Asimov, suggested Kaplan, an agronomist. Zimma produced Goldfarb, another doctor, and then Klein the singer and Zhelkov the psychologist appeared. That closed the list. By then other Jews in the camp had heard about them, and begged to join, but they would accept no more. It was the other Jews who called them the minyan: the minimum number of Jewish men who must meet together before a service can be held. The ten.

At their first meetings they talked about communism. Avramov lectured, and the rest asked questions, dialectically pure questions about the dangerous fallacy of Israel and the gratifying decline in Judaic religion; questions one could address to the hidden microphone that Gabrilovich found within minutes of entering the hut. After four weeks the microphone was withdrawn; the Uzbek had found the tapes both boring and pathetic. Obviously these men hoped to have their sentences reduced by proving how deserving of rehabilitation they were. But the Uzbek knew they would never be released.

So did they. When the microphone went they talked about the world as it should be, not as it was. Avramov told them how the world need never hunger, Zhelkov told them how the human mind could develop into an instrument beyond their comprehension, Kaplan how the desert in Israel could blossom, quite literally, like a rose. Asimov related stories, Klein sang. Without books or writing materials they created something new with their voices, part seminar, part magazine. Then Gabrilovich discussed survival, their own – how to hoard their food, their sleep, their strength, to give them the best possible chance to avoid the terror of the hospital and a slow but certain death. It was Daniel, always the bravest, who asked the question: How many of us want to survive? To their surprise, their joy, they found they all did, so long as they could meet together, and that night Klein prayed. He alone was Orthodox, he alone knew the words, but that night when Klein prayed they all prayed with him and from him took lessons in their own religion.

Daniel let two more weeks go by before he talked of escape. He had never spoken before, and at first they did not want to hear him, but Daniel had two persuasive arguments: his gold rented their meeting place, now, inevitably, nicknamed the synagogue, and on escape he was the expert, and a rule of their society was always to listen to the expert. He disarmed them at once by saying that it was inevitable that most of them would fail, but even they would achieve the reward of a quick death. For the others, the successful ones, there would be a chance to get out of the country, and if they succeeded, they could tell of their suffering and contribute to the arrival of the world as it should be. That was a debt they would owe to God. Asimov agreed at once; he was by far the youngest, and the enormous odds frightened him least. With the others it took time, but in the end they all agreed, even Kaplan, who at fifty had no chance at all. Two things persuaded them: the fact that it was a moral – even a religious – duty, and the fact that if they failed, as most of them would, death was their only punishment, and death, so long as it came quickly, was the only release that would ease them once the minyan was disbanded.

Even so, the magnitude of their task, when they began to examine it, appalled them. The camp was at Volochanka, two hundred miles inside the Arctic Circle. In its bitter winter no human being could survive outside the camp, in summer the guards were doubled, dogs roamed the spaces between the huts all night, and searchlights played at random, without predictable patterns. There were, besides, two tangles of barbed wire and machine guns mounted at each corner of the camp's perimeter. The guards, armed with Tommy guns and clubs, used skis in winter and Mongolian ponies in summer. And it was all waste, all display. Until the ten men began plotting together, none of the prisoners, even the crazy ones, had even thought of escaping. There was nowhere to escape to.

They began by nourishing and training their bodies. Daniel taught them how to exercise, Klein how to develop their breathing, Gabrilovich how to work their muscles to the utmost limit of their capacity. They pooled all their possessions except Daniel's gold – that would be needed after their escape – and used them to buy food. They were ruthless about this: when food could not be bought it was stolen, and to steal prisoners' food at Volochanka meant agonizing death at the hands of other prisoners, if they were caught. Here, too, the Mosaic law operated. A life for a life. To take a man's food *was* to take his life. But they succeeded, and grew strong. Goldfarb taught them hygiene, and they survived the wave of typhus that swept the camp in the spring. Chance alone had kept them alive as a group through the January influenza epidemic, and they thanked God for it. Asimov developed into a bold and cunning thief and stole worn-out tools, hinges, screws that Zimma patiently transformed into wire cutters and weapons. That winter a guard fell in love with Asimov, who submitted and brought his presents into the common pool to buy food. Kaplan found a suitable patch of ground and grew flowers in it and the camp thought he was crazy as the summer slowly waned, the nights grew shorter and almost disappeared.

The break was planned for July. There

were only two hours of darkness in Siberia then, and Kaplan's flowers had reached the state they needed. Nightshade, most of it, but there were other ingredients. One day he picked them all, as the camp jeered, and let them wither, then he and Goldfarb set to work extracting the poison that would deal with the dogs. It was Zhelkov who fed the dogs. They loved him. Whatever he fed them, they would eat... Zimma had his own plans to deal with the power cable. They might work, and they might not – insulation was impossible even to steal, but Zimma had agreed to tackle the job, and the risks were his own. God might yet let him live. They had their escape route planned, their rallying point in the forest that Daniel had mapped out for them already memorized, their hopes and prayers centred on a boat that might take them to Vadso, in Norway, eight hundred miles away. Then Zimma cut his leg in the mine, and he knew that he, who by his laughter had started the movement, would not see it through to the end. The cut was not serious, but it turned septic and there were no medicines. It grew worse and he found it harder to work, his strength faded. But every day until the escape he staggered to work. On the last three days he gave the others his food. And he was happy. God had been generous. Even if he had decided not to let Zimma live, at least he had simplified the problem of cutting the power supply.

On the night of the break nine of them assembled in the hut and waited for Kaplan, whose job it was to bring the poison for the dogs. This they needed desperately, but even more they needed his presence. Without him they were not ten; there could be no ritual prayer. It was strange how important prayer was to them. Zhelkov had lectured on it once, not stating a theory, but verbalizing the question that nagged in all their minds, except the Orthodox Klein's: Why do we need the prayers when we none of us believe in God? They had decided at last that the answer was in their Jewishness, which the ritual, the prayers, the Hebrew tongue all made manifest. But there was more than that, and they knew it, though what that 'more' was they never could define. To the end the question nagged at some of them, though Zimma, Klein, and Daniel joined Kaplan in his faith. But now, all alike, believer and non-believer, waited for Kaplan and their prayers.

He came in at last and they moved toward him in a wave of impatience and relief. What had delayed him? Was anything wrong? Why did he have to be late on this night of all nights? It was Daniel who called them to order. Daniel was leader now. He took Kaplan to the window and examined him in its light. Beside Daniel's huge, slab-muscled body, Kaplan's wiry toughness looked frail.

His face was grey and there was a bruise already darkening his cheekbone.

'Tell it,' said Daniel.

'I was bringing the poison,' Kaplan said, 'and a guard stopped me.'

'He found it?' Klein asked. Daniel motioned him to silence.

'He wanted me to fetch water. I was too slow for him. He hit me – and kicked me. Here.' He pressed his hands to his stomach. 'Daniel – I don't think I can do it.'

'You must,' said Daniel. 'Each man has his place. You know that. Without you we cannot go.'

'I can stay behind and help Zimma,' Kaplan said.

'Then you will die.'

'Of course,' said Kaplan.

Daniel turned to Goldfarb. 'Look at his stomach,' he said.

Goldfarb's hands were deft and tender as he looked. The bruise was enormous and they had nothing for it. 'It hurts,' Kaplan whimpered.

'Does it hurt too much to pray?' Daniel asked, and Kaplan stood then, and Klein led them in prayer.

When they had done, Daniel sat down beside the older man, and his voice was gentle. 'Kaplan,' he said, 'it must be tonight. We are ready *now*. Tomorrow and every day that follows, little by little our courage will go.

Our food will be found, our tools will be discovered. It has to be tonight. And please do not stay behind with Zimma. It is brave, but it is also foolish. If you want to die, volunteer for the wire.' Kaplan bent his head.

'Please do not hate me,' he said.

'How can I hate you? How can any of us? We need you, Kaplan.'

Then Kaplan said, 'Very well. I will come,' and the others crowded round to thank, to praise, and Daniel gave him some vodka, the only painkiller they had, from his carefully hoarded store. Kaplan raised his glass, and drank to their endeavour. Six hours later he, Daniel, and Asimov were declared missing; the rest were dead.

Chapter Two

Craig accepted his third drink and watched as Thomson put in the ice, added whisky, and then ginger ale. His quantities were generous. At one time Craig would have hesitated when the third drink was offered, needing the assurance that it was safe to accept, that his mind and body would not be called upon to work for him with a speed and certainty that a third large Scotch could impair, perhaps with fatal results. But now Craig ran no risks, and so he accepted the third drink without hesitation. It was easier to. Thomson was an overforceful host. But then Thomson was an overforceful everything. He had the flat above Craig's in the elegant block in Regent's Park, and that, Craig thought, was the only possible reason why he'd been invited to the party. The best way to keep the neighbours happy was to invite them too. He didn't mind; parties were boring, but he was always bored anyway. At least at a party you had company.

Thomson produced films for television. He had noisy friends who did noisy things and a seemingly endless supply of young actresses who looked intense and called Craig 'darling' and were nice because Craig might turn out to be in the business, and if they weren't nice he wouldn't offer them a job. Craig knew that in television terms this passed as logic, so he played fair most of the time and admitted he didn't do anything. Only with the very pretty ones did he linger for a while, make them wonder, before the shocking truth came out. He was nothing, not even an adman, and not even ashamed... He sipped his Scotch and looked from a very pretty one to the bracket clock on Thomson's not quite Regency table. It was seven thirty. Time to go out to dinner. After he had dined Loomis wanted to see him, but he wouldn't care if Craig were late, not any more. Loomis saved his anger for the important ones, and Craig was no longer important. The thought was consoling. Craig had known another man whom Loomis had considered important, and that man was incurably insane. He shook the ice in his drink and put it down on a coaster, dead centre. The girl he was talking to – Angela, was it? Virginia? Caroline? – noticed the power in the hand, the ridges of hard skin across the knuckles, along the edge of the hand from wrist to fingertip. And because she was a sensitive girl, she also noticed the boredom of the man and resented it. A man who stood six feet tall, a wide-shouldered lean-hipped man with mahogany-coloured hair and grey eyes that made her think of

Scandinavian seas, had no right to be bored. Not when she was talking to him. Suddenly he smiled at her, and the face, that had been only strong before, was suddenly handsome.

'You're very nice,' he said. 'Very nice indeed.' The words distressed her, though they were kindly meant. 'Look,' he said, 'why don't I introduce you to those people over there? Two of them are producers, and one's a casting director.'

'You don't have to be so bloody polite,' said the girl. 'I'm not a hag yet.'

She left him in a flurry of anger, her miniskirt riding over impeccable thighs, and Craig went to say good-bye to his host.

Thomson was hurt. He said so noisily, and at great length. The whole idea of the party, he explained, was for Craig and a few kindred spirits to get together. Have fun, enjoy themselves, talk to a few girls.

'I've done all that,' said Craig. 'It's time I was off.'

Thomson wouldn't hear of it. There was a second, and very exciting reason why a favoured few had been asked along. He'd hoped to explain it later over a few sandwiches and a mouthful of champagne. As a matter of fact that girl he'd been talking to would be staying. Wouldn't Craig like that?

'Very much,' said Craig. 'But I really have to go. You know. Business.'

The word was one which Thomson had

never taken lightly, and he responded to it at once.

'Just give me five minutes, old man. That isn't too much to ask, is it?' And Craig agreed that it was not.

He found himself hustled into a room called a study, which was mostly Morocco leather, on books, on the writing desk and chair, even on the wastepaper basket. Thomson shut the door on him, disappeared, then re-entered almost at once with a short, squat young man and a trayful of Scotch. The squat young man it seemed had written a play, and Thomson needed a backer... Craig discovered it was even later than he had thought. He said so, and turned to the door.

The squat young man said, 'I'm an artist. I create things. Surely I have a right to a hearing?'

His voice was unbelievably harsh. Nothing it could say, not even 'I love you,' would sound like anything but a threat.

'Some other time,' said Craig. 'I have enjoyed meeting you.'

The squat young man put a hand on his arm.

'Look,' he said. 'I used to be a wrestler. I've done time for assault. You're going to hear me now.'

Craig looked at Thomson, who had the baffled look of a conjuror suddenly realizing that his best trick is about to misfire.

'Is he sober?' he asked.

'He's had a few,' said Thomson.

Craig looked at the hand on his arm.

'A year or two ago if you'd done that I'd have broken your arm,' he said.

The hand slid up the muscle of Craig's arm, and fell at once to his side.

'Some other time, when I'm not so busy,' Craig said, and left.

Thomson downed a drink quickly, looked in scorn at the wrestler turned playwright.

'And you thought he was a fairy,' he said.

Craig dined on salad, sole veronique, and a half-bottle of Chablis, and as he dined he thought of the squat young man. The violence of his own reaction surprised him.

Their tactics, after all, had been perfectly reasonable in terms of the world they lived in. He'd made no passes at girls, therefore he was queer, and because he was queer the squat young man had put his hand on him. There were better ways to handle that situation than to talk of breaking arms. And yet it had happened at once: the flat threat thrusting at them both, escaping his conscious control. He could have done it too, even now. Without disarranging his tie he could have broken both their arms; or their necks. Craig shivered. He didn't want that feeling, not any more. Nor did he want to see Loomis, but he went. The fat man was power: irresistible power to those who had worked for him, and Craig had served him for five violent years.

Queen Anne's Gate looked well by night. The street lights softened the clean lines of the buildings to a pretty romanticism that made the street remember its elegant past with nostalgia, but Craig's thoughts were with the present. He ignored the row of brass plates: Dr. H. B. Cunnington-Low, Lady Brett, Major Fuller, the Right Reverend Hugh Bean. They were precisely the sort of names that belonged in Queen Anne's Gate – but they didn't exist. Craig pressed the bell marked 'Caretaker' and waited till the door was opened by a muscular man in overalls. Somewhere about him, Craig knew, he carried a Smith and Wesson .38 revolver and a commando knife. The caretaker held his job because he could use them.

'You're expected, Mr. Craig,' he said. 'You're to go straight up.'

Craig climbed the stairs to the flat marked 'Lady Brett' and went inside. The caretaker watched him go in. Lady Brett's flat was Craig's office, and Craig had no business there when Loomis had summoned him at once, but the caretaker made no move to interfere. Craig might be slowing up and drinking a bit too much, but he had a judo black belt and an expert's knowledge of karate, and the caretaker had to practice unarmed combat with him once a month. He never antagonized Mr. Craig if he could help it.

The office was neat and tidy, the way his secretary Mrs. McNab always left it. And, anyway, there wasn't much work sent to him now. The place wasn't all that hard to keep in order. He looked through his 'In' tray, but nothing had been added since he left: there was no helpful memo from Mrs. McNab. Whatever Loomis had in store for him would come as a surprise. The fat man liked surprises, when he delivered them. Craig went along the corridor and tapped on the door that was of panelled mahogany, polished silken smooth. There was an indeterminate growl from behind it, and Craig went inside, into a perfect establishment set-piece with a superb stucco ceiling, sash windows, and overstuffed furniture covered in flowered chintz. Behind a Chippendale desk Loomis sat in a buttoned leather armchair that was the biggest piece of furniture Craig had ever seen, and yet it fitted the big man so exactly that a Savile Row tailor might have measured him for it. Loomis was vast, a figure of enormous power that had slopped over into fat, with pale, manic eyes, an arrogant nose, and white hair clipped close to his skull. When Craig first met Loomis the white hair had been dusted with red, but now the red had gone.

'Pour coffee,' said Loomis, 'and sit down.' For Loomis the invitation was cordial.

Craig poured coffee from a vacuum flask – it was black, bitter, scalding hot – then sat on the arm of one of the chairs. It was bad enough facing Loomis, even if he were in a good mood, without being three feet below him.

'I've been thinking about you,' said Loomis. 'Thinking a lot. I'm beginning to wonder if you still fit in here, son.' Craig waited; there was a lot more to come.

'You've done some nice jobs for us,' Loomis said, 'and I don't deny it. You kill people nice and tidy, and you got a few brains as well. But the last job spoiled you – or at least I think so. Do you still dream about it?'

'No,' said Craig, and it was true. The best and most expensive psychiatrist in the country had laboured for weeks to stop those dreams.

'Think about it?'

'No,' Craig said again, and this time it was a lie. When you have been tortured by having electric shocks run through your penis there are times when you think about it, no matter how hard you try not to.

'I don't believe you,' said Loomis, 'but it doesn't matter. You finished that job and I'm grateful to you, but I don't think you're ready for another one.'

'Nor do I,' said Craig. He put his cup down quickly before his hand began to shake.

'You do nice paperwork, but I got too many fellers for that already.' He paused. 'Experts,' he said, making the word an insult. 'I'm beginning to wonder if I can use you at all.'

'You can hardly just let me go,' said Craig.

'No,' Loomis agreed. 'I can hardly do that. Nobody ever leaves my department – once they sign on.' Craig waited again.

'I been thinking of sending you to the school,' Loomis said. 'Training the young hopefuls. You're the kind of feller they'll be up against, once they get into the field – or you were. But I dunno. You're not exactly cut out to be a schoolmaster, are you? On the other hand, I got nothing else to offer. We better make it the school. I tell you what,' he said. 'I'll make you a sort of graduation exercise. Go down there tomorrow, have a look around, but don't let the students see you. Pascoe will pick out the ones who are ready, and you can set up test situations for them. See if they're any good. See if you're any good come to that. Like the idea?'

'No,' said Craig.

'I didn't think you would. You can go down there tomorrow. I'll tell Pascoe to expect you.'

The school was in Sussex, an isolated Eliza-bethan manor house in fifty acres of grounds enclosed by an eight-foot granite wall. There were always two men at the gates, and they were armed. Closed-circuit television warned them of every approaching car, and day and night Alsatians roamed the grounds. They were good dogs; Pascoe had trained them himself. The nearest village was seven miles away, and the villagers had kept well away from the manor house ever since the dogs had caught a poacher ten years ago. The villagers believed that the manor house was a nursing home for wealthy, dangerous maniacs, and Pascoe did all he could to encourage that belief. Once he'd even faked an escape: a red-bearded schizoid armed with a crowbar, trapped in the snug of The Black Bull just before opening time; dogs and straitjackets and a tremendous smashing of glass. It had cost Pascoe fifty pounds in breakages, and the village had never forgotten.

His pupils were driven hard. They had to be: there was a great deal to learn. The school existed only for the benefit of Department K, and those who worked for Department K were specialists of the highest order. Their business was destruction – of plans, of aspirations, of life when the need arose. And those who wished to serve Department K had first to master many trades. In the school Pascoe had a language laboratory, a small-arms range, a unit dealing with arson and sabotage, a gymnasium, and a garage. There were daily sessions in unarmed combat, there were visiting lecturers who taught safe-breaking, the extraction of information, the use of the knife, the improvisation of weapons, the picking of pockets, on every conceivable subject from desert survival to everyday life in the Soviet Union. There was a course on how to resist methodically applied pain to the limits of physical and mental strength. At the end of each course – and courses were held only when there were a sufficient number of likely candidates – the school turned over to Loomis a handful of men and women who were afraid of nothing but their master's power. If they disobeyed, defected, or used their skills against anyone but the targets Loomis selected he could have them killed, and they knew it.

They had been deviously recruited, those who served Loomis: from the Intelligence Services some of them, or the Special Branch of CID; from the armed forces, the universities, the business desk, and the factory floor. Some, not many, from prison. One of Loomis's experts spent his whole working life reading photostatted personnel files acquired via his cover as director for the Unit of Psychological and Statistical Research. Likely candidates were spotted, observed, tailed, unknowingly interviewed, and tested. Loomis's expert was good. Of the candidates he spotted, perhaps four per cent reached the school, and after that they belonged to Department K forever, whether they reached the standard of field operative or not. Loomis's security was absolute. No one who knew about the department ever left it alive.

Craig waited at the gate while one of the men on duty examined his pass. The other one wasn't in sight, but he'd be there, Craig knew, with a gun on him. The man he could see handed back the pass and said, 'Straight on up to the house, please, sir. And don't get out of the car till Mr. Pascoe comes to fetch you. There's dogs about.' He went back to the gatehouse, pressed a button, and the gates swung open. Craig drove the Lamborghini through and at once the gates were closed. As he drove slowly up the drive, the car whispering, Craig spotted the dogs. They used cover like leopards, and they followed him all the time. He reached the main doors of the house, switched off the engine, pulled up the hand brake, and waited. The six dogs settled in a great arc round the car, ears back, the hair on their necks bristling. If he left the car they would kill him, for all his skill, and Pascoe wasn't there to meet him; Pascoe was enjoying the fact that Craig was helpless in the face of something that he, Pascoe, had created.

He appeared at last, and whistled to the dogs. At once they moved off back into the grounds and their endless patrol. Craig got out of the Lamborghini and moved up the steps, not hurrying, to where Pascoe waited. Pascoe had been a colonel in military intelligence and a liaison officer with the maquis, and had survived three months in a Gestapo prison. He was tall, thin, whipcord hard, and proud of his school. The people he turned out were the best there were, except that Craig had been better than any of them. Craig was the only Department K operator who had never attended the school. Pascoe detested him.

'You do yourself well,' he said, and looked at the Lamborghini, its insolent scarlet blaring at a bed of soft Mayflowers. Craig walked past him into a hall that held a Shiraz rug, a Jacobean chest, an oil by Stubbs.

'You don't do too badly yourself,' he said. 'For a schoolmaster.'

Pascoe's hands clenched. Sooner or later they always did, when Craig appeared. He had never met the man who could beat him, until he met Craig. The thought was bitter to him. Then he remembered what Loomis had said to him over the scrambler phone. Craig was getting past it. The fists loosened, became hands again.

'Can I get you something?' he said. 'A drink?'

Craig looked at his watch.

'I'm not quite that far gone,' he said. 'Eleven o'clock in the morning is a shade too early, even for old dipsos like me. Where are all the pupils?'

'At a lecture,' Pascoe said. 'They won't know you've been here.'

'Can I see them?' Craig asked.

'Of course,' said Pascoe. 'They're watched all the time.' He took a key from his pocket, inserted it into the back of a television set, and switched on. As its picture formed Craig saw five men and two women listening to a doctor. He was explaining how to set a broken arm. Craig thought he had never seen such an intensity of concentration.

'No one-way glass?' he asked.

'Certainly – if you'd prefer it,' Pascoe said.

He took the key from the set, then led the way toward the lecture room. Set in one wall of it was a mirror, and behind it Craig stood. From his side the mirror became a window, and he looked at the seven faces, the set of their bodies, the way they used their hands. After the lecture they went to the target range, and again Craig watched, unseen. Then it was unarmed combat, and he watched them on the dojo mat. Lunch then, with Pascoe presiding, the meal conducted with the formal stiffness of an embassy reception, butler and footman wary for mistakes with glasses, forks, knives, as Craig spied on them. After lunch Pascoe held his class in situations. You have to get information out of a man, but you must make no noise. What do you do?... You pretend to speak no Russian, and the KGB have trapped you into showing a knowledge of Russian. What do you do?... You have a message that must be delivered; a live drop. The courier who turns up seems impeccable – and yet you are not quite sure. What do you do?... Craig eavesdropped, and ate sandwiches.

By the end of the class he had made his choice. He went to Pascoe's office, and Pascoe joined him.

'They're in the language lab for half an hour,' he said. 'After that I really should turn them loose for a bit or they'll start to wonder.'

'The one you called David,' said Craig. 'David Branch. I'd like a copy of his file. And the fair lad – Andrew Royce.' He paused, and Pascoe said:

'You were asked to pick three.'

At last Craig said, 'The rest of the men were pretty average.'

'And the girls?'

Slowly, reluctantly, Craig said, 'The tall one had possibilities.'

'Joanna Benson? I quite agree,' said Pascoe. 'They're the three I'd have picked myself.'

He went to a cabinet and took out three files. Craig signed for them.

'How do you propose to organize these tests?'

'You tell these three they've graduated. I'll take David first, then Joanna, then Andrew. Loomis will see them at the department – and give them their first briefing. For them it'll be the real thing. That way we'll know what they'd really be like – if and when.'

They walked back to the hall, and then on to the sun-warmed steps. At once the dogs appeared, then waited as Pascoe walked with Craig and saw him to his car. Craig slammed the door and Pascoe whistled; the dogs clustered round him.

'I'll keep them here till the gates close,' Pascoe said.

Craig switched on and the engine exploded with life, then muted at once to murmured power.

'I hope you won't hurt my students too much,' Pascoe said.

'I hope they won't hurt me,' said Craig.

Chapter Three

Loomis gave the American lunch at his club.
Years ago Loomis had decided that that was
what Americans liked: the secret places of the
Establishment, the byways that led to the
corridors of power, the shabby leather of
libraries, the mahogany bar, and pink gins
before lunch with a man who had once been
an admiral on the China Station. Then a traditional lunch – smoked salmon, roast beef
and Yorkshire pudding, gooseberry fool,
washed down with draught bitter. The
American was a gourmet, and the food at
Loomis's club was appalling, but Loomis had
allowed for this. It made the American de-
fensive. He had come to ask a favour after all.
Loomis ordered the beef underdone, then
asked for an extra portion of sprouts. Even
the waiter was awed by this: the sprouts at
Loomis's club were notorious.

Throughout the meal they talked of horses.
Loomis had once served in a cavalry regiment and had hunted at Melton Mowbray;
the American owned a ranch in Arizona and
bred quarter horses. Their talk was detailed,
impassioned, and very boring to others, as it
was meant to be, and the American was

grateful for it. It helped distract his mind from the appalling food. When they had finished the meal, Loomis said, 'If I were you I wouldn't try the coffee here. It isn't all that good,' and to the end of his days the American couldn't decide if he were serious.

'Tell you what,' said Loomis. 'Come into the little library. I got a picture of Jumbo there. Horse I rode with the Quorn in '33. Seventeen hands and jumped stone walls.'

The American said carefully, 'If you're sure it's all right?'

'It's perfect,' said Loomis. 'Nobody can disturb us there.'

They got up, and the headwaiter bowed as they left.

'I hope you enjoyed your meal, sir,' he said.

'Amazing,' the American said. 'Absolutely amazing.'

'You don't get grub like that in the States,' said Loomis. The American shuddered.

The little library was drab and oppressively hot. It was also safe. Loomis began talking at once.

'We got your request,' he said, 'and I've been looking around. You want some pretty talented lads.'

'We do,' the American said.

'I thought you had some,' said Loomis. 'The ones I met seemed to know what they were doing.'

'We've had trouble in the Middle East,' the American said. 'Big trouble. There's a leak somewhere and we haven't plugged it yet. Anybody we sent could get blown.'

'We've had trouble too,' said Loomis. 'We've fixed it for now, but we can't use anybody that's known there. It would have to be a new face.'

'That's perfectly okay,' the American said. 'Provided it's somebody you have faith in.'

'I have faith in them all,' said Loomis. 'I made them. But I made them my way. Trouble is they don't understand your system. As a matter of fact, neither do I.'

The American hesitated. What he had to say now was painful to him, but it was an order. It had to be said.

'We would take it as a favour if your department would handle the whole operation,' he said at last.

'Ah now, wait a minute. This is a biggish exercise,' said Loomis, 'and I'm a bit short-handed, d'you see.'

They began to bargain and the American discovered that Loomis had the ethical standards of a horse trader.

At last he said, 'Sir, I realize that we're asking you to mount a big operation, but what you're asking is far too much. After all, you can't give us any guarantee of success, now can you?'

'I think I can,' said Loomis. 'You can pay

for the whole bag of tricks COD.'

'Would you care to amplify that, sir?'

Loomis said genially, 'Ah, I forgot. You used to be a lawyer, didn't you? Put it this way. If we fail, you give me nothing. If we succeed, you give me the lot. That do you?'

'You guarantee success?'

'I guarantee it,' said Loomis. 'You want to draw up a contract?'

'Your word is acceptable,' the American said.

'So's yours,' said Loomis. 'When d'you want us to start?'

'Just as soon as you can. This one's urgent.'

'It'll take a week or two. I'm running some tests. I got to find the right operators.'

'You think you'll need more than one?'

'Bound to,' Loomis said. 'I gave you a guarantee, didn't I? You got stuff I need, son. I got to have it. That means using a decoy.'

'An expendable decoy?'

'We're all expendable in this business,' Loomis said, surprised. 'Surely you know that by now.'

This time the American was sure Loomis was not joking. He got up, took a framed photograph from the wall, and passed it to the American. It was of an enormous and very handsome horse.

'That's Jumbo,' he said.

'Don't you have one with you up?' the American asked.

43

Loomis grinned, a vast and evil grin. 'Certainly not,' he said. 'Security burned 'em all. Want to stay for tea?'

'I'm sorry, I can't,' the American said. 'I have to be in Paris this evening.'

'Paris,' said Loomis. 'I pop over there myself now and again. Nice place. But you can't trust the grub.'

He saw the American out, went back to the main library, spread the *Financial Times* over his face, and sprawled out motionless. Around him the sleepers whinnied and snorted. They reminded him of Jumbo... The Americans would pay if they had to, but only if. The information he had asked in payment was too high a price to be paid willingly. That meant two sets of risks – the operation itself and the chance of the Americans snatching the prize at the last minute. The men who brought this off would have to be good. So would the decoy... And the decoy was expendable... Pity, that... Loomis slept, and his snore was thunder.

David Branch had not expected to like his first assignment. He had imagined himself being too much aware of the danger, too much *afraid*, if one were honest, to be able to enjoy applying the skills he had learned with so much labour; but it wasn't like that at all. He'd met Loomis and the task had been explained to him, and of course he'd chosen to be taken on as Craig's secretary. That was also pretty good. A nice room in an enormous flat, delicious meals, excellent wine, and not too much to do. Craig had made a disreputable fortune, and he got his money's worth in the way of comfort. He also had a secret. Something to do with Morocco, and some shady French manoeuvres of ten years ago, when the sultan abdicated. Loomis wanted that secret: Branch had to get it.

At first, the job looked easy. Craig had nothing in safe deposits, nothing – except money – at his bank, and no safe in the flat. Moreover, Craig was a man who was easily bored, and hence always involved in small, trivial expeditions: to art galleries, to the movies, the theatre, new bars, new restaurants. Branch should have had all the time he needed, but he never did. Too often Craig forgot things and telephoned him to fetch them, or asked his cook to come in early and prepare a special dish, or simply got bored with what he was doing and left the movies halfway through the film. He moved very quietly too, and he was big. The hell of a size. Branch found consolation in the thoroughness of his training, but as the days slipped by and the deadline drew near the feeling of enjoyment left him. He began to worry if he would ever find that damn piece of paper.

Then one day his luck was in. Craig took him out to dinner and proceeded to get quietly, unobtrusively drunk. It was hard for Branch to stay sober, but his terror of Loomis helped, and he managed at last to get Craig talking about Tangier in the old days. Craig talked at length.

'Used to be a smuggler,' he said. 'Used to do all kinds of jobs. Made a bit of money – went into shipping. Did I tell you I was in shipping?'

'Yes, sir,' said Branch. 'You did. But I never knew you were in Tangier.'

'Ought to do a book about it,' said Craig. 'You could write it for me.'

'I couldn't do it without the facts.'

'Gotemallathome,' said Craig. 'Show you. Gemme taxi.'

Branch got one, and Craig fell asleep in it. He woke him up and got him into the flat – he was hell to carry – and talked about Tangier and the book. Craig's hands flopped aimlessly towards his pockets. 'Must find my keys,' he said. 'Drunk. Make me a cup of coffee, will you?'

Branch made it and came back carrying the cup, to find Craig on his feet, holding his keys.

'That's better,' Craig said. 'I must have had too much to drink. You shouldn't let me drink too much, David. It isn't good for me.'

'I'm sorry, sir,' said Branch. Craig lurched toward him, took the coffee and sipped, then scowled. 'Lousy coffee,' he said.

46

'I'm sorry, sir,' Branch said again. 'I made it just the way you like it.'

'I don't like this,' said Craig. 'Here, you taste it.' He held out the cup. 'Go on.'

He gestured again, and Branch took the cup and sipped warily. As he did so, Craig stumbled on the carpet and finished up behind him, then his right hand struck at the nerve in Branch's upper arm, paralyzing it, his left clamped on the cup, pushing the lip across Branch's mouth so that his head tilted back and he had to swallow. Had to. The pain was so much. And when the coffee was down it was too late to struggle, and anyway Craig held him in a hammer lock, and even breathing was agony.

'I'm sorry,' said Craig. 'You're just not up to it, son. Four times you left signs you searched the place. And the way you ask questions is far too clumsy. You were wrong about the coffee, too. You shouldn't have drugged me till you knew which key to use.'

He could have said more, but Branch was asleep. Craig waited. Branch had a lot to tell him before he telephoned Loomis.

'I'm sorry to bother you like this,' Joanna Benson said.

'That's perfectly all right,' said Craig. He opened the door and stood aside. 'Come in, won't you?'

Her entrance was pleasing. She wore a

47

ranch mink and a Balmain dress, her diamonds were real, and she handled her height with confidence. Craig led her to the sitting room and she stood, uncertain. She looked beautiful in her uncertainty.

'Please sit down,' he said.

'Oh no. I couldn't possibly. I mean it's very late, isn't it?'

'Nearly one o'clock,' he said. She was doing much better than Branch.

'Oh dear,' said Joanna.

'How can I help you, Miss–?'

'Benson. Joanna Benson. Oh gosh – you do know who I am, don't you?'

'You're my next-door neighbour but one.'

'That's right. We've met in the lift, haven't we?'

'I'm flattered you should have remembered,' said Craig.

'You're very nice,' said Joanna. 'The thing is I've lost my key. I'm locked out. And I wondered if you could help me?'

'Gladly,' said Craig. 'Are you sure you won't sit down?'

This time she did so, and loosened her coat, and her body was there, decked out and jewelled, the merest hint of a promise. Really, thought Craig, she's awfully good.

He went to the telephone.

'What are you doing?' she asked.

'Calling the hall porter. He has spare sets of keys.' He put the phone down. 'No. Wait

48

a minute.' He walked toward her, and her eyes were wary.

'Are you sure you didn't overlook it?'

'Certain,' she said.

'It might be in your bag,' he said. 'Just as well to make sure.'

She took the bag – it was a small thing of crocodile skin, with diamond clasps – and tipped it on to the table beside her. Lipstick, make-up, lighter, cigarettes, change purse, and wallet. No key. And no pockets in the mink. She was very thorough.

'I'll ring for the porter,' he said, and did so.

'You've been awfully kind,' said Joanna. 'I'm sure I'm keeping you up. I did see your light on as I came in, and the people next door to me seem to be asleep.'

Very nicely done. Very nice indeed.

'It's no trouble,' he said.

'I don't want you to think I'm as stupid as this all the time,' said Joanna. 'But at least it means we've got to know each other.'

'But we haven't. Not really. My name is–'

'John Craig,' she said, and added hastily, 'it's on your door.'

Then the porter came up with the passkey, and she stood up to leave. She left the mink open and it swirled round her, making her very rich, very desirable. Craig walked with her to the door, shut it, came back, and poured himself a drink.

This one was ahead of Branch. Everything she'd done so far proved it. She'd handled the whole thing with just the right amount of reserve – and of promise. If he'd been a normal man he'd have lain awake all night working out ways of meeting Joanna Benson next day, but he wasn't normal. He'd never be normal again, after what they had done to him. Women were an irrelevance now, or worse. An inconvenience. He looked and acted so male, and they expected him to do something about it. Their instincts were stronger than the squat young man's. They knew he had no time for men. What they didn't understand was that he had no time for anybody, not any more. A woman had betrayed him, and a man had almost destroyed him in one of the most agonizing ways anyone had yet devised. After that, it was better to be on your own, except that on your own life was so lonely and so boring.

He made no attempt to find her, and she left him alone for two days, but on the third she came to call on him again. It was four o'clock in the afternoon and she was dressed in jodhpurs and hacking jacket, and she held her key in her hand. Not one woman in a thousand looks well in jodhpurs. Joanna Benson was the one. The gamine effect was there, as it should be, but she looked invincibly feminine. The best of both worlds.

'I'm not in trouble this time,' she said. 'I.

came to ask you to dinner. Tomorrow.'

Damn Loomis, he thought, and his postgraduate exercises. And damn this girl who was so sure he would accept because her legs were long and her breasts were rounded. You were only safe on your own. Once you let them get near, hurt inevitably followed.

'I'm afraid I haven't been too well,' said Craig, and hesitated. 'But it's very sweet of you. I'd be delighted.'

They dined with well-drilled friends: a rising young barrister and his wife, whom Joanna had been at school with. The wife, Rosemary, had obviously been carefully briefed by Joanna. They were there simply as window dressing, and behaved accordingly. Craig was the target, the victim. There could be no doubt that Rosemary approved. She did everything but wink at Joanna from the moment Craig entered the room. The husband, too, was impressed, and left it to Craig to pour the drinks, test the temperature of the wine. Joanne had no talent for cookery, and said so at once. The food had been ordered and was excellent. The wine she had attended to herself. It was superb, as was the brandy that followed. Joanna wore a short evening dress of black chiffon and looked very lovely, and, after the brandy, very slightly drunk. At midnight, the barrister remembered the baby sitter, and Craig, too, got up to leave. He felt no surprise when he did not succeed. This time Rosemary all but winked at him.

Joanna poured more brandy and Craig realized that she was nervous as well as drunk, but she moved well even so, the short skirt swirling round her long, beautiful legs... And how, Craig wondered, do we get back to my flat? Why don't we just stay here, or are we saving my place for next time? Joanna moved about, stacking dishes and glasses, and as she moved she talked, about how lovely London was at this time of year, and how Regent's Park was the loveliest thing in London.

'To see it by moonlight,' Joanna said. 'It really excites me.

'There's a moon tonight,' said Craig.

'But we can't see the park from here.'

'We can from my flat,' said Craig.

'So we can,' said Joanna. 'Darling, would you mind?'

Craig didn't mind, and Joanna loaded glasses and cups on a tray, Craig carried the coffeepot and brandy bottle, and they moved with exaggerated stealth to his door, went quickly inside. The 'darling' was a fact now, the business of carrying the coffee and brandy a small intimacy, a game for lovers. Craig switched off the lights and pulled the curtains wide. Below them the park was a vast silver-point, elegant yet shadowed. Joanna sighed.

'I know it's trite,' she said, 'but it makes me think of Hermia and Helena and that ridiculous mixup in the wood. Don't you think so, darling?'

'I think it's beautiful,' said Craig. And dangerous. Those pools of shadow are always dangerous.

The girl made a slight, inevitable movement, and she was in his arms. Her lips on his, the touch of her lightly clad body, were meaningless to him, but he returned her kiss with a simulated passion that the strength of his arms underlined. She gasped as he held her.

'You're very strong,' she said. Her body wriggled as she spoke. He sensed her fingers unhook, ungrip, and the black chiffon drifted downwards like a black cloud. She wore fashionably little beneath it. Mechanically his hands stroked the cool softness of her back, but his mouth could kiss no more.

'Don't you like me?' asked the girl.

Craig said, 'I'm sorry. I'm afraid I don't feel very– '

He allowed himself to sway on his feet. She grabbed him. It took all her strength to get him to a chair, but at last she did so, and he collapsed into it, and she looked down at him. In the moonlight, it was hard to read her face.

'Pills,' Craig whispered. 'In my pocket.'

He fell back, and at once she took his

wrist, felt for his pulse, but the benzedrine he had taken took care of that. It was racing. For a long moment she looked at him, then drew the curtains together and switched on the lights: Craig made no move. She put on her dress and began systematically to search the flat.

Craig let her look for three minutes. She was quick, methodical, and sure, and wary always of him lying in the chair. She held her handbag with her, too, wherever she went... In time, this one would be deadly. At last she found it necessary to get his keys. They were in his right-hand trouser pocket, and she had to move him. She came up to him, wary as a cat, but he lay quite motionless. Reluctantly she put down her handbag, grasped his shoulders, and heaved. He was too heavy for her. She swore, and heaved again, and this time he came up in a quick surge of power, and one splayed hand pushed under her chin, one held her right arm away from her bag. Joanna found that movement, any movement, brought instant agony. She stayed still.

'You did very well,' said Craig. 'Very well indeed. But you should have checked to see where my pills were first ... I haven't got any.' The hand under her throat moved, brought her to her knees. He let her numbed arm go, reached for her bag, took out the little Beretta automatic. 'And you should have kept hold of this,' he said. 'All the time. It was the only chance you had.'

Andrew Royce made no attempt to reach him at all. No dinner invitations, no call to read the gas meter or chat in a bar. Instead, Royce studied the outside of Craig's flat, then worked in the gym every day, and with one of the experts who had visited the school. The expert's field was burglary, and he was a master. Loomis observed his plans and said nothing to Craig. Royce's choice of methods was his own.

He chose a night when Craig went to bed early. Patiently he waited for the lights in the flat to die, then climbed, steady, not hurrying, his body protected by shadow from the dying moon. He found the window of the spare bedroom and felt for burglar alarms. There were none. No wires, no photoelectric cells. The tools the expert had taught him to use worked admirably, and the window catch yielded to him in minutes. Cautiously then, he greased the side of the window, let it slide open, and was inside. Once in, he pulled a mask over his face and moved silently to the door of Craig's bedroom. Royce had considered the problem of the sleeper from the beginning. Loomis had impressed on him how important the document was. Inevitably, it would be hidden. That meant either a long search or forcing Craig into telling him where it was. In either case Craig would have to be put out of action first. Royce looked at the cold chisel he'd used on the window, then dropped it into his pocket. The chisel was dangerous: he might hit too hard. For a job like this it was better to use the hands.

An accident saved Craig. As Royce opened the bedroom door and eased, slowly, noiselessly round it, the phone rang. Craig woke up at once and Royce saw him stir. He leaped for Craig, and his hand, held like an axe blade, struck down with controlled force. (On no account must the man be killed, Loomis had said.) But Craig had flung the covers aside already and the blow was smothered in bedclothes. Royce followed it up with his fist, and the punch caught Craig on the side of the neck, the impact an immediate eruption of pain. Craig groaned, fell back, and Royce leaped for him, but Craig's fall became a spin that took him out of the bed and on to the floor. He scrambled to his feet and the pain stabbed at him, slowing him so that Royce too had time to roll free.

Royce was younger and faster than Craig, and he had not been hit. He was wide awake, and Craig had been asleep. He leaped in again, anxious to get it over, but Craig swayed away from the three-finger strike he aimed at him, and countered with a chop that smashed just below his ribs. Royce groaned and lashed out with a karate kick aimed at the groin. Again Craig swayed, and the shoe scored along the edge of his thigh, but his hand smacked under the heel even so. He levered and pulled, and Royce spun like a top in the air, then his arms smashed down, absorbing the impact of his fall, but Craig still held on to his foot, and any attempt at movement was agony. Craig looked at the masked face on the floor. This was Andrew, he had no doubt, and Andrew was fast and young and tricky – and mad because he'd been beaten. If he let him go, Andrew would immediately start again, and Craig had taken two blows already. Still holding the foot, he limped forward, then his own bare foot flicked, the hard edge seeking the nerve at the base of the neck, and Royce's body stiffened, then relaxed. The phone rang again. Craig picked it up.

'Is that the Mercury Mini Cab Service?' said a voice that would stand no nonsense. 'I rang you a minute ago and nobody answered.'

'You see it's a bit difficult,' said Craig. 'We're not on the phone.' He hung up. He hadn't finished yet.

Craig rang the bell at the Queen Anne's Gate and the porter answered.

'You're expected,' he said, then watched Craig climb the stairs. It was some satisfaction to know that he was limping. Loomis

57

made no mention of it, but for once Craig was glad to sink into an overstuffed armchair and watched the red, eagle-beaked face glower down at him.

'Branch won't do?' he asked.

'Not at maximum risk,' said Craig. 'He gets excited. It makes him obvious.'

'And the girl? This Benson person?'

'Good,' said Craig. 'Subtle. And she doesn't overdo it. She'd have made it with another man.'

Loomis nodded. 'And Royce?' he said.

'Excellent,' said Craig. 'Strong and fast. Tough-minded. A good brain too. He worked it all out.'

'Worked *what* all out?'

'The exercise,' said Craig. 'He knew there was a good chance this was a test, so he came in from outside – when I was asleep ... I like that. And he knew he'd have to clobber me. Hurt me maybe. That didn't bother him. Even if I turned out to be on his side. He'll do well.'

'Weaknesses?'

'He hates being beaten,' Craig said. 'It makes him angry. But it won't happen often. He'd have beaten me – if it hadn't been for that phone call.'

'You think I could use those two then?'

'I know it,' said Craig. Loomis sighed, and Craig thought of whales wallowing.

'Would they break easy?' he asked.

'Ask the psychiatrists,' Craig said.

'Oh I will, son. Over and over I'll ask them. But just now I'm asking you. You've had what you might call first hand experience.'

'They'll break eventually,' said Craig. 'Everybody does. But they'll last as long as most.'

'Good,' said Loomis. 'They can be your assistants then. I got a job for you.'

'A month ago you said I was finished,' said Craig.

'I was wrong,' said Loomis. 'It's happened before. Twice. You showed I was wrong the way you handled those three. Royce in particular. And the Benson person. Women can't get at you, son. Not any more.'

'Royce and I won't get on all that well,' said Craig. 'Not after what I did to him. And the girl – she's bright. Maybe she knows about me. I couldn't work with her if she knew.'

'They won't work with you,' said Loomis. 'They'll assist you by being decoys. If they see you in the street they won't look at you twice.'

'What's the job?' said Craig.

'You're going to Turkey to pick up a feller,' Loomis said. 'And when you've got him you're going to take him to Israel. But first you're going to New York. There's people in New York can tell you all about this feller. Name of Kaplan. The Russians want him too.'

'That's why you're setting up decoys?'

'That's why,' said Loomis. 'They got him in one of their "Most Urgent" files. You know what that means.'

'It means he's going to die,' said Craig.

'That's not our business – provided we get him to Israel first. And that's your job. I'll send you the file we got on him. Work on it in your office. It doesn't leave here... You fly to New York on Thursday. That's all on file too... You better get on with it, son.'

Craig levered himself out of the chair and limped to the door. He felt old and battered and very tired. Three days in the gym would help, but not enough. The savage concentration of strength he had once summoned at will, was gone, perhaps forever.

'Why me, Loomis?' he asked.

'You're not what you were,' said Loomis, 'but you're still the best I've got for this sort of caper.'

'The KGB are after him. "Most Urgent." That means they'll be after me too.'

'Not if we use decoys,' said Loomis.

'They're just out of school. What chance will they have?' said Craig.

'Very little,' said Loomis. 'But that isn't your business.'

Chapter Four

The Kaplan file was thin. Aaron Israel Kaplan had been born in Riga in 1915, the son of a rabbi, and the family had moved to Moscow just before the Revolution. By 1932 he was a Komsomol leader and a biology student at Moscow University and had broken with his family; by 1936 he was researching in agricultural method at the Lenin Institute, and had begun a crash course in water engineering. His overriding interest was the cultivation of crops in dry areas, and papers he had written on this had gone as far as the Central Committee when the war came. In 1938 his father had died, but Kaplan had not been present at the funeral. During the war Kaplan had fought with distinction as a political commissar attached to an infantry regiment that had finished up in East Germany. After it he had gone back to work at the Lenin Institute, at first with success. He had survived the Lysenko scandal, and once again the Central Committee had read his papers. There was talk of financing a scheme of his – a capital investment of seven million roubles. He had nine assistants, limitless opportunity for research, and access to the Institute's papers, no matter how highly classified. Then, quite suddenly, he had crashed. His scheme was dropped, his research team broken up. Then his membership at the Institute was revoked, his car and dacha taken from him. For three months he worked as a factory hand, then he was arrested, tried, and sentenced to Siberia. His sentence was 'indeterminate,' which meant he stayed there till he died. The camp he went to, Volochanka, was the hardest of them all. His sentence had never been revoked, and yet he had been reported in Turkey. He was one of three brothers. One had been killed at Stalingrad and the other had left Russia with an uncle in 1922 and was living in New York – Marcus Kaplan, 189 West 95th Street. The most recent photographs of Kaplan had been taken in 1939 and had all the fuzziness to be expected of a black and white print taken with a box camera, ineptly handled. It suggested that Kaplan was tall, scholarly, and thin, but his features were anonymous.

Craig turned the page. There followed a note in Loomis's small, neat writing: 'For further information on Kaplan consult his brother and Laurie S. Fisher, the Graydon Arms, 145 East 56th Street.' On the next page was a description of Volochanka. Craig wondered how any man could possibly escape from such a place. After that there came key information about Turkey, the sort of stuff he would need to get Kaplan out without the Russians knowing, but no information about where he was. Even Loomis didn't know that. That had to wait until he got to New York, and then Laurie S. Fisher would tell him, if he thought him good enough. The file didn't tell him why Kaplan was important, either, but that wasn't Craig's business. Craig's business was to get him to Israel. He telephoned Sanuki Hakagawa at the house in Kensington and made an appointment for that evening, then went back to the file and read it through again and again. Gradually the information it contained began to stick. In two days he would never need it again.

The Hakagawas had the ground floor and basement of a house off Church Street, one of a series of Edwardian monsters of salmon-pink brick relieved with stone painted a glittering white. The exterior was fussy, ornate, blatantly opulent, the interior furnished with the same spare elegance of Japanese who still lived in the traditional style so far as London would let them. Sanuki opened the door to him, slim and ageless in a sweater and jeans.

'Please go down to the gymnasium,' she said. 'Shinju is waiting for you.'

Craig went down the steps to the changing rooms. There was a judo costume waiting for him, and a black belt. He changed slowly, allowing his mind to achieve the state of wary relaxation essential before a fight with Shinju Hakagawa. When he went in the Japanese was already waiting for him, on the dojo mat. Craig joined him on the mat and the two men bowed in the ritual of greeting.

'What style shall we fight?' Hakagawa asked.

'We'll just fight,' said Craig.

It was like very fast chess, every move played out to the limits of strength, every throw a potential opening to the checkmate that could end your life if you didn't get up, or counter, in time. At the end of twenty minutes Hakagawa signalled a halt, and both men were steaming with sweat. Hakagawa produced towels, and they dabbed at their sweating bodies, then knelt, facing each other on the mat.

'You have been drinking too much,' said Hakagawa. 'You are slow. This time I could have killed you.'

'I'm old, Hak,' Craig said.

'Not as old as me. I am fifty-four years old.' Craig looked at the squat, bullet-headed Japanese. His face was astonishingly beautiful and almost unlined.

'Show me your hands.'

Craig held out his hands and Hakagawa very carefully examined the lines of hard skin along their edges, and across the knuckles.

'You have neglected them,' said Haka-gawa. 'Suppose I asked you to punch the board.'

'I couldn't do it,' said Craig.

'It will take you two weeks to get your hands right. You will practice here every day.'

'I can't,' said Craig. 'I go to New York in three days.'

'I will give you the address of a master there,' said Hakagawa. 'You must become right again – or karate is finished for you.'

'Become right?'

'You do not mean it any more,' Hakagawa said. 'It is in your hands, but not in your mind. You are becoming what boxers call a gym fighter.' He paused, and looked at Craig in affection. 'Until your mind changes you will never beat me again. When it changes, you will beat me every time. Shower now. You drink too much.'

Each evening until he left, Craig fought with Hakagawa. His hands began to harden and his speed and stamina increased as he sweated the alcohol out of his system, but his mind remained the same. He could not beat Hakagawa. After the second defeat he went back to the department and booked a session on the firing range. He used the gun he'd always preferred, a Smith and Wesson .38, and that skill at least had not deserted him. Over and over he aimed and fired, and each time he scored a bull. The PSI who ran the place, an ex-gunman himself, looked on and was happy. Craig never gave him any problems. Craig began to relax, until the thought hit him: no matter what you do to a target, you cannot make it feel.

He went back to his flat and worked doggedly on his hands, punching and striking at the thin bags of hard sand. When he had had enough, he went to the phone and called Sir Matthew Chinn. Sir Matthew was the very eminent psychiatrist who had treated him after he had been tortured. Craig spoke to a housemaid, a butler, and a secretary. They were unanimous. Sir Matthew was unavailable for at least six weeks. Craig wondered if Sir Matthew's unavailability were Loomis's idea. Sir Matthew had not wanted Craig to work for the department ever again, but Loomis had insisted. He was insisting now. From time to time Craig hated Loomis, but there was no sense in it really, he thought. There was nowhere else for him to go.

New York began in the Boeing 707, and Craig was grateful for it. There was a hell of a lot of New York to get used to. The flight was all dry martinis and chicken à la king and the toasted cigarettes he could never learn to enjoy. There was a movie, too. Hollywood money, Spanish location. All about the war in Greece. It was bold, noisy, and totally inaccurate. Craig calculated that if the hero had behaved in reality as he did on the screen he would have been shot dead twenty-three times. He enjoyed the movie. It was right that he should. According to his cover, he was an advertising man sent over to study American techniques; not the ulcer-gnarled, thwarted genius advertising man, the extrovert, jolly kind, the kind that actually likes war movies that gross six million. After the movie he read a paperback about rape in Streatham, then abandoned that for *The New York Times*. The race riots were going to be late this year on account of the cool weather; the President needed another hundred million dollars for Vietnam; the longshoremen were going to strike after all, and baseball would never be the same without Mickey Mantle. Craig slept till Boston.

The run-in was slow and easy, the way Craig liked it, the wheels settled gingerly on the tarmac like a fat man in a hot bath. Craig remained seated and refrained from smoking as the signs and hostess told him to do, then queued, briefcase in hand, to be smiled at, wished a pleasant stay, and walk into the humid, infrequent sunshine of Kennedy Airport, the quick-fire politeness of immigration and the ultimate, grudging acceptance of the world's worst customs officers that he was not carrying heroin, marijuana, or fresh fruit.

He joined another queue then, for the helicopter, and the lazy, clattering journey through the concrete canyons of Manhattan, to look down at the cars like beetles, the human beings like ants, except that these ants, these beetles, scurried only in the pre-destined straight lines that the avenues and streets laid down for them. The helicopter waltzed slowly down the sky and Craig marvelled at the great ranks of skyscrapers, tall, thin giants that were sometimes elegant, sometimes ugly, sometimes – so quickly you grow blasé in New York – just dull. Then the clattering died and he was on the roof of the Pan Am Building, and down or up New York was all around him as far as the Hudson River, and only the sky was closed to the scurrying ants below.

He took a cab to his hotel, an ant himself now, alive and scurrying inside a beetle. The taxi driver talked about the humidity, only fifty but still climbing, and what the figure would have to be before the race riots started. Seventy? Seventy-five? Eighty? Meteorology and social science welded together to form an irrefragable law.

'What this city needs,' said the taxi driver, 'is one hundred percent air conditioning. Just one big unit all the way to Queens. Then we might have some peace in the summer.'

Craig, sweating in the back seat, agreed with him. They had found him a hotel in the

East Forties, and it was the kind he liked; old, with a lot of leather, and pictures on the walls that related to people who had actually lived, actually achieved something in the hotel. There was a man waiting for him too, a single-unit committee of welcome, A. J. Scott-Saunders of the British Embassy. A. J. Scott-Saunders was lean and exquisite, his tie was Old Harrovian and his manner distant, which impressed the desk clerk and overawed the bellboy who took Craig's bags to the elevator, opened the door of his suite, and demonstrated lights, taps, and air conditioning like a saint performing all his miracles at once. Craig handed over money. and A. J. Scott-Saunders sighed.

'I'd like some ice,' said Craig, 'soda water, and ginger ale.' The bellboy went, and until he returned Craig kept up an uninterrupted flow of conversation about his trip, the food, the movie, and as he talked searched the suite for the kind of bugs unobtrusive enough to be smuggled into an exclusive hotel in the East Forties. There weren't any. When the bellboy returned he handed over more money and poured drinks from his duty-free bottle.

'You do yourself well,' said Scott-Saunders.

'When you're in the advertising game you have to,' said Craig.

Scott-Saunders looked disgusted and

opened his briefcase.

'I have here fifty thousand dollars emergency money,' he said. 'The money is to be used at your discretion.' The thought obviously caused him pain, and the pain intensified as Craig counted it.

'All there,' said Craig, and waited. Scott-Saunders sipped Scotch and water.

'Have you got anything else for me?'

'Isn't that enough?'

'I didn't mean money,' said Craig.

Scott-Saunders looked surprised, his best yet.

'What else could I bring you?' he asked.

'Equipment,' said Craig. 'You know. Machinery.'

'I'm very much afraid I don't know,' Scott-Saunders said. 'Money was all I was told to bring. Money – and two requests: one, spend no more of those dollars than you have to; two, keep away from the British Embassy. I trust I make myself clear?'

'Transparent,' said Craig, and Scott-Saunders flushed, finished his drink, and made for the door. Somehow Craig was in his way, which was strange. Scott-Saunders could swear that he had scarcely moved.

'I've done this sort of thing before,' Craig said. 'Have you?'

'Never,' Scott-Saunders said.

'You have a regular man for this job?'

'We do,' Scott-Saunders said. 'He was

busy today.'

Craig let him go. The regular man was busy, so they'd sent him an idiot with the right accent who knew nothing about equipment or machinery. That meant no gun. Loomis had always been very anti-guns in the presence of allies, but this was carrying a prejudice too far. Admittedly a gun was no good unless you were prepared to use it, but then he, Craig, was prepared, and Loomis knew it. It would seem, Craig thought, that the fat man doesn't trust me anymore.

He called Laurie S. Fisher and got no answer, then tried Victor Kaplan. A voice like that of a method actor playing Bertie Wooster told him that Mr. Kaplan never returned to his apartment before seven. Craig showered and changed, and there were still three hours to kill before Kaplan got home. He sealed the fifty thousand dollars in its manila envelope, took it down to the desk, deposited it, asked how to get to Brooklyn, and discovered for himself the blood-and-iron realities of New York's subway system. Even the damp heat of Brooklyn was preferable to it, but nevertheless he walked slowly, cautious not to sweat too much, to the old brownstone house with the wide stoop, and grudged the effort needed to try to push his way past the throng of men sheltering on it.

They were all large men, large enough to make Craig's six feet and hundred and ninety pounds look skimpy. It took Craig some time to realize that, like him, they were waiting to get in. In England they would have formed a queue. At last one of them, who wore a single gold loop earring and hair dyed pink, put a hand on his chest.

'They're not hiring light heavies today,' he said.

Craig looked around him. On all sides, giants towered. It was like being lost in a primeval forest.

'I came to see Thaddeus Cooke,' he said. 'I think he's expecting me.'

At once the giants opened up and let him through, then resumed their restless milling. Craig wandered down a corridor lined with open doors. In each room that he passed, giants were wrestling – in pairs, in tag teams, in groups – and with each set of wrestlers was a smaller man screaming directions: part referee, part choreographer. Craig walked on till he came to a door on which the name 'Thaddeus Cooke' was painted, and below, in the same neat lettering: 'Keep Out. This Means You.' He went inside.

The man behind the desk was sleeping peacefully, feet up, thumbs hooked into his belt. He was tall, slender, and apparently ageless: his hair, close-cropped and bristling, could have been pale gold, could have been white, the lines on his dark skin the result of weather or of age. He slept soundlessly, but woke almost at once as Craig walked into the room. Very blue eyes looked into Craig's, but the man didn't move; only there was a wariness, even in his relaxation, that told Craig at once: This one is good.

'Got a good business,' the man said suddenly. 'Wrestlers. I train 'em. Book 'em. Promote 'em. Branch out on the coast. Same deal. Only there we do stuntmen and fight arrangements too. Doin' well. TV helped. You know what I grossed last year?'

'No,' said Craig.

'Hundred and fifty thousand dollars. It's not Standard Oil – but it's enough. For me anyway. I've got a hobby – now I can afford it. Know what it is?'

'No,' said Craig.

'Sleepin'. That's why I put that notice on the door. Maybe you can't read?'

Craig said, 'I can read.'

The man sighed and put his feet down, stood up. He wore a rumpled silk-tussore suit from Saks that must have cost three hundred dollars; his dirty unpolished shoes were hand sewn, English imported. The tie twisted almost to one ear was one Craig recognized as that restricted to former pupils of Eton College.

'I better throw you out,' he said. 'It'll hurt you, son, but we all have to learn sometime.'

He moved forward slowly, easily, and for a moment Craig decided to let him do it – or try to. It would be the best practice he could buy. But it would also be noisy, and very noticeable. He backed off.

'Shinju Hakagawa sent me, Mr. Cooke,' he said.

The easy movement stopped, and Cooke became once more a tired and happy tycoon.

'You're Craig?' he said. Craig nodded. Cooke's eyes moved over him warily. 'John Craig. He says you're maybe going to beat him one of these days... You know, I always thought I was the one who'd do that. Come into the gym.'

Craig moved back to the door, but the other man shook his head.

'No,' said Cooke. 'Not in public, son. One of us is going to find this embarrassing.'

Cooke's gym was a small, square room, its one article of furniture a dojo mat. Craig and Cooke changed and faced each other across it, bowing in the ritual way as Craig noticed the strength in the other's slimness. He was pared down to undiluted power, and with it, a dancer's speed and precision. Craig moved warily forward, and as he did so, Cooke leaped at once into the air, aiming a snap kick that would have ended the fight then and there if it had landed. But Craig dived beneath it and whirled round, ready, as Cooke landed and aimed a fist strike at his belly. Craig grabbed his wrist and threw him, and Cooke landed in a perfect break-fall, rolling over to avoid the kick of Craig's follow up, his grab for Craig's foot just missing as Craig pirouetted away. Time and again they attacked each other and ran into a countermove that just, and only just, prevented success. They fought, each of them, in silence and speed, and with all their skill, and they fought a draw. After twenty minutes Cooke signalled a halt.

'You're not ready for Shinju – not yet.' he said. 'But one day you're going to be – if you go on improving.'

Craig said nothing; his exhaustion was total.

'Bet I know what you're thinking,' said Cooke. Craig looked up. 'If I'd gone on for another two minutes I'd have licked you. That what you were thinking?'

'Yes,' said Craig, 'I was.'

'Know why I didn't?... Because I couldn't, son. You're the best I ever saw. What kind of business you in?'

'Advertising,' said Craig.

Cooke stared at him. 'Figured you were,' he said.

'Did you?' said Craig.

'Sure. You talk so damn much – what other business could you be in? Tell you something else.' Craig waited. 'If you ever decided you didn't like me – you'd kill me. D'you hate much?'

'Not often,' said Craig.

'Come in when you like, son. Any time. I ain't saying I'll teach you much, but I ain't too proud to learn.'

He walked with Craig back through the gym and paused near a mountainous Negro who appeared to be disemboweling a fat Greek with his bare hands. The Greek's yells were piteous to hear. Suddenly the Greek brought up his knee, and the Negro hit the canvas like a house collapsing.

'Constantine,' said Cooke severely, 'that wasn't nice. You want me to take Blossom's place?'

The Greek broke at once into a babble of broken English, all of it apologetic.

'You just watch it, that's all,' said Cooke. 'You too, Blossom.'

The Negro twitched in response. and Cooke walked on. 'Sometimes they mean it,' said Cooke. 'I can't let 'em fight if they mean it.'

'Why not?' asked Craig.

'Why,' Cooke said. 'They're valuable, son. Can't let 'em go damaging each other. They cost too much money.'

At five thirty Craig reached the Graydon Arms. It was an apartment building, neat, unobtrusive, and wealthy, its air conditioning Arctic, or at least Siberian, Craig thought, as the sweat congealed on his body. Kaplan's Siberia had not been so elegant: maplewood desk with ivory telephones, a desk clerk out of a Frank Capra movie, dark-blue carpet, pale-blue walls. In front of Craig three matrons and what appeared to be two lifeguards with clothes on – so bronzed they were, so golden their glinting hair – talked of vodka martinis as they walked to the lift. Craig told himself he was disguised as a lifeguard, and followed, and the desk clerk looked on and sighed, but made no move to stop him. Perhaps, thought Craig, he wants a vodka martini too – or a matron.

The lift whispered its way to the ninth floor, and by the time they arrived Craig found that vodka martinis and matrons alike were at his disposal, but he stayed on, and went up to the penthouse, and Laurie S. Fisher.

The door to the penthouse was of mahogany and polished till it glowed. A splendid door, a door belonging to a Georgian house; craftsmanship and artistry nicely blended. It made Craig feel good, even patriotic – just to look at it. Except that it was very slightly ajar. Laurie S. Fisher of the Graydon Arms was a wealthy man. He had to be, if he owned the penthouse – and wealthy men in New York don't leave their doors ajar, not even slightly ajar. Craig examined the door and the gap between slowly, with extreme care. No wires, no bugs. Just a door that should not have been open. He pushed it gently, using his knuckles, and it swung wide. Craig took a deep breath and jumped inside, swinging in the air as he moved, hands clawing for whoever hid behind it. There was no one. He pushed the door shut and looked around the apartment. An empty hall, an empty drawing room, an empty dining room, all furnished with a deliberate, conscious good taste, a neat blend of modern and Georgian pieces that had cost Laurie S. Fisher a great deal of money. Craig moved on to an empty bedroom. Its occupant was a devotee of science fiction, stock-car racing, and bull fighting. About seventeen, Craig thought, with a preference for English clothes conceived in Carnaby Street. Away – to judge by the books lying about – at one of those schools Americans call private, and the English, with a subtler, sharper irony, public. He passed on to the master bedroom. Fitted cupboards, pictures of horses, wall-to-wall carpet, a TV set high in one wall so that a man could lie down, relax, and look at his leisure. Or a woman.

A young woman, about twenty-eight, well-nourished, a mole on her right hip, once operated on for appendicitis. Not visibly pregnant. Blonde. Blue eyes. Probably of Scandinavian origin. And beautiful. Very beautiful. And dead.

Craig looked at the naked body without ruttishness or embarrassment. There was a faint stirring of pity, no more. In a sense she had been lucky. One shattering blow to the nape of the neck and – nothing. Oblivion. Everything finished. No more worries about beauty parlours, Italian shoes, Lord & Taylor dresses. He touched one slender foot – it was still warm – then turned to the small heap of clothes on the bed. Her purse was there, and it was empty. He left her and went into the bathroom.

Laurie S. Fisher hadn't died nearly so quickly. He had been tortured by experts, and they'd been in a hurry, but even so it must have taken an hour, maybe more. Craig marvelled that a man could hold out for an hour, even a man as strong as Fisher had undoubtedly been. And handsome too. They hadn't touched his face. He'd been gagged with a hand towel while they – while they – Craig turned away to the toilet basin and was violently sick, his body shuddering, then methodically cleaned and flushed the basin, ran the tap till the water was cold, washed his face, and drank from his cupped hands. In the end, Fisher had talked, then they'd killed him as they'd killed his girl. One sudden, longed-for blow. The boy in the private school would be a man very soon, he thought, and turned his mind to the problem of leaving. But no one stopped him, no one came back to make sure that Fisher and his woman were dead. Why should they? They were experts, technicians. The man who had killed knew that Fisher and the woman were dead the moment he unleashed his hand.

Craig stood in the hall, recalled each movement he had made. The door pushed with his knuckles, the toilet flushed, the tap turned with his handkerchief. Nothing else. He used the handkerchief on the door again, and left it as he had found it, very slightly ajar, then ran down three flights of stairs and took the elevator to the mezzanine floor, where there was a cocktail lounge and Scotch whisky.

He drank two, taking his time, making himself look relaxed, even bored, and grateful that the lounge was busy. Grateful also that it had a separate door to the street... He should have left after one, but his whole body screamed for the stuff. Things had been done to Fisher that had once been done to him, and Craig needed to drink for a long, long time if he were to forget what he had seen. But he couldn't forget.

After the second drink it was six thirty, and at seven Marcus Kaplan might be home, so the method actor had said. And at his home there might be experts, technicians, waiting to do to Kaplan what they had already done to Fisher and the girl.

Craig walked out, not hurrying, toward Fifth Avenue. It was hotter than ever, and there were no empty cabs. (That's a thing to remember about New York, Loomis had said. They don't have empty cabs. Only full ones.) But he needed to walk anyway. And there was time.

Kaplan's apartment house too was smart and well kept, but then Kaplan was in millinery, and men who do well in millinery tend to do very well indeed. Craig reached the building at five to seven. Nobody seemed interested in it except its Negro doorman. There were no waiting cars, no loiterers; but the windows across the street could conceal a sniper, if they wanted Kaplan dead, if Fisher had told them all they needed to know. The roofs too. There was good cover, and too much of it. Suddenly Craig shivered, in spite of the damp, unrelenting heat. His face was known. He also had been in a Most Urgent file. Maybe they'd made it active again. He looked in a shop-window next to the apartment house. It held a display of hunting clothes, with pump-action shotguns and rifles brutally arranged to underline the masculinity of those who bought such very expensive clothes. The rifles were the best of their kind: telescopic sights, light action, a trigger you squeezed so that it didn't jar your arm. Craig felt as if he had a target painted on his back. From across the street you couldn't miss – but at least he could use the window as a mirror and watch what was happening.

At seven five a Lincoln Continental drew up and the doorkeeper sprang into action. Craig turned and moved slowly forward. The car contained a Puerto Rican chauffeur and a fat passenger, already dismounting. The fat passenger was exactly like his brother, plus fifty pounds weight. Craig moved faster. As Kaplan left the Lincoln he was completely masked from across the street, Craig on one side of him, the doorman on the other. 'Mr. Kaplan?' Craig said.

'That's right,' said Kaplan, and looked up at Craig. His eyes were bright, alert, and, Craig thought, wary.

'I've got a message for you,' Craig said. 'From Aaron.'

The wariness in the eyes intensified.

'You better come in,' he said without enthusiasm.

Another crowded elevator, fast, air-conditioned, careful not to let the stomach lag. Kaplan got out at the nineteenth floor. (No New Yorker lives lower than the seventeenth floor, Loomis had said. They only have sex when there's a power cut.) Kaplan stood by the elevator and looked down the carpeted corridor. There was no one else there.

'What's Aaron's full name?' he asked.

'Aaron Israel Kaplan. Last heard of in Volochanka.'

'Okay,' Kaplan said, less enthusiastically than ever. 'We'll go to my apartment.'

He led, Craig a half step behind him, and almost too late Craig remembered his trade.

'Mr. Kaplan,' he said, 'are any of these apartments to let?'

'No,' Kaplan said at once. 'There's a waiting list. Very desirable apartments.' He frowned. 'Maybe you're thinking of the Boldinis.'

'Am I?' said Craig.

'Number 37,' Kaplan said. 'But they're in Maine. They go there every summer. Lucky–'

By this time they had reached Number 33, and Kaplan thought that Craig had gone mad, for the deferential but very strong Britisher promptly knocked him down, a deft, efficient trip, and leaped over his body, hit the door of Number 37 just as it had begun to open. There was a sound like that of a large, wet sack hit with a paddle, and Craig was through the door. Kaplan, bewildered but courageous, groaned himself upright and followed. Inside the Boldinis' apartment Craig was grappling with a man who held a gun. As Kaplan entered the gun went off, and Kaplan observed a vase he had detested for years shatter to fragments inches from his hand, but instead of the dull boom of the explosion there was a small, soft plop. Craig struck at the gunman and he groaned. Kaplan moved into the room, noting that Craig was gathering his strength to finish the fight. It was suddenly important that he observe just how this was done. He moved clumsily, and Craig saw him, his concentration weakened. The gunman wriggled from Craig's arms and through a window, then leaped crazily down the stairs of the fire escape. Kaplan still watched attentively as Craig scooped up the gun and ran to the window. From below came the fading sounds of shoe leather on metal.

'I'm sorry,' Kaplan said.

Craig leaned in from the window and turned.

'It's all right,' he said.

'I didn't think I would put you off–'

'You wouldn't have,' said Craig, 'except that there's another one behind you – and it's you they came for, after all.'

Kaplan spun round. There was a man lying on the floor, and he had a gun in his hand. Right there in the Boldinis' apartment, a gunman lay flat on his back, automatic in hand, and he, Kaplan, stood amid the ruins of that damn ugly vase. That was as fantastic as the gunman. The Boldinis had worshipped that vase. Paid over a hundred dollars to have it shipped from Hong Kong, and now here was this Englishman crunching over it, bending down to look at this – gangster I guess you'd call him. Craig's face told him nothing at all – but when he turned the gunman over, suddenly Kaplan knew he was dead, even before he looked up and saw the set of teak shelves near the door, with their hard, sharp edges, one of them just the height of a standing man, and that one covered in what looked like jam. Kaplan turned away.

'Well, well,' said Craig. 'How very careless of him.'

He went quickly through the man's pockets. Money, a packet of Marlboros, book matches, a dirty and much-used handkerchief. And on the floor a Browning Hi-Power automatic with a silencer. Thirteen shot. His unlucky day.

'You killed him,' said Kaplan. There was amazement rather than accusation in his voice.

'That's right,' said Craig. He unscrewed the silencer from the gun he'd picked up, then stuffed the silencer into his pocket, the gun into his pants' waistband, and opened the door, using his fingernails only. The corridor was still empty.

'At least you haven't got nosy neighbours,' said Craig. 'Did you touch anything?'

Kaplan shook his head. Craig jerked his head at the door and Kaplan left, Craig followed, still a little behind, and to the right. The way the bodyguards walk on television, thought Kaplan. The only crazy thing was he still wasn't scared. He still couldn't believe it was happening.

Inside Kaplan's door the manservant waited to take Kaplan's hat and tell him that

Madam was having a cocktail in the drawing room. Craig looked the man over. The voice was phoney, but a splendid phoney; rich and plummy as fruitcake. The man himself, lean and rangy in his white mess jacket, with cold, expressionless eyes that noticed the bulge at Craig's middle, and became more expressionless than ever.

'Cocktail?' said Kaplan. 'Sounds like a good idea. We'll have one too.'

He led the way and Craig found himself shaking hands with a plump and hennaed matron who took one look at her lord, and blamed it all, whatever *it* was, on Craig.

She thinks I've had him out drinking, thought Craig, and waited for the introductions.

'This is Mr. Craig, honey,' said Kaplan. *So he knew I was on my way here.*

'How d'you do?' said Mrs. Kaplan, uncaring. 'Hetherton, mix the drinks will you?'

Craig looked over his shoulder. Hetherton had exchanged the mess jacket for a swallowtail coat that fitted badly on the left-hand side. Craig asked for Scotch on the rocks, and Hetherton mixed it and passed it to Craig with his left hand. When Craig took it with his right, Hetherton began to look happy. Kaplan accepted a modest vodka martini and at once said, 'Business, Ida. I'll take Mr. Craig to the study.' This was the merest routine, and yet, Craig thought, she still hates me. She knows there's something wrong.

'Will you be needing me, sir?' Hetherton said. His right hand, Craig noticed, was adjusting an already impeccable tie, six inches away from his gun butt.

'No, no,' said Kaplan. 'Mr. Craig and I are old friends. We'll look after ourselves.'

Hetherton bowed and relaxed still further. Craig assumed he had the place bugged.

The study was small, untidy, and masculine, more den than study, full of small cups that Marcus and Ida Kaplan had won at bridge tournaments, and larger cups that Marcus Kaplan had won at skeet shooting. There were also two huge and highly functional lamps. Kaplan tossed off his martini and promptly refilled it from a bottle in the base of one of them.

'Scotch is in that one,' said Kaplan, pointing. 'Help yourself.'

Craig twisted the base and pulled, as Kaplan had done. Inside the lamp was a bottle of Red Hackle. He freshened his drink.

'The trouble with Ida is she worries too much,' he said, then began to shake as the fear hit him, and from his mouth came a travesty of laughter. 'No, that's not right – is it Mr. Craig? The trouble with Ida is she doesn't worry half enough.' The laughter resumed then, shrill and crazy. Craig leaned forward politely. 'You can stop if you want to,' he said, but the laughter went on. Craig reached out and his fingers touched, very lightly, Kaplan's forearm, found the place he needed, and pressed. Pain seared across Kaplan's arm, terrible pain that stopped at once as his laughter died.

'You see?' said Craig.

Kaplan said, 'I see, all right.' His body still shook, but his voice was steady. 'You really got a message from Aaron?'

'Mr. Kaplan, you know I haven't,' said Craig. 'I've come for your information'

'Again?' said Kaplan. Somehow Craig's body stayed immobile.

'Again,' he said.

'But I gave it to the other two.'

'Which other two, Mr. Kaplan?'

'Mr. Royce,' said Kaplan. 'And that nice Miss Benson. They took me on a trip in a motor launch. Taped the whole thing.'

'So they did,' said Craig. 'Now tell it all to me.'

Kaplan told it and Craig listened, and remembered. When he had done, Craig said:

'Thank you. You've been very helpful'

Kaplan said. 'Helpful. Yeah. Is it going to find my brother?'

'It's possible,' said Craig.

'I'm fifty-nine,' said Kaplan. 'I haven't seen him since I was twelve years old – and he was seven. But he's my brother. I want him found.'

Craig said, 'So do a lot of people. Friends and enemies. If the friends find him first – you'll see him.' Before Kaplan could speak, Craig said, 'Do you know a man called Laurie S. Fisher?'

'Sure,' said Kaplan. 'He's the guy who got me into this thing – whatever it is. Flew me out to his ranch in Arizona. And that reminds me – what in hell are we going to do about the Bol–'

Craig's voice cut across his. 'Mr. Kaplan, I met you on your doorstep, you invited me in, and we talked. I'm grateful for the time you spared me, but that's all that happened.'

Kaplan looked down at the arm Craig had touched, where the memory of pain still throbbed.

'Jesus,' he said. 'You're a cold-blooded bastard.'

'If I'm to find your brother I'll have to be.' Craig put down his glass. 'Thanks for the drink,' he said. 'I never drank from a table lamp before. It was delicious.'

'Okay,' said Kaplan. 'I get it. Keep my mouth shut or you'll tell Ida.'

'Is it really so important?' said Craig.

'It is to me,' said Kaplan. 'And to her too. Looking after me – all that. You don't care about all that crap. Right?'

Craig said, 'You've had a shock, and I handled you roughly. I'm sorry.'

'Where I was brought up we used to have

a saying,' said Kaplan. 'With you for a friend, who needs enemies?'

'Not you, Mr. Kaplan,' said Craig. 'You already got them.'

He left quietly. Sounds from another room told him that Thaddeus Cooke's *corps de ballet* were performing on television, and that Mrs. Kaplan approved. Craig kept on going and met Hetherton in the hall without surprise.

'How long have you been with him?' Craig asked.

'Three weeks, sir,' said Hetherton. 'May I ask–'

'Department K,' said Craig. 'M-I6.'

'Ah,' said Hetherton.

'Ah, is right,' said Craig. 'Stay on a while, Hethers, old top. He needs you.'

Hetherton said in quite a different voice, 'There's been nothing out of line so far.'

'Number 37,' said Craig. 'The Boldinis. They're away in Maine. Somebody broke in and smashed a vase. Then somebody else broke in and smashed somebody's head. And somebody had a gun. With a silencer. Like this.' His hand dipped into his pocket, showed the silencer, replaced it. 'It's a good silencer, and Kaplan's a hell of a target. If I were you, old top, I'd put him on a diet.'

He went back to his hotel room, and wrote down what Kaplan had told him. He was hungry and tired, but that didn't matter.

The hunger sharpened his memory and the tiredness could be ignored. It was all a matter of will. When he'd finished he read it through three times, then repeated it back to himself. Twice his memory failed him, so he read it three times more. When he'd got it right he lay down on the bed and slept at once, waking two hours later as he'd willed himself to do. Again he repeated Kaplan's message. It came back word-perfect. The only thing wrong with it was it didn't tell him enough. One picture postcard sent from Kutsk, in Turkey, and a message about a rabbi they'd both known as children. And Kaplan had lost the postcard. Craig screwed the paper into a twist, set fire to it, and dropped the pieces into a metal trash can. When they had burned out he flushed the pieces down the toilet and went out to eat.

By now it was close to midnight and New York was much too quiet. (If Cinderella had lost her glass slipper in New York, Loomis had said, her foot would have been in it at the time.) He found a place that sold him clams, steak, and beer, and a piece of apple pie that reminded him of Tyneside. When he asked for coffee with caffeine in it, the waiter reacted as if he were a junkie. He walked back through the silent canyons, glittering with light, their only occupants in pools of shadows, men, always in groups, waiting, watching, men inhibited by his size and the way he walked, the suggestion of power to be used at once and to the limit if they tried to hurt him.

Craig went back to his hotel room and remembered that Loomis, detestable as he was, was invariably right. The thought reminded him of the equipment that hadn't been supplied, and Benson and Royce's visit to Kaplan. But he'd got equipment anyway, a Smith and Wesson and four rounds, and a Browning Hi-Power. And Benson and Royce were problems he could do nothing about... Craig slept.

Chapter Five

They came for him at four in the morning, the dead hour when reactions are slowest and sleep at its most profound. They were good men, there were enough of them, and they didn't get too close. Craig, worn out as he was, heard them just three seconds too late. By then they were in his bedroom and one of them had flicked on a torch, its brilliant bar of light hitting him full in the eyes. Craig flung up one arm, and in the dazzling silence heard the click of a safety catch. A voice said, 'You know what I'm holding, Mr. Craig?' He nodded. 'Just keep looking this way and maybe I won't use it.'

He looked into the light. Behind him someone was moving very softly, someone poised for a blow. At the last possible second Craig swerved round. The hand shielding his face shot out in a fist strike. He felt muscle and flesh give under his hand, then a second man struck, a single blow behind the ear with a life preserver of plaited leather, and Craig collapsed at once. The lights went on then, and three men dressed as ambulance attendants set up a stretcher, loaded him on to it. A fourth man clung to the bedrail, his fingers solicitous where Craig's fist had smashed into his belly. He was a young, strong, fit man. Had one of those prerequisites been missing, Craig's blow would have crippled him or killed him. When Craig was on the stretcher, one of the men gave him an injection of paraldehyde. It was vital that he shouldn't move for twenty minutes. After that, two of them carried out Craig; the third supported the one he had struck. It would be an hour at least before he could walk by himself.

Craig woke up in a bed that was five feet from the floor, a hard bed on an iron frame that was the only thing in the room except for a chair. He wore a nightshirt of some kind of coarse linen, his wrists and feet were tied to the bed by canvas straps, and there was a bandage round his forearm. His head ached vilely, the drug made his stomach heave, and his wrists and ankles were already sore. He had no doubt that shortly he would regard his present position as one of luxury, and shut his eyes at once, trying to buy time, to prepare his body and mind to resist what was going to be done to him. That he would tell what he knew eventually was inevitable; any man can be broken, and if you've been broken once before it's that much easier the second time. But it was Craig's business to escape if he could, and hold out if escape were impossible. Des-

94

perately he tried to drive his mind and body away from what was coming, but the memory of Laurie S. Fisher was too strong. Beneath the bandage gauges recorded the sudden spurt of his pulse, the increase of perspiration, and in the next room a doctor saw these things recorded on instrument dials, and nodded to the man beside him. Craig was ready.

The man who came into Craig's room was tall and lean. His clothes were elegant, his face at once weatherbeaten and scholarly. He stood looking down at Craig for twenty seconds, and Craig remained immobile, though the dials in the next room leaped as he waited.

The tall man said at last, 'I think we should have a talk, Mr. Craig.'

Craig opened his eyes then and looked at him: perhaps the most difficult thing he had ever done.

The tall man said, 'I think we can dispense with the formalities of outraged innocence, don't you? Your name is John Craig, you work for Loomis in Department K of M-I6, and you're here to find out about a man called Kaplan.'

Craig said, 'My name is John Craig – yes, but I'm an account executive for Baldwin-Hicks. I'm here on advertising business. I never heard of Department K. Or Kaplan.'

Believe your cover story all the way, they

had taught him. Know it. Feel it. Belong to it. Even when they begin to hurt you. Especially then. Even if the other side knows you're lying, it'll help you to hold out.

'Yes of course,' said the tall man. 'And you didn't go to see Kaplan's brother today?'

'Of course not,' said Craig. 'I never heard of Kaplan.'

The tall man pressed a buzzer and two other men came into the room. They wore the white smocks of hospital orderlies, but Craig knew them at once for what they were. In the next room, the dials on the instrument panel moved up further.

'You went to an apartment block on West 95th Street,' said the tall man. 'Kaplan lives there. Don't waste our time, Mr. Craig. We *know.*'

'I went to see an advertising man,' said Craig.

The two men in white moved closer to the bed.

'And did you go to the Graydon to see another advertising man?' the tall man asked.

Craig said, 'I don't know what you're talking about. I don't know what you're doing here.'

One of the men in white took his arm, held it firmly, and the other moved up close. Something flashed in the room's hard light, and Craig whimpered at a brief stab of pain, before his mind told him they had injected him again. Pentathol, he thought. Truth serum. The only way was to blank out your mind, think of nothing that would make sense to your questioners. Methodically he began to recite the days of the week in Arabic, over and over again, saying them harder and harder as the tall man's questions came. It would be so easy to answer the questions, and such a pleasure to talk about the terrible thing he had seen. But his business was to recite the days of the week in Arabic. He went on doing so.

Suddenly the tall man had gone, and in his place was another, chubby and benign, with hexagonal rimless glasses that made him look like a cherubic gnome.

'Hi,' he said. The seven words went on and on in Craig's mind. He said nothing.

'What you doing?' said the chubby man, and settled down in the chair. The dials had told him all he needed to know. This one was terrified. 'Counting sheep? Reciting poetry? French irregular verbs? They try all kinds,' the chubby man said, then rose suddenly and stood over Craig, the chubbiness gone, and in its place a squat power, as he noticed the tension in Craig's hands.

'You're not comfortable,' he said. 'Let me tuck you up properly.'

His hands stripped away the sheets, and Craig gabbled his seven words as the other man lifted the smock and looked at the marks on his body, the sweat soaking from him so that the bed sheets were wet.

'My, my,' said the man. 'Somebody certainly didn't like you. Somebody certainly hurt you all right. You must be a very brave man. And strong too. I admire you, sport, I really do.'

The voice continued, softly, gently, and Craig saw him grow chubby again, fat and well meaning and anxious to help as he told Craig how brave he was, and asked him how he managed to withstand such terrible pain. Slowly, inevitably Craig listened, and answered, the seven words falling like pierced armour from his memory. The chubby man knew all about pain – and cared. On and on Craig talked, and gradually the chubby man's questions moved from Craig's agony to Laurie S. Fisher's, and Craig wept as he remembered what had been done to him.

'And you really didn't see who did it, John?'

'No,' said Craig. 'I thought it was the KGB, but–'

'But what? Go on. You can tell me.'

'You're the KGB, aren't you?'

'Just a research team, John. Asking questions about the problems of pain. Kaplan now. We heard there were two hoods in the Boldinis' apartment. Were they going to hurt Kaplan?'

'They were going to kill him,' said Craig.

'Only I killed one of them instead.'

'And the other one got away, right? You should have killed him too, don't you think so?'

'Noise,' said Craig. 'People.' Suddenly he felt very weary.

'Please, John,' said the chubby man. 'Don't go to sleep just yet.'

Craig said, 'They weren't – executives. Not like the ones who got Fisher. *They* were your best people. The two I met were just hired guns. Not worth killing.'

'Or hurting, John?'

Craig said, 'I don't like hurting people. I don't like being hurt.'

'John,' said the chubby man, 'I think you're in the wrong business.'

'That too,' said Craig, and slept.

The tall man came out of the shadows and looked at Craig as the two orderlies left. 'Well, well,' he said. 'The best in the business.'

'You take a blade, you sharpen it and sharpen it till it'll split a silk scarf drawn across it. Then one day you drop it on a stone floor. After that it'll still cut bread, but the silk scarves are safe. They stay in one piece.'

'Damn your parables,' said the tall man. 'What about Fisher?'

'He didn't do that to Fisher. He couldn't. Anyway, he told us the truth. He found him.'

'And the girl too?'

'And the girl. She was a Scandinavian type, just like he said. Mai Olsen. Fisher met her–'

'I know all that,' the tall man said, and turned back to Craig. 'What do you think?'

'Of John? He can still fight, still kill if he has to – but he can't cut silk scarves.'

The tall man turned away.

'Get rid of him,' he said.

There were rats. He could hear them scuttering about the floor, running up the legs of the bed, ducking beneath the bedclothes every time he turned his head to see them. He'd never actually seen one, but they were there all right. He could feel them. From time to time they bit him in the arms. Not that it mattered. The bites didn't hurt: they were just reminders that the rats were there. And there was another one – probably a baby he thought – that hid behind the pillow and bit him behind the ear. A baby rat. Brown fur, naked tail, scrabbling paws. He could imagine it perfectly, but it didn't disgust him – only it *was* a nuisance. Biting like that. The trouble was he couldn't stop it, because his hands were tied. Better to sleep, if the rats would let him.

Suddenly a bell sounded, deferential but insistent. A telephone, he thought, an American telephone. Only there weren't any telephones, not in that room where they'd talked about the pain. The ringing went on, and Craig woke, the rats disappeared, their scrabbling the hum of air conditioning, their bites the ache in his arms and head. As he woke he noticed that his arms and legs were stretched out as if he were still strapped down. Cautiously he reached for the telephone at his bedside, and pain stabbed behind his ear.

'Noon, Mr. Craig,' said the voice of the girl at the switchboard.

'I beg your pardon?'

'It's noon,' said the voice again, acidly patient. 'Twelve o'clock. You left word for a call.'

'Oh yes,' said Craig. 'Thank you.'

'You're welcome,' said the girl. The words meant, 'Jesus. Another lush.'

He rang room service for breakfast and a bowl of ice, and spent a long time bathing, showering, soaking the pain from his body. The mark of the thing they'd clipped to his arm was red and angry, but it would soon go. The one behind his ear was another matter: purple, exotic, and with a lot of life left. He'd have to tell absurd lies about backing into a shelf, or something. Then he remembered the gunman he'd slammed against the wall with the door. The lie wasn't so absurd.

The waiter came and he tipped him, wrapped ice in a towel, and put it on the bruise, then ate his breakfast. He found it strange that he could be so hungry, when his life was finished. He was no danger at all, so far as they were concerned. So much so that they hadn't even bothered to kill him. To them, he wasn't even a joke. Doggedly he tried to remember the questions they had asked, but all he could remember was pain, and Laurie S. Fisher, and a fat little man looking at where he too had been hurt. He also remembered a tall man, but that was all. Craig finished his coffee and began to dress and pack. If he really was finished. Loomis would have to know. He booked a seat on a plane for the next night, the first flight he could get, and went back to bed. No rats, no dreams, no arms and legs in a Saint Andrew's cross. When he woke up he felt better, remembering the man he'd hit in the stomach, the way he'd saved Kaplan's life. He remembered, too, the information Kaplan had given him, word for word. There might after all be some point in staying on, in order to find out who had decided that Craig was finished. In tracking them down. After all, the night clerk at the hotel should be able to give him some sort of a lead.

But the night clerk, when he came on duty, knew nothing, except that Craig had come back very late with two friends, and he'd had a little – difficulty in getting up to bed. In fact the two friends had helped. That would be around six in the morning. Must have been some party, Mr. Craig. Sure he remembered the ambulance, but that had been for another guest, two floors below Craig. The way the clerk had heard it, he'd called a doctor, and the doctor had diagnosed a perforated appendix and called a hospital. He didn't know what hospital. No. But the ambulance looked classy. Craig thanked him and gave him ten dollars in hard currency, taxpayers' money, then went back to his problem. The Yellow Pages told him just how full of hospitals and nursing homes New York is. Moreover, there was Loomis to be considered. He'd got Kaplan's information, and Loomis would want to know about that, as well as the fact that he, Craig, was a failure. Craig ate dinner in the hotel and slept for twelve hours.

Next morning he felt better than ever, and had found a way to solve his problem. He would call on Thaddeus Cooke, and have another fight. If he won, he would stay on. If he lost, he would report back to Loomis.

Cooke beat him three times in seven minutes, and looked almost as horrified as Craig.

'Mr. Craig,' he said, 'you must have got problems since I saw you last. Why, man, I tell you, they've even got down into your feet. You got to solve them, Mr. Craig, or you ain't goin' to be no good at this game any more. I tell you honest, the way you're doing now, you couldn't even lick Blossom. At least' – he thought it over, and made one concession – 'not if Blossom was set for you. You go on home – get those problems licked. Or take up golf.'

Craig went. Not home, not immediately. There was plenty of time for the plane. But he had to see the Kaplans again. There was a good man looking after them, and there'd be others backing up and all that, but the Kaplans didn't *know*. It was true that Marcus Kaplan had seen a man killed in the Boldinis' apartment, but they didn't, either of them, know Fisher was dead, or what had been done to him before he died. It was up to Craig to tell them that these things happened; that people got hurt, or were even destroyed, and yet were allowed to go on living.

The doorman was off duty when Craig arrived, but the apartment building seemed quiet enough, not at all the kind of place where a man had been killed. No cops, no spectators, no crowds of sightseers. Perhaps that was just the heat. (If Lady Godiva rode down Fifth Avenue in July nobody would watch, said Loomis. The sight of that poor horse sweating would kill them.) He went up to the Kaplans' floor. The Boldinis' door was unguarded, but Craig moved on more quickly and rang the Kaplans' bell. Nothing happened, so he kept on ringing, over and over. Hetherton wasn't going to keep him out.

But it wasn't Hetherton who stood there. It was a girl. A small girl, long-legged, brown-eyed, swathed in the most enormous sable coat Craig had ever seen. Just to look at her made Craig melt in sweat, but she looked happy enough about it and hugged the coat to her body with her arms. What she was not happy about was Craig, whom she apparently cast as an intruder, maybe even a prowler.

'I called to see Mr. Kaplan,' said Craig. 'My name's Craig.'

'I'm sorry,' the girl said, 'he's not at home right now.'

She made to close the door, and Craig did not try to stop her, but said quickly: 'When will he be back?' The girl hesitated.

'Three weeks – maybe a month,' she said. 'He and Aunt Ida are on a vacation trip.' So that was all right. The CIA could move when they had to. They'd taken the Kaplans away.

'Thanks,' said Craig, and turned to leave. He'd taken three steps down the corridor when the girl called out: 'Just a minute.' He went back to her.

'You've hurt yourself,' the girl said. 'Behind your ear.'

'Miss–?'

'Loman,' said the girl.

'Miss Loman – I know it.'

'Sort of a crazy place to hurt yourself.'

'It happens,' said Craig. 'I stumbled and banged my head on a shelf.'

The brown eyes looked puzzled and faintly amused, nothing more.

'You'd better come in for a minute,' she said. 'You look awful.'

She led the way to the Kaplans' living room and sat, still wearing the coat. The air conditioning wasn't on; Craig looked at her again, and began sweating seriously.

'You know why I asked you in?' she asked. 'I figured you couldn't be a prowler. You have a British accent. So it's okay. Can I get you something?'

'No thanks,' said Craig. 'But I'd like to ask a question. Two questions.'

'Go ahead,' the girl said.

'Is Mrs. Kaplan your aunt?'

'No,' said the girl. 'Just an old friend of the family – so I call her Aunt Ida. What's the other one?'

'Why are you wearing a fur coat?'

Miss Loman blushed a fierce, unpleasing pink. As Craig watched, she got up, looked in the mirror and brushed at her face with one hand, still clutching her coat with the other.

'Oh, shoot,' she said. 'I hate doing that. You see, Mr. Craig – the Kaplans went away

106

just this morning, and they asked me to close the apartment up for them. And Aunt Ida has the most fantastic furs, so when I found a new one–'

'You just had to try it on,' said Craig. 'But aren't you hot?'

'I'm dying,' Miss Loman said. 'If you'll excuse me, I'll hang it up.'

She rose, still clutching the coat, tripped over a footstool, and flung up her hands to steady herself, and the coat swung open. Beneath it she was quite naked, and very pretty. She whirled round from Craig, and he remembered another girl in swirling fur, a very bright girl, and pretty too. As pretty as this one. When Miss Loman had finished swirling she held the coat in place, one-handed. The other one held the telephone. Craig hadn't moved from his chair.

'You're absolutely right,' he said. 'Much too hot to try on fur coats. How fortunate I'm not a prowler.'

Miss Loman laughed and put the telephone back on its cradle.

'You British,' she said. 'How do you get to be so diplomatic?'

'Practice, I suppose,' said Craig, and got to his feet unhurriedly. 'When you write to the Kaplans, tell them I said they should take care of themselves.'

'I will,' she said, and followed him to the door. When he reached it, she called out:

'What's your first name?'

'John,' he said.

'Mine's Miriam. Tell me, John – did you think I was pretty?'

'Delightful,' said Craig. 'Absolutely delightful.'

When he left she was blushing again.

He went back to London on an Air India Boeing 707. Curry, and hostesses in saris, and breakfast served an hour before landing, and when the plane touched down it was lunchtime. He hadn't slept at all and felt bone-weary. Passport control and customs were separate purgatories. His world was finished, and waiting for him now was Loomis, with a thousand questions, and after them one fact: Loomis could hardly just let him go. It was conceivable that Loomis would have him killed. But even so, he had to call him. Loomis would know he was back anyway. He took a taxi from the airport to a pub he knew. It was not a very nice pub, but it had one valuable asset: from it you could see Queen Anne's Gate. He bought a drink, and went to a phone booth. First he got Loomis's secretary, then the fat man came on.

'That was quick. Get what you wanted?'

'Most of it,' said Craig. It was true enough.

'What's that supposed to mean?' Loomis said.

'I saw the Kaplans. And a young friend of theirs. A girl called Miriam Loman. Not Fisher. He was dead when I reached him.'

'Ah,' said Loomis. 'You better come and see me. Tomorrow morning.'

'Can't it be today?'

'No. I got a lot on today. Tomorrow morning. Ten sharp.'

Loomis hung up. At six o'clock Joanna Benson left Department K. Ten minutes later, Royce left too.

He went back to his flat, taking his time, but nobody was watching it. Craig, it seemed, was past all that. You just pointed him in whatever direction was necessary, wound him up, and off he went. When the job was over he just sat around waiting till the next time – or until he was thrown away. Craig discovered that he was very angry, and the anger surprised him. There was no fear in it; only rage. If Benson and Royce were so bloody marvellous, let them get on with it. *He* wasn't going to sit around while Loomis made up his mind whether he should live or not. And yet what else could he do? If he bolted, Loomis would be after him in earnest. For Loomis there was no such thing as an ex-agent, only a defector waiting for a new master. The new master might be offering money, or merely a cessation of pain, but sooner or later he would appear, Craig knew, if Loomis didn't act first. But Loomis always had acted first, in the five times it had happened, and Craig knew it well. He had executed one of them himself. The anger yielded to despair.

The only logical way out was suicide. A lot of whisky and a massive dose of chloral hydrate, painfully hoarded over weeks of sleeplessness. That would be easy, painless, almost desirable. His life was finished anyway: his ability as an agent gone, his zest in women gone, the booze he despised his only pleasure. It was right that it should help to kill him. Even if Loomis let him live it would kill him anyway. He looked at the whisky decanter, then went into the kitchen and found a fresh bottle. The chloral hydrate tablets were in the bathroom. They could wait...

When the phone rang the bottle was a quarter empty and Craig was in the bathroom, counting the tablets. Twenty-three, that was more than enough. He poured the tablets back into their bottle and noticed that his hand was still steady. The discovery didn't please him: he wanted to be really drunk before he swallowed the damn things, so drunk that he couldn't change his mind even if he wanted to. He put the tablets in his pocket and went back to the drawing room and the view of the park Benson had liked so much. The phone shrilled at him still. He picked up first his glass, then the phone.

'Craig,' he said, and swallowed.

'Where you been?' said Loomis.

'The loo,' said Craig. 'I'm allowed to. You gave me the night off.'

The words came out with the right insolence, but he was terrified.

'You drinking?' Loomis asked.

'I've had a couple.'

'Don't have any more. Come here instead. I want to talk to you.'

'But you said–'

'I changed my mind,' Loomis snarled. 'I'm allowed to. I'm the boss.'

He hung up then, and Craig finished his drink reflexively, without thought, then realized what he had done and put the glass down, very deliberately, still looking at the park. Benson had really liked that view, he thought. But then she was young and healthy and quite sure she wasn't going to die: that kind could afford to like things. He went back to the bathroom, and noticed on the way what a big mistake the last drink had been. He was staggering. He ran the water cold, stuck his head under it, and thought. The tablets were out now. If he took them, Loomis might send a man round – they'd find him and have him pumped out before they had a chance to work, and Craig had no intention of being as vulnerable as that to Loomis, if Loomis were going to let him live. He had to get away, have time to think – but in London Loomis was the master. There was nowhere to hide from him. And out of London? The seaports were watched, and the airports too. Always. And the men who watched them knew Craig. They'd know at once which ship, which plane – and at the other end Loomis's men would be waiting. Men who'd spot him at once, though he'd never seen them before.

'Sods,' Craig said aloud. 'Bloody *sods.*' And the words came out in the hard, flat accent of his childhood. And as he said them, he remembered. There was a way.

Getting there involved two tubes, a taxi, and three buses, and time was important. But even more important was to know you weren't followed, and by the time he reached the boatyard he was sure. It was in Wapping, behind a dirty back wall and a sagging door that waited in crumbling patience for the demolition squad. But inside it was neat, tidy, craftsman like, filled with every kind of pleasure craft from dinghies to trimarans, and every one built with patient skill. Arthur Candlish did well out of sailing boats, and paid his taxes on them. His other incomes were all tax-free. He listened in silence, a slow, big-boned man of fifty, as Craig talked. Candlish's slowness was not stupidity, but it helped when others thought it was. Craig told him his life was in danger, and he had to get away.

'Who's after you?' Candlish asked. 'The coppers?'

'No,' said Craig. 'Not the coppers. These lads mean it.' And Candlish smiled.

'You brought a feller here once,' he said. 'Big fat feller. I did a job for you. Is that him?'

Craig nodded, and Candlish sighed. 'I'll charge you nowt, John,' he said. 'But there'll be others, and it'll cost money to beat him.'

'How much?' asked Craig.

'A thousand quid.'

'Fifteen hundred,' said Craig. 'I'll pay in dollars. You're entitled to your share.'

'I couldn't take money off ye,' said Candlish. 'I knew your da.' He paused, and Craig marvelled for the hundredth time that twenty years of London hadn't modified Candlish's voice in the slightest, so that he had only to speak to carry Craig back at once to his childhood: the cobbled streets, the gulls and docks, the cold, grey-glittering sea.

'Where?' Candlish asked, and Craig had dreaded the question. 'Ireland,' he said.

Candlish went out and Craig saw him dismissing his men, then at the telephone. There was no other way. He'd realized it there in Regent's Park, when he looked at Joanna Benson's view. He couldn't kill himself. Not now. Maybe if he'd been left alone and got drunk enough he'd have done it *then*. Maybe. But he couldn't try again. And he couldn't just drift, waiting for Loomis to find him. All he could do was finish the job, and do it well enough for Loomis to lay off him till the next time. That meant going back to the States and finding Marcus Kaplan – and getting more information. There had to be more. That was why the Americans had him, but he could be found.

Candlish came back. 'We'd better make a start,' he said.

He rose and put on a bowler hat of antique design that made him look like a bookmaker with a taste for religion.

'That fat friend of yours won't have forgotten me,' he said.

Loomis missed him by seven minutes. When he arrived the boatyard was locked up tight, and a sign outside said **closed till further notice.** Nobody had seen Craig, nobody had seen Candlish. The staff – three men and a lad – were on holiday, and Mr. Candlish had probably gone up North to see his relatives...

Mr. Candlish, in fact, was driving to Holyhead in a fish lorry, and Craig went with him as his mate. They stopped in the suburbs for Craig to have his photograph taken, and were met outside Holyhead by a young man in an Aston Martin DB6 who had Craig's new passport – not too new, not too blank, the American visa exactly as it should be. Craig found that his name was John Adams, and that he was a general dealer.

'Useful that,' said the young man. 'You can deal in anything you like. Early Picassos or army surplus. Two hundred and fifty quid please.'

'Send me the bill,' Candlish said.

'Anything you say, Mr. Candlish.'

The Aston Martin roared and disappeared, nervous at being so far from London, and Candlish drove on down to the docks. In place of the fishing boat Craig had expected there was an elegant power launch complete with owners – a thin Manchester cotton broker and his fat Salford wife – Craig and Candlish were the crew.

'Six hundred quid they want – and a hundred and fifty for the lorry,' said Candlish. 'It's a bloody scandal.'

There was satisfaction in the thought that A. J. Scott-Saunders had provided the money.

They sailed at once, and made for Cork. There was relief in handling a boat again, the relief of knowing that one skill at least had not deserted him – and the realization of what waited for him in the States killed his need for alcohol. The fat lady from Salford could cook, too, and the weather was clear and bright. The trip at least was bearable, and more than bearable when Arthur started to talk about the old days, about the father Craig could scarcely remember. He took the wheel while Arthur slept, and when it was his turn, found that he too could sleep. Four healing hours that left him alert, ready, as the boat ran into a small, empty cove and Candlish and Craig prepared to go ashore in the dinghy. The thin man and fat woman said nothing, but their eyes on Craig were hungry. Money was going ashore. A lot of money.

Craig took the oars and Candlish cast off. The sea gleamed in the morning sunlight, bright and diamond-hard, without the Mediterranean tenderness Craig knew so well.

'You'll have to watch those two,' said Craig.

'I'll watch them.' Candlish's voice showed no trace of worry. 'They're a bit scared of me, John.'

Craig was still laughing as the dinghy beached. They walked ashore dry shod.

'Straight up to those cliffs,' said Candlish. 'Get to the top and you'll find a bit of a path. Follow that and you'll come to a farmhouse. There'll be a Volkswagen there. Take it.'

'Stolen?'

Candlish chuckled. 'Your own car, lad. All in order. There's papers to prove it. Just leave it where you want. When the police find it – you'll be miles away.' It wasn't a question. He

116

had no doubts of Craig's ability. 'Good luck, John.'

Craig scrambled ashore. 'Thanks,' he said. 'So long.'

Candlish watched as Craig went up the beach to the cliff. A good lad. A hard one to get on the wrong side of. He touched the inside of his jacket, and the hundred-dollar bills crackled like music. That fat bitch would be happy when he paid her. Slow and easy he rowed back to the launch.

Craig found the Volkswagen waiting, a road map open on the front seat, and drove at once to Cork and breakfast in a hotel. Bacon and eggs and tea, and a waiter who talked because he felt like it, because it was a beautiful morning. Craig went next to a travel agency, and then bought clothes, a suitcase, shoes, and set off for Shannon across the cheerful Irish landscape, the improbable green grass and whitewashed cabins unreal as a film set. And why not? The Irish were all actors anyway. That didn't make them any less efficient when they wanted to be, Craig thought, and drove the Volkswagen with care. He daren't risk an accident.

At Shannon, Ireland stopped and Mid Atlantica began. Even the tea tasted different, at one with the plastic and insurance machines and flight calls. Craig boarded an Aer Lingus Boeing at five o'clock. Nine hours later he was in Chicago, and it was eight p.m. Two hours after that he was at Kennedy, and it was eleven p.m. He went into New York by bus, and found a hotel in the West Forties in downtown Manhattan, and slept for fourteen hours. When he awoke it was time to find Miss Loman.

He rang Marcus Kaplan Inc. and asked for him by name. When a secretary's voice told him he was on holiday, he said:

'My name is Adams. John Adams. I had rather hoped to see Mr. Kaplan.'

'I'm sorry, Mr. Adams. We have no way of contacting him right now.'

'Oh dear,' said Craig, very British, 'it's about clay pigeon shooting. What I believe you call skeet shooting over here.'

'That's right,' said the girl, and the voice was weary now, long-suffering – a secretary too often involved in her boss's obsession. Skeet shooting to Kaplan was like a fix to a junkie. She didn't dare get in the way. Get off the hook, her instincts said. Fast.

'You might try Miss Loman, sir,' she said. It was that easy.

She lived in Greenwich Village, on the ground floor of a house in Grove Street, with a small brick yard where a maple tree somehow survived and even gave shade. When Craig called she had been sunbathing, and had to put on a robe to answer the bell's ring. When she saw who it was, she blushed again.

'I'm sorry,' said Craig. 'Did I disturb you?'

'No,' she said. 'I was in the yard. Do you want to come out?'

He followed her, thinking how young she was, how easy her movements, with the ease that comes from knowing, really *knowing,* that nothing can ever go wrong, nothing can really hurt all that much. There was a chair under the tree, and she waved him to it. She sat on a Lilo that lay in the full glare of the sun. She was still blushing.

Craig said, 'What's wrong?'

'It's ridiculous,' Miss Loman said. 'Every time I see you I'm like this. Maybe you think I don't *have* any clothes... I was sunbathing.'

'Go ahead and sunbathe,' said Craig. She hesitated. 'Look, Miss Loman, I can't be a prowler. I'm British.'

She giggled then, took off the robe, and lay down. She wore a tiny bikini and her body was sleek with suntan lotion. A small, luscious body that would one day be fat, but that day was yet to come. A woman's body, thought Craig, who had never subscribed to the theory that women were failed men and ought to look like it.

'I've come to ask about your uncle,' he said.

Miss Loman pouted. 'He's fine,' she said. 'But he's not my uncle.'

'I'm sorry, I'd forgotten that,' said Craig. 'Just an old family friend, isn't he?'

'That's right.'

'Is your father in the millinery business too?'

'My father's dead, Mr. Craig. So's my mother. Marcus brought me up. Supported me.' She hesitated. 'He's supporting me now. I got bored being a secretary.'

'You know where he is?'

She swung round to look at him, her body's movements forgotten. She was wary of him now. 'I can't tell you,' she said.

'He's in danger,' said Craig. 'He could be hurt.' She got up and backed away. Craig sat on, under the tree.

'Just who are you?' she said.

'You weren't surprised at what I said. You knew it already,' said Craig.

'And how did you know I was here?' She hesitated, then – 'Adams. You rang up Marcus's firm, didn't you? Called yourself Adams.' She took a step backwards, then another. 'I want you out of here.'

Craig sat on, and she retreated further.

'Marcus knows where his brother is,' Craig said. 'Maybe you know it too.'

The words stopped her.

'His brother's dead,' she said. 'He died in Volochanka prison.'

'He's alive,' said Craig. 'He escaped from prison – God knows how. The story is he's in Turkey.'

She began to move again, and Craig, still

slouched in his chair, suddenly had a gun in his hand. It moved up slowly from her waist to a point between her eyes.

'Look at it, Miss Loman,' said Craig.

'I'm looking,' she said. 'You'd never dare–'

'Miss Loman, you don't believe that,' said Craig. 'Come and sit down.'

Slowly, her eyes fixed on the gun's black mouth, she obeyed. Craig still didn't move.

'There's a question you missed,' he said. 'You should have said, 'Who the hell are you, anyway?''

'Who the hell are you, anyway?'

'British Intelligence. M-I6. Department K,' said Craig.

'You'll have to leave here sometime. I'll call the police–'

She stopped. Craig was shaking his head. 'Why wouldn't I?'

'All sorts of reasons. If you did that – I'd kill your uncle. Or you. Or both.'

'But that's crazy.'

'Miss Loman, you're up to your neck in a very crazy business. There's another reason. Your uncle wants to see his brother.' Her eyes looked into his then, for the first time ignoring the gun. 'You know that's true, Miss Loman.' She nodded. 'I'm the only one who can find him.'

'You think you're so good?'

Craig said wearily, 'I have to be. If I don't, I'm a dead man myself.'

He stood up then, and the gun disappeared in a blur of speed. She looked up into flat grey eyes that told her nothing at all.

'Where's your uncle, Miss Loman?'

'Miami Beach,' she said. 'The Portland Arms.'

'Any skeet shooting there?'

'Yes,' she said. 'But nobody goes there now.'

'We will,' said Craig.

He moved then, and took her arm. She could sense the power, carefully controlled, in his hard hands. There was something else too. He was trembling, but her body meant nothing to him. She was sure of it.

'I meant what I told you,' he said. 'If I don't get Kaplan, I'm dead. And if I die, Miss Loman, I'm going to have company.' He paused. 'I'm sorry.' he said, 'but I'll have to watch you dress.'

To her amazement, she realized the apology was genuine.

Chapter Six

He wouldn't let her pack. She wore the new dress Marcus had bought for her birthday – a drip-dry thing in glittering yellow, and her handbag was big enough to contain a spare pair of stockings, bra, and pants. He let her take them, but that was all, then they walked together down the street, the pretty girl and the attentive beau who was taking her out to lunch.

'Nothing's more conspicuous than a suitcase,' he said. 'Even if your neighbours aren't nosy.'

They took a cab to the air terminal and a bus to Kennedy. He paid for everything in cash, and seemed to have plenty. All the way he was polite and attentive, and she realized that in other circumstances this man would have been attractive to her, tremendously attractive, in spite of the threat of cruelty behind the politeness. Perhaps even because of it. But he was unaware of her as a woman, she knew, and the thought irked her, even then.

Only once did she almost panic and try to get away. They were in the departure lounge, waiting for their flight call, and a cop walked by, the kind of cop you needed in a situation like this. A big one, big and mean, not the kind who helps old ladies across streets. She stirred in her seat, ready to run, to scream maybe, but Craig was as fast and as sensitive as a cat. His left hand reached out and touched her arm, and pain scalded through her. He let it go, and she saw that his right hand was inside his coat.

'No,' he said. 'Not yet.' She sat very still. 'I had to do that to your uncle once,' he said. 'You're a hard family to convince.'

Then the flight call came, and they went out to the 727 and he was polite and attentive all over again as he sat by her side. It should have felt like a nightmare, she thought, but it wasn't. She knew that everything he had told her was true, and she was very frightened. For the first time in her twenty-three years of life, death was real to her. She did exactly what he told her, and the smiling, polite man watched her as intently as ever. When they touched down at Miami he bought her a meal, then took her to the car-rental firm that tries harder, and watched as she hired a Chevrolet coupe with the money he had given her. She drove, and he made her pull up on the road into town, slipped something into her hand. 'Here,' he said. 'Put it on.'

It was a wedding ring. Slowly, hating him, she put it on her finger.

'Don't be sentimental,' Craig said. 'That's a luxury, believe me – and we can't afford luxuries. You're alive, Miss Loman. Be thankful.'

She drove on, and he made her pull up at a supermarket. They went inside and he bought whisky, sandals, a shirt and jeans for her, and for himself, toothbrushes and a zippered travelling bag. They went to a motel then, and he booked them in for the night, saying little and sounding, when he did speak, like a New Yorker. The woman at reception hardly looked at him, at her not at all. The unending soap opera on the transistor radio had all her attention. Craig thanked her even so, and they drove past the dusty palms, the minute swimming pool to cabin seven. She switched on the air conditioning at once as Craig carried in the bag. The plastic-and-vinyl room was as glittering and unreal as a television ad, but the chairs were comfortable and the twin beds still had springs. Craig opened the bag, took out the whisky, and mixed two drinks, offered one to her. She shook her head.

'Suit yourself,' he said, and took off his coat and sprawled on the bed. She saw for the first time the supple leather harness of his shoulder holster, the gun butt that looked like an obscene extension of his body. Her eyes misted with tears.

'Not yet,' said Craig. 'You can cry later.

Drink your drink.'

'I hate you,' she said.

'I know. Drink your drink.'

The whisky was strong, and she choked on it, but the tears left her.

'Get your uncle on the phone,' he said, 'and tell him exactly what I say. Tell him you're with me – and he's not to worry about you if he does as he's told. Then tell him to meet us at the skeet-shooting place – does he know where it is?'

She nodded. 'He was at the championship here five years ago.' she said.

'Tell him to be there in an hour.'

She looked up the Portland Arms in the phone book, and did just as he said. Aunt Ida was at the beauty shop, and that made it easier. Her uncle took a lot of convincing.

'Craig?' he said. 'That tough Englishman?'

'You're to meet him at the skeet-shoot – in an hour,' she said.

'Honey – you know I can't do that.'

She said quickly, 'Marcus, you've got to. If you don't – I'm all right now. But if you don't – maybe I won't be. I'm not fooling, Marcus.'

'He's with you?'

'Yes,' she said. 'He's with me. Marcus – please do as I say.'

Craig took the phone from her.

'That's good advice, Mr. Kaplan,' he said. 'If you harm that girl–'

'It'll be because you didn't turn up,' said Craig. 'Drive carefully.'

He hung up. She was looking at him in loathing. 'I don't believe it,' she said. 'The first time I met you – I liked you.'

'It doesn't matter,' he said. 'Get changed.'

'Here?'

'In the bathroom, if you're shy,' he said. 'Just do it. And hurry.'

When she came back she wore the shirt and jeans. The gun lay on the bed, near her hand, and her eyes went to it at once.

'Go on,' said Craig. 'Pick it up. Shoot me.' She didn't move. 'Go on. Get the gun.'

She leaped for it then, and the speed of his reaction was terrifying. He came at her like a diver, and a hard shoulder slammed her into the bed as one hand pinioned her gun hand, the other splayed beneath her chin, thumb and forefinger pressing. She forgot the pain that made her drop the gun, forgot the pain in her breast where his shoulder had caught her, and thought only of the agony the thumb and finger made, crushing nerves, choking out breath.

'Please,' she gasped. 'Oh, please.'

He let her go, and the intake of air was an unavoidable agony to her. He picked up the gun and dropped it near her hand.

'Want to try again?' he said. She shook her head. 'Poor Miss Loman,' said Craig. 'But I had to do it, you know.'

'Why?' she said. 'Why?'

'To show you you can't win. Look at my hands, Miss Loman.'

He held them up in front of her, and she saw the hard ridges of skin from fingertip to wrist, and across the knuckles.

'I can break wooden boards with these. With my feet, too. It's called karate. I'm a Seventh Dan black belt. There are only five men outside Japan who can beat me – and they're not in Miami. Miss Loman, we're not taking the gun.' He moved his hands closer to her. 'Just these.'

'You're hell on women,' she said.

'And middle-aged furriers. I want you to remember that.'

She drove him to the skeet-shoot club, through downtown Miami, past the resort hotels and the restaurants and the pastel-blue Atlantic. Traffic was light, the tourist season was over, and they made good time. Craig sat back easy and relaxed, drinking in the wealth of the place. There was so much of it, and it went on for so long. They left it at last, and got into country-club land, golf-club land, where shaven grass was as obvious a sign of wealth as a Cadillac or a chinchilla coat, and stopped at last before a building of glittering white stone, of the kind that she had called Hispaniola Baroque that time she had kidded Marcus about it, when he'd shot there five years ago – a glittering white building with pillars and pilasters and mullioned windows, and miniature cannon on its embrasured roof. All it needed, she'd said, was Long John Silver limping down the stairs, a parrot on his shoulder. Marcus had laughed then. He wasn't laughing now.

They left the car to a Negro attendant in white, a scarlet cummerbund round his waist, and walked up the steps toward him, Craig on her right. When they reached him Craig's left arm went round her waist, his right hand held out to Marcus, who hesitated.

'Take it,' said Craig, 'or I'll hurt her.'

His fingers moved, and the girl gasped. At once Marcus's hand came out to him.

'Great to see you again,' Marcus said. 'How are you?'

'Fine,' said Craig, 'Everything's fine. So far. Let's get on with the match, shall we?'

They went inside the building then, through a low, cool bar to the gun room, where Kaplan signed for two guns and ammunition, then picked up one gun as Craig took up the other. With the gun in his hands, Kaplan changed at once. The gun was something he knew; it gave him confidence, even courage.

Craig said, 'You walk ahead, Miriam. Lead the way while Marcus and I talk.'

She did as he bade her at once, without question, and Craig followed, the shotgun under his arm, English style, the muzzle aimed at a point behind her feet, but Marcus knew, capable of tilting to her back in less than a second. He had been warned about shotgun wounds, knew what they could do to her at such close range. His courage receded.

'Guns are useless things,' Craig said, 'unless we're prepared to shoot. Don't you agree, Mr. Kaplan?'

'What do you want me to do, Craig?'

'Tell me where your brother is.'

'I don't *know.*'

They reached the shooting range then, and Miriam waited till they came up, ready to work the treadle that would fire the skeet.

'That's a pity,' said Craig.

'For you it certainly is.'

'For all of us. You see I know you're lying, Mr. Kaplan. And if you go on lying, I'm going to kill Miriam here.'

'You're crazy,' Kaplan said.

Craig said, 'I'm desperate, certainly. And I mean it.' His hand moved onto the safety catch of the shotgun, the barrel came up. 'I'll kill *you,*' said Marcus.

'Maybe,' said Craig. 'You've never done it before... And even if you did, she'd still he dead.' Kaplan didn't move.

Craig said, 'Mr. Kaplan – if I don't find your brother, I'm dead anyway.' His finger moved to the trigger.

'Marcus,' said the girl, 'he means it. For

God's sake tell him.'

'Outside Kutsk,' Kaplan said. 'In Turkey. He sent me a postcard from there eight months ago. That's the first time I heard from Aaron in twenty-five years. I told you that.'

The gun barrel dropped.

'You told Miss Benson and Mr. Royce too?'

'Yes,' said Kaplan. 'A man from the CIA asked me to.'

'What else did you tell them?'

'Things,' said Kaplan. 'Family things. You know. About my father, my uncle – all that. The way things were in Russia. So Aaron would know they came from me.'

'Does Miss Loman know these family things?' Kaplan nodded. 'Then I won't bother you about them,' Craig said.

Kaplan looked up. 'You mean you're not going to let her go?'

'How could I?' said Craig. 'You'd tell the CIA.' He raised the gun again. 'Just be quiet and everything will be fine.'

Kaplan stood immobile, his hands clenched round the shotgun. The CIA had warned him so carefully: no one but Royce and Miss Benson must be told the things he knew about his brother. To tell anyone else would be to betray his country, and Kaplan loved his country, not because of what it was, but for what it would become. His was a questioning, suspicious, and demanding love, but it was real; real enough for him to die for it. He had seen this, in his daydreams: Major Kaplan, USAAF, in a dogfight with Messerschmitts; Commander Kaplan, USN, steering his tincan to intercept a Jap cruiser. In the reality of his warehouse he had acknowledged the silliness of his daydreams, but not his right to the dreams themselves. Only he had never daydreamed Miriam's death. His hands loosed their grip.

'This CIA man, Laurie Fisher–' said Craig.

Kaplan looked up. 'You know him?' he said.

'I've seen him once,' said Craig. 'He was the one who told you to take a vacation?'

'Yes,' said Kaplan.

'It was good advice,' said Craig, 'but from now on stay in a crowd. If you think I'm rough, Mr. Kaplan, you should try the KGB – like your brother.' He paused, then added: 'Let's see you shoot, Mr. Kaplan. That's what we came for, wasn't it?'

Miriam worked the treadle, and the skeet balls shot out, small and travelling fast. Kaplan fired, pumped the gun, fired, pumped the gun, over and over. The first two missed, the next eight were smack on the target.

'You're brilliant, Mr. Kaplan,' said Craig. 'If you could keep emotion out of your shooting you'd be deadly. Me, please.'

Miriam worked the treadle, and Craig shot: the first two misses, then eight hits. He grinned at Kaplan.

'We must have a play-off sometime,' he said.

'So you're just brilliant, like me?' Kaplan said.

'No,' said Craig. 'I'm deadly. But I've never shot skeet before.'

They left Kaplan at the clubhouse, and she drove back to the motel. On the way they were picked up by a blue Buick sedan that followed them decorously through the Miami traffic. It was still with them when they turned off for the motel. Craig sighed.

'Drive on a bit,' he said. 'Make this thing go.'

The Chevrolet moved from fifty to seventy, then on to eighty, and the Buick was still there. When the girl slowed down, so did the Buick's driver. Craig sighed again.

'That Buick's following us,' said the girl. Her incredulity was touching.

'Start to slow down,' said Craig. 'Wait till we get near a lay-by, then cut your motor and coast in.'

She did as he said, and the Buick slowed too. When they went into the lay-by, the Buick slowed even more, then entered it in front of them. By that time Craig had got out of the car and was looking at its offside rear tyre. The man who got out of the Buick was young, broad-shouldered, Florida brown. He walked back to the Chevrolet and smiled at Miriam, a warm and friendly smile.

'Having trouble, folks?' he asked.

Before she could answer, Craig said, 'Yeah. Look here,' and the tall young man leaned toward the tyre.

Craig's body uncurled like a spring, and the tall young man went down to a back-handed strike. On the way down he met Craig's knee, and after that the concrete, then Craig went through his pockets, hefted him into the trunk of the Buick, and threw its ignition keys into the bushes.

Miriam stared at him, her mouth open in a silent scream. 'Let's go home,' said Craig.

She fought for words that refused to come, and at last gasped out, 'You killed him.'

'No,' said Craig. 'He'll live. And he's out of the way for a while. Drive on.'

She obeyed at last, and they made for the motel.

'Who was he?' she asked.

'No card,' said Craig. 'Licence said Harry Bigelow. Just fifty dollars cash, a big smile and a Colt .38. Harry Bigelow, CIA.'

'You're so sure?'

'We're lucky it was,' said Craig. 'The KGB wouldn't play it like that. And neither will Harry – not any more. To start with there'd probably be two of them – tailing your uncle. When we left they'd split up. The better one would take Kaplan. I got the apprentice, poor kid. It all looked easy, didn't it?'

'Horribly easy.'

Craig chuckled. 'It isn't usually. But your Uncle Marcus was routine – so they thought. So they gave some of it to a new boy. It won't happen again. The CIA knows its stuff.'

And so does Loomis, Craig thought; yet he's risking a new boy.

'What now?' said the girl.

'We go back to the motel,' said Craig, 'and ask for a nine-o'clock call tomorrow morning. But that's because we're sneaky. Actually we leave tonight.'

'Where to?' Miriam asked. 'Back to New York?'

'Eventually,' said Craig. 'First we go to Caracas, Venezuela, then the Azores, then Rome, then Istanbul, then – if you're a good girl, back to New York.'

'But you can't,' Miriam said.

'I'm doing it.'

'But I haven't got my passport.'

'I picked it up for you,' said Craig. 'While you were dressing.' Suddenly she started to blush again. 'What's the matter?' he asked.

'I've got to go to the john,' said Miriam.

135

Chapter Seven

The tall man's name was Lederer. His cover was that of investment counsellor in the firm of Shoesmith, Lederer, and Fine. The chubby man with hexagonal glasses was called Mankowitz. His cover was that of consultant psychologist, and was worth a hundred thousand dollars a year. Some of those dollars he invested on Lederer's advice. It was an excuse for meeting, and Lederer's advice was good. They met in Lederer's office as Craig and Miss Loman landed in Caracas. Both men liked Lederer's office. It was in Wall Street, on the eighteenth floor of an aging skyscraper, it had a kind of brown-leathered, New England dignity, and it was not bugged. The last, negative virtue was the most desirable of all, but the others also had charm. For Lederer they represented a continuity of life: prep school in New England, Harvard, a home in Long Island, a summer place in Maine. For Mankowitz they had all the charm of novelty. Enormous leather chairs, Hogarth prints, period furniture; there was even a humidor, and the cigars it contained were Havana, and quite illegal in the States, no matter where your allegiance lay. He took one and pierced it with a device that might have been used for extracting confessions. Lighting it was a ritual that occupied two minutes and three matches. When it was drawing Lederer said:

'Craig got to Marcus Kaplan.' The chubby man looked up, surprised. 'He took the girl with him. Miriam Loman. They met at some skeet club Kaplan uses. It seems likely that Kaplan told Craig all he wanted to know.'

Mankowitz sucked on his cigar like a fat child with a lollipop.

'You gave us the wrong advice,' Lederer said. Mankowitz pouted.

'I didn't give you any advice,' he said. 'I gave you facts. Craig as an agent was finished. That was a fact. He's too scared of pain. That was a fact. He'd lost his drive – another fact. And the way Fisher was handled threw him – also a fact.'

'In Miami he put through a nice, smooth operation. He wasn't scared and he didn't panic.'

'Then something's happened to him,' Mankowitz said.

'What?'

The fat man's shoulders heaved in a comprehensive shrug.

'How do I know? For that sort of guessing I need a crystal ball.'

'I'd be obliged if you'd use it,' said Lederer,

and Mankowitz pouted again.

'I can tell you a possibility,' he said. 'But that's all it is.'

'Tell me a possibility.'

'Somewhere Craig's got the idea that he's got nothing else to lose. He's so far down he can only go out – or up. Craig isn't the type to go out. So he's started to hit back.'

'But you saw him a couple of days ago. What could have happened since then?'

'He went back to London,' the fat man said. 'It's possible he saw Loomis.'

'Inevitable,' Lederer said.

'Maybe Loomis rejected him. The archetypal father-figure rejected him. That means he's absolutely alone.'

'Except for the girl.'

'The girl is expendable. For Craig, now, everyone may be expendable. And he is expendable to everyone. Hence his need for a hostage. Nobody loves him any more.'

'That's why I let him take the girl,' Lederer said. 'The way he is now, he might just do the job for us.'

'You can keep track of him?'

'Oh yes. He's booked through to Rome. He stops over at the Azores. If he makes Rome, he goes on to Turkey. We've got plenty of chances to pull Loman out if we have to.'

'It might be wiser not to take them,' Mankowitz said. 'If Craig's recovered his skill as a result of – whatever has happened, he'll need the Loman girl to find Aaron Kaplan. Then we can take over.'

'Not in Turkey. Turkey's a little difficult for us at the moment.'

'Then get him out of Turkey. Surely there are ways?'

Lederer thought for a moment, watching the thick coil of cigar smoke plume into nothingness as the air conditioning got it.

'There's a man called Royce and a girl called Benson. They're after Kaplan too. Craig won't want to meet them. Perhaps we could use that. I'd like to. It would make the whole thing so much neater.'

'It would make Loomis mad too.'

Lederer smiled. 'There's that also, of course. And when Loomis is angry he's at his most vulnerable. Yes. That's the way we'll play it.'

One of Lederer's phones rang. He had three on his desk and one on a side table, an old-fashioned piece of ivory, inlaid with gilt, that belonged to Paris in the naughtiest nineties. Most people thought of it as decoration, but it worked, though its number was unlisted. He walked to it now, and picked it up.

'Yes?' he said. The phone squawked briskly, then went dead. He hung up and turned to Mankowitz.

'Craig's recovered remarkably,' he said. 'Yesterday he clobbered a CIA man.'

The journey was a gruelling one, and by the end of it the yellow Orion dress had lost its glitter. Beside her, Craig looked as indestructible as ever, in his crumpled suit, the shirt that had stopped being white the day before. Rome was behind them now, and they were on an Al Italia Caravelle, headed for Istanbul. She had a confused memory of meals that were always breakfast, of sound systems that shouted first in Portuguese, or Spanish, or Italian, then in English; of uneasy sleep and only half-awake wakefulness as one plane or another screamed across the Atlantic, Spain, the Mediterranean, Italy, and now the Middle East. All the way he had been kind to her, considerate for her comfort, easing the strain of travel that seemed to touch him not at all, so that in the end she had slept against him, her head resting on the hard muscle of his shoulder, and he had sat unmoving, hour after hour. Once she had awakened, and found him looking down at her. There had, she thought, been a kind of pity in his face, but it had disappeared at once, the blank mask taking its place as he settled her down again, put his arm across her shoulders, the most impersonal arm she had ever felt. It was there now as the plane strung islands like jewels below them: Limnos, Imroz, Samothraki, before the long ride down to Gallipoli, Marmara, Istanbul. He shook out one of his rare cigarettes and lit it left handed.

'Are we nearly there?' she asked.

'Soon,' said Craig.

'Boy, could I use a shower,' she said. The arm quivered, she looked up and saw that he was laughing. 'What did I say?' she asked.

'Miss Loman, Miss Loman, how American you are.'

'Well of course I'm American,' she said, 'and anyway, I wish you'd stop calling me Miss Loman.'

'Never spoil a professional relationship for the sake of a little politeness,' said Craig.

She looked up at him, but his face as usual told her nothing. He concentrated on the pleasure the cigarette gave him.

'Professional relationship?'

'We're colleagues,' he said. 'We may not want to be, but we are.'

The No Smoking sign came on then, and it was time to fasten seat belts.

The customs, she thought, were disappointed in them. They carried so little luggage, but currency control cheered up appreciably when they saw the dollars he carried. They walked through the bright impersonality of the arrival lounge, and already she felt bewilderment, even resentment. The Middle East resembled the Middle West far too much. He guided her out to a clouded sunlight that added to her resentment – they had better weather in Chicago – and took her to a long line of taxi cabs. This too was Middle Western, but twenty years too late. An unending line of museum pieces: Fords, Chevvies, Oldsmobiles, even a salmon-pink Cadillac that reminded her of the pictures Marcus had in his album; the kind of cars they made when Detroit started rolling again, just after the war, before she was a year old, battered now, their paint peeling, the shark's grin of chromium turned yellow, or nonexistent, but as American, she thought bitterly, as Mom's apple pie. Only the drivers were different, but there the difference was so marked it almost compensated for the rest. Miriam had never seen taxi drivers before who promised so much in so many different languages.

Craig let his glance move across them, taking his time. To her they all seemed alike, swarthy, noisy, not very clean, but Craig found one at least who was different, and walked toward him, a tubby and excitable man with an ancient Packard that smelled of nothing more terrible than coarse soap, recently used. Craig spoke to him in a language she didn't recognize, but which she presumed to be Turkish, and the taxi driver grinned and answered him in a speech that lasted until they drove away from the cab rank and were on the highway to the city.

From time to time Craig butted in for a word or two, and once they both exploded with laughter, then the driver gave up at last and concentrated on passing everything else on the road. As he did so, he twiddled with the radio, and station after station wailed out the music of the Middle East. For some reason this annoyed the driver, who twiddled even harder, but the radio was obstinate.

'So you speak Turkish too?' she said.

'No,' said Craig. 'That was Greek. There are thousands of Greeks in Istanbul.'

'You've – worked in Greece?' she asked.

'During the war,' he said. 'My war. You weren't even born then.'

'You're still fighting,' she said, and yawned. She couldn't help it. 'Where are you taking me?'

'This fellow knows a place,' he said, and she remembered the laughter, and willed herself not to blush. 'It's quiet and it's clean, and the food's good,' he said. 'I'll wake you when we get there.'

But in fact she woke long before, as they drove into the racket of the new suburbs, and the even worse racket of the old city: old cars, even older buses, horse-drawn carts, mules, and people, once even a small, bunchy herd of sheep that threaded their way through streets that grew narrower and narrower, past tall, shuttered houses, with now and again a glimpse of the dome and minaret of a

143

mosque, until at last they turned a corner, and in front of them was the Golden Horn, blue and gleaming, the ships bobbing on it like birds. She looked and cried out, 'My God, it's marvellous.'

'You should have brought your camera,' said Craig. The driver abandoned his war with the radio and turned to grin at her, then flung out a hand as if offering the blue water, the purple-hazed hills beyond, white houses embedded in them like pearls. He spoke again, and again Craig laughed.

'He says it was a Greek city first,' he said. 'And in many ways it still is.'

He settled back as the car just scraped through a narrow cobbled street, turned a corner, and stopped at last in a tiny square, one side of which was a long building of wood that seemed to have emerged at the whim of generations of owners. Parts of it seemed wholly isolated from others. There were three roofs and four entrances, and everywhere tiny, shuttered windows. It was painted a fading green, but the white of its balconies still dazzled. There was a charm about the place that she found hard to define. It certainly didn't lie in its design or proportions – only there was a rightness about it; it belonged there, opposite the tiny Orthodox church and alongside the great warehouse that looked like a Sultan's palace. Their driver picked up the canvas bag and led them through an entrance, past a sign that said, in Turkish and Latin script, Hotel Akropolis.

They were in a cool room then, low, dim, marble-tiled, with a battered desk and a fat woman behind it who could only have been the driver's sister. Craig signed the register, and handed over his passport. Nobody asked for Miriam's and the fact annoyed her even as it consoled. Then an aged crone appeared, and led them through a maze of corridors, and flung open a door with a flourish. Inside was a huge room with an enormous canopied bed, more marble flooring, and a vast wooden fan like the paddle of a steamer that stirred the sluggish air when the crone pressed the switch. Off the bedroom was a bathroom with a copper bath built on the same scale as the bed, and a huge copper shower suspended above it. The crone looked at it in wonder that people should waste so much time in being clean, then went back to the bedroom again, prodded the mattress, and grinned. Here at least was luxury that made sense, and she said so to Craig. It cost him a quarter to get rid of her.

Miriam watched him take off his coat. The gun harness was still there, but the gun was in the waistband of his trousers. He took it out, checked it, laid it on the bedside table. The time was four thirty, and she was dizzy with fatigue.

'You want to bathe first?' he asked. She nodded. 'Go ahead.'

'Are we sleeping together?' she asked.

He looked at the bed. 'Looks like it,' he said. 'Don't worry, Miss Loman. I'll control my bestial desires.'

She flinched at that and went into the bathroom. When she came back, she wore a towel tied round her like a Hawaiian *pareu*, covering her from shoulder to thigh.

'Very pretty,' he said.

'I've washed my dress.'

'Tomorrow I'll buy you a new one. Which side of the bed d'you want?' She got in on the left. The gun was close to her hand. 'I'll bet it isn't loaded,' she said.

'You'd win,' said Craig. 'Little girls shouldn't play with loaded guns. They go off.'

'Please,' she said. 'I'm not a child. Don't treat me like one. It's bad enough being here—'

'You're on your honeymoon,' he said. 'That's what I told them downstairs. You're nervous and shy, and you might try to run away. Don't try it, Miss Loman. Nobody speaks any English for miles around. They'd just bring you back and embarrass you.'

She began to cry then, and still crying, fell asleep.

When she woke it was daylight, and she was alone. She got up quickly, and the towel fell from her. She ran to the door – it was locked

– and then to the bathroom. Her dress was dry, and she put on bra, panties, and dress with clumsy haste, then prowled the room. There was no sign of the gun, no sign that Craig had ever been there. She had no memory of him in the bed. The thought should have been a comfort to her. She wondered what Ida would say if she knew how her Miriam had spent the night, and the thought made her smile, until she remembered Marcus, and the look on his face when Craig had taken her away. She loved Marcus as he loved her, unquestioningly, without reservation. A fat, middle-aged milliner had no business to possess such a capacity for love. It was a wonderful thing, no doubt, but one day it would destroy him.

She went out on to the tiny balcony and looked down. The Bosphorus was below her, the ships tied up to the stone quays, the racket of the port unending: stevedores, lorry drivers, even policemen milling about, and not one she could talk to, not one who could understand a word she said, even if she could escape from the hotel. She picked up her handbag and looked in the change purse. A five-dollar bill, three dollar bills, two quarters, and seven pennies. And Craig must be carrying thousands of dollars. Suddenly there was the sound of music, American music, below her. She leaned over the balcony and looked down. A small, dark man was washing the windows of the floor below. There was a transistor radio hooked to his ladder, and it was playing 'Stardust' very loud. It had to be loud to compete with the racket of the port, but the volume couldn't mar the clean drive of the trumpet. She began to feel better.

When he came back, his arms were filled with parcels. She lay on the bed, not sleeping, and he looked so like Hollywood's version of the wholesome American husband at Christmas time that she smiled.

'There should be a sound track playing "Jingle Bells",' she said.

'I bought you some clothes,' he said. She sat up then, angry.

'Did it ever occur to you I might like to choose my own?' she asked.

'Perhaps you'll like these, Miss Loman,' he said. 'It's possible.'

She opened the parcels, adored everything he'd bought her, and hated him even more.

'I'm hungry,' she said.

'Lunch is on its way up,' he said.

The feeling of frustration grew inside her. She had never known anything as hateful as this massive and very British competence.

Lunch was moussaka, grilled swordfish, salad and cheese, and a white wine she decided she detested, then drank three glasses of it. After it, she felt well and wide awake for the first time since she'd left the aircraft.

'You're looking well,' said Craig, and again the intuitive competence enraged her. She watched in silence as the crone poured Turkish coffee from a battered brass pot and left them.

'This food will probably make me ill,' she said. 'You know what we Americans are like – if the food's not flown in from home we go down with a bug.'

'Ah,' he said. 'I'm glad you reminded me. I bought you some pills for that.'

She slammed down her coffee cup.

'I hate you,' she said.

'That's obvious – but it doesn't matter, so long as we don't let it get in the way. You ready to go?'

'Now?'

'We haven't a lot of time,' he said. 'And Kutsk is five hundred miles away. Are you frightened?'

'Horribly,' she said. He nodded.

'Me too,' he said, and caught her look of surprise. 'No matter how often I do it. I'm always frightened. So are all the others – except the nuts, and they don't last very long. Being frightened's part of the game, Miss Loman.'

'This isn't my game,' she said.

'Poor little innocent bystander,' said Craig. 'Get your things together.'

The Greek taxi driver had found Craig a Mercedes, a battered 200S that had nothing to recommend it except its engine, but that was astonishing. He drove Craig to the outskirts of the city, and again the girl had glimpses of the other Istanbul, the five star dream world of the tourist – Haggia Sophia, the Blue Mosque, the Dolmabace Palace – that gave way too soon to the narrow caverns of streets, first shops, then houses, then the dusty wastelands that fence in all big cities: abandoned cars, billboards, the first ploughed field. The driver pulled up at last by a bus stop and made another speech. At the end of it, he shook hands with Craig, then got out.

'He hopes we'll be very happy,' said Craig.

'That's nice of him,' the girl said. 'He's not to know it's impossible, is he?'

When she looked back, the driver was waving to them, teeth flashing.

Turkey turned out to be mostly dry hills and plains, waiting for water. That, and terrible roads that the Merc took with more philosophy than she did. And mosques of course, mosques in every village and town, built of everything from mud to marble. There were almost as many mosques as sheep. The car ate up the miles to Ankara – this was Turkey's main highway, the one they kept repaired – and Craig drove quickly, yet with caution, saving his strength for what was to come. When darkness came the girl drowsed again, and woke to more street lights, and Istanbul was nearly two hundred miles away. Craig drove slowly now, following the directions the Greek had given him, and stopped in a wide avenue, lined with olive trees that whispered softly even in that still night. He led the drowsy girl to the doorway, rang the bell, and again there was the babble of Greek, another crone, another vast bed with cool, white sheets. Then supper came: olives, lamb kebab, rice and fruit, and a dark, acrid wine that Craig drank freely. The whisky stayed in his bag untouched. Then after supper came Turkish coffee, and the sound of the crone running a bath. She took the first bath without asking. This time there were bath salts, the talc he had bought her, and a dressing gown, a scarlet kimono he had chosen that did a lot for the plumpness of her body, made her taller, more elegant. She went back to the bedroom.

He was standing, half turned away from her, practising with the gun, drawing it, aiming, the muzzle a pointed, accusing finger, then putting it back in the holster, repeating the process over and over, then switching, the gun in the waistband of his pants, pulling it, aiming: and the whole thing so fast that the gun seemed to unfold in his hands into the hardness of death. He saw her, but didn't stop until he was satisfied, the sweat glistening on his face, pasting his shirt

151

to his body. The girl thought of boxing champions she had seen on television, the endless training sessions devoted to just such a skill in hurting the man who faced you.

'You work so hard at it,' she said.

'I'm still alive.'

He left her then, and this time took the gun with him to the bathroom.

He'd bought her a nightgown, yellow like her dress. It lay on the bed, and she picked it up, looked at it. Pretty. She pulled the cord of her kimono, felt the smooth silk slide from her, felt her naked body react to the coolness of the room. She was sleepy again, but sleep was a luxury and her world was poor. Her world was two hard hands and a terrifying speed with a lightweight Smith and Wesson .38. And beyond that the certainty of danger, probable pain, the possibility of death.

I'm twenty-three years old, she thought. It can't happen to me. It mustn't.

She turned, and the mirror on the wardrobe showed her a pretty, plump girl, her nude body in a showgirl's pose, holding a splash of yellow to bring out the honey gold of her skin. She jutted one hip and admired the result. In twenty years she would be fat – maybe in ten – but now she was, not beautiful maybe, but pretty. And desirable. Surely she was desirable? She put a hand to a breast that was firm and rounded – and cold. The cold was fear.

He came in from the bathroom wearing pyjamas, carrying his clothes. This time the gun went under his pillow. 'Who can hurt us tonight?' she asked.

'The Russians,' he said. 'My people. Yours.'

'Mine?'

'Not the CIA,' he said. 'They're not bad, but they're not up to this one. For this, your side will use Force Three.' He frowned, trying to explain it to her. 'Look, the Russians have the KGB. But for really nasty jobs – like this one – they use the Executive. That's blokes like me. And Force Three – that's me too, ten years younger, in a Brooks Brothers suit.'

'All to find Marcus's brother?'

'You know what he did,' said Craig.

She pulled the sheet more tightly around her.

'Betrayed the Revolution,' she said. 'They sent him to Volochanka. But he escaped, so they want him dead.'

'They have the easy job,' said Craig, and she shivered. 'Your people want him alive.'

'*Marcus* wants him alive.'

'Because he's his brother. The Americans want him alive because he can perform one miracle.'

'Only one?'

'It's a good one,' he said. 'He can turn sea water to rain water. Cheap. He can make the desert blossom. He's America's present to the underprivileged world.'

'And why do you want him alive?'

'So that I can stay alive too,' said Craig. 'If I've got him, everybody will be my chum.'

'With all that opposition – you think you can do it?'

'It's not much of a chance, but it's the only one I've got.'

He put the light off and got into bed. Before he could turn from her, her arms came round him, her body eased against his. He put up his hands and found that she was naked.

'Miss Loman,' he said, 'you're making a big mistake.' Her mouth found his, her hands tore at his pajama jacket, then she found herself pulled away from him. He was gentle about it, but his strength was too much for her.

'Please,' she said. 'Please, Craig.'

He got out of bed, switched on the light again, and looked down on her, her bare breasts tight with love, then he lit a cigarette and his hands were shaking.

'Miss Loman,' he said. 'What the hell are you playing at?'

'I don't love you,' she said. 'I never could love you. But I may die tomorrow. That scares me – it scares us both.' She wriggled out of the sheets, her body supple in youth, but the logic she offered was ageless. 'We need each other. Now,' she said. 'It's all there

154

is.' He turned away from her. 'Am I that hard to take?'

'No, Miss Loman, you're not,' he said. 'But my interest in women ended a year ago. They have a machine that does that. All very modern. It gives you electric shocks.'

'Oh, my God,' she said.

'Maybe I'm wasting my time staying alive, Miss Loman.'

'Who did it to you?'

'A man who hated me. In our business, we stir up a lot of hatred. I nearly died. They tell me I was crazy for a while. Then they patched me together – the surgeons and psycho experts – and sent me after the man who did it.'

'Did you kill him?'

'No,' he said. 'He had to live. But he wanted to die. Very much.' He came to her then, and he looked at her body and smiled. His hand reached out, smoothed the hair from her brow.

'I'm sorry, Miss Loman,' he said.

'Couldn't you just hold me?' she said. 'I'm so alone, Craig.'

He put the light off. She heard the rustle of cloth as he removed his pyjamas, then he lay on the bed beside her, took her in his arms, kissed her gently. Her hands moved across him, and her fingertips told her of what he had suffered, the knife wound, the two gun shots, the flogging. His body was marked for life, but the strength inside him had overcome everything that had been done, until the last, most appalling pain had left him alone, uncaring, with only one emotion left, the fear of death. Her hands moved down, over the hard belly. Her body rubbed soft and luscious against him.

'I'll make you,' she said. 'I'll make you want me.'

There was a compassion in her hands and lips that went beyond the ruttishness of fear, a gentle understanding that knew nothing of the game without rules he'd played for far too long. Even now, in the very offering of herself, this girl was on the side of friendship, of life.

His mind loved her for it, but his body would not respond. Could not. She touched him, and his flesh remembered the pain and only the pain, but he willed himself not to cry out, or move away. She was offering him compassion: the least he could do was accept it. Suddenly Craig decided that, whatever happened, Miriam Loman wouldn't be killed. Her compassion was too rare, too precious a commodity to be squandered before its time. And with that realization, the memory of the pain receded, and she became not just the embodiment of a virtue but a woman too, and Craig realized, as he needed her at last, that his frigidity had become a kind of necessary selfishness, a protection against the involvements women always demanded, this one not least, and yet how could one repay such compassion except with involvement? His hands grew strong on her, and she rolled back, then pushed up to meet him, brave in her passion.

'There, my darling, you see?' she said, then, 'Yes. Oh, please. Please.'

When they had done, they bathed together, then lay down cool on the rumpled sheets. She smiled at him then, a grin of triumph.

'You didn't believe it was possible, did you?' she said. 'And I made you.'

'You made me.'

'That's something isn't it? After what they did to you? You ought to say, Thank you, Miss Loman.'

'Thank you, Miss Loman.'

'That's a good boy.' She kissed his mouth. 'A *very* good boy. You can call me Miriam.' She stretched out, feeling the hardness of his leg against hers. She felt marvellous: relaxed, fulfilled, yet still engrossed in her body's responses to his. There was just one thing–

'I don't want you to think I do this sort of thing all that often,' she said.

'I don't.'

'You mean I wasn't much good?'

She made a joke of it, but the anxiety to please was there, would always be there.

'You were perfect,' he said. 'That's how I know you didn't do it often.'

'Just one man,' she said. 'One nice Jewish boy. I adored him. And he went to Israel.'

'Does Marcus know?'

'I hope not,' she said. 'I never told him. He'll never know about you either. You bastard. You drag me here, kidnap me, then let me rape you. And tomorrow you'll probably get me killed.'

'No,' said Craig. 'You won't die, and it wasn't rape – or kidnapping either.'

She said quickly, 'I feel great – but I'm still scared.'

He turned to her then, and his hands were gentle on her, coaxing yet slow, as she had been to him, till the girl cried out aloud, her arms came round him, taking him to her.

Chapter Eight

They drove through Kirikkale, then on to
Kayseri, climbing the foothills of the Taurus
Mountains. The road was bad now, the pave-
ment giving out for long stretches, but the
Mercedes took all it was given, and came
back for more. They passed hamlets of mud
and stone, tiny fields wherever there was
water, and where there was not – scrubland,
goats, and sheep. Gas stations were a rarity,
and whenever he passed one Craig filled up
the tank, paying in Turkish lire this time.

Once a police car followed them, then shot
past them, waving them down. The girl was
frightened, but Craig was unhurried, and
wound down his window as the two policemen came up to him, thin and hard and dark
as gypsies. One of them spoke a little French,
and asked them if they were lost. Craig said
they were not. They were going to Iskenderun to consider the possibility of making a
film there. The policeman was impressed,
and gabbled to the other man in Turkish,
then asked if Craig had ever met Brigitte
Bardot, and Craig said no, but he'd met a
man who had. The policeman asked if they
were American, and Craig said they were.

His partner then took a deep breath and said, 'Hey, Joe. Gimme some whisky and a broad.' Craig applauded then, and scowled at Miriam till she applauded too. The French-speaking policeman then explained that his partner had fought in Korea, Craig handed round Chesterfields and they were free to go.

They drove on sedately to the next bend, then Craig put his foot down. 'My God,' said the girl.

'Take it easy. They were bored and they wanted cigarettes. When trouble comes, it won't be wearing a uniform.'

It came at Volukari, eighty miles farther on. Craig had stopped yet again for gas and the girl had gone into the fly-festooned shack beyond it that said cafe. He sat and waited, looking at the town that seemed to be in training for its next famine. Tired houses, unpaved streets, people who owned nothing but time, but in time they were millionaires. The women, he supposed, were bored at home; it was a crowd of men and boys who watched his tank fill up: the big excitement of the day. And then they had another excitement: the peremptory blast of a horn, the squeal of tyres that longed for tarmac and met only dirt, then an E-type Jaguar went by, and the crowd exploded into comment. Four foreigners in one day. If things kept up at this rate they'd have to organize a festival. Miriam came back, and the crowd settled down to watch again, careful not to miss a single detail, the flick of her skirts, the glimpse of knee before the door closed. Craig's mind was elsewhere; he was thinking of the E-type. The man driving it was Andrew Royce, the girl beside him Joanna Benson.

'I've just seen two more film producers,' he said, 'and we're both after the same property.'

He had no doubt that Royce and Benson had seen him.

They drove on into the evening, through Iskenderun, on past a little beach where somebody optimistic had built a little white hotel, with beach umbrellas and fairy lights and a couple of discouraged palm trees like thin old ladies. It seemed like a good place to stop if you drove an E-type, but there was no sign of it. Instead they picked up an elderly Fiat truck that rattled along behind them, then dropped slowly back as they drove round the bay and came at last to Kutsk, a gaggle of fishermen's huts huddled round a mosque, with one larger building, just as dirty, just as decrepit as the others, coffeeshop, bar, and restaurant combined. With any luck, it would be the hotel, too.

'Welcome to the Kutsk Hilton,' said Craig.

He got out and stretched stiffly, near exhaustion, not daring to yield to it. The E-type could cover a hell of a lot of country,

161

even this country. He took the girl's arm and led her inside the coffeeshop.

She found herself in a world of men. In Turkey, she realized, a man's business was to drink coffee; a woman's was to make it. The silence that greeted her was absolute, and she moved closer to Craig. The room was long and narrow, with deal tables and chairs. One unshaded light bulb competed unsuccessfully with cigarette smoke and flies. The room smelled – had smelled for twenty years – of cigarette smoke, sweat, and coffee. It reeked of coffee. The proprietor, a chunky man who smelled like his property, came up and stood in front of them without enthusiasm. Around him his customers looked on, like men pleased with themselves at being in on something good. Craig tried him in Arabic, French, and Greek, with no reaction. In the end he resorted to pantomime, and the patron nodded his understanding and relaxed enough to jerk a thumb at a table. The villagers relaxed then; the show was over. Someone switched on a radio, and they began at once to shout over it as a woman brought plates of fish stew, bread, and water to Craig's table. The girl looked at it dubiously.

'Eat,' said Craig. 'It'll be good.'

It was, and Miriam discovered how hungry she was. Craig ate left-handed, and watched the door. When the stew was gone, the woman brought coffee, and with it an aging man who smelled of fish walked up to Craig and bowed, then began making noises with his mouth. At first the girl thought he was singing, then realized, incredulously, that he was speaking English, but English of a kind she had never heard before. Craig pulled over a chair and signed to the woman to bring more coffee. The aging man went on talking English with a combined Turkish and Australian accent. He had fought in Arabia in the First World War and been captured by Australian Cavalry. Was Craig an American, he asked, and when Craig said he was English he was delighted, or so Craig deduced. 'Good on you, cobber' were the words he used. He went on to make it clear that, what trouble Russia hadn't made, America had, and asked how he could serve Craig. A room? Of course. His son owned this appalling coffeehouse, but it had one room for Craig and his wife. A good room. Almost an English room.

He led them to it. It was behind the coffee room and the racket was appalling, but it was clean. Craig remembered where he was, and made a long speech in praise of the room. The aging man was delighted.

'You know your manners, sport. My oath you do,' he said, then bowed again. 'My name is Omar.'

'John Craig.'

Still remembering his manners, Craig made no move to introduce Miriam as his wife or anything else, and Omar, remembering his, didn't look at her.

'Sorry I wasn't around when you came in,' Omar said. 'I was sleeping.' He yawned. 'You come far?'

'Ankara,' said Craig, and Omar's eyes widened. Craig might have said the moon.

'You have business here?' he asked.

'Maybe,' said Craig. 'Perhaps we can talk tomorrow?'

'Too right,' said Omar, and turned to the door.

'D'you get many English here?' Craig asked.

The aging man giggled.

'Before today I hadn't set eyes on a Pommy for fifty years,' he said, and left them.

Craig locked the door. When he turned round she was removing her dress, but her eyes were angry.

'Why do I have to be British?' she said.

'You don't like us?'

Again the blush came. 'Oh you,' she said, then the anger came back. 'I love my country.'

Americans, he thought. With their passion for precision. Love is a pure word: colour it red, white, and blue. When would they get away from primary colours?

'Usually I'm quite fond of the old place, sometimes I adore it, sometimes I absolutely loathe it.' Was it possible to be as ambivalent as that to a fact as enormous as America?

'If you love it you want to help it,' he said. 'And you can help it best by letting Omar think you're British.'

'You're treating me like a child again.'

'No – an innocent American,' he said. 'I'm a wise European.'

'And decadent too?'

'You tell me,' said Craig.

'Henry James would have loved this one,' said Miriam.

'Who?'

She sighed, came up to him, put her arms round his neck and kissed him.

'Would a wise European help an innocent American take off her bra?'

They came in soundlessly, surely, the way they had been taught – the man at the window, the girl at the door. It was early morning, half-light, but that was light enough. The man carried a 9-millimetre Walther automatic, thirteen shot, a stopper. The girl had a .32 revolver, a neat little job with a cross-checked butt. Nobody ever stopped anything with a .32. The girl was a dead shot. They stood holding the bed in their crossfire, waiting for their eyes to adjust to the dark, picking out the masses of the shapes on the beds, ears strained for the faint sound of breathing in the most profound sleep of the night. Suddenly the light came on, and behind them a voice they knew and detested said, 'Pascoe would have been proud of you.'

Joanna Benson froze, Andrew Royce began to turn.

'No,' said Craig, and Benson stayed still. Miriam Loman sat up in the bed, frightened, bewildered, and pushed away the bolster she had lain against.

'Guns on the bed,' said Craig. The armed man and woman made no move to obey, and Craig, by the light switch, risked a quick look at Miriam. The terror was still there.

Omar's voice said, 'Your gun on the bed, Mr. Craig.'

He stood in the doorway; in his hands was a single barrelled shotgun. It was old, but serviceable, and it pointed straight at Miriam.

'I'll drop your sheila, Mr. Craig,' Omar said.

The Smith and Wesson landed at Miriam's feet, and Royce scooped it up, slipped it into his pocket and turned to Craig.

'Thanks, Omar,' he said. 'Come and join us, Craig.' He gestured with the Walther. 'Come on.'

Warily, ready for a blow, Craig moved forward. The shotgun still pointed at Miriam's breast.

'You lied to me, Omar,' he said. 'You disappoint me.'

'No,' Omar said. 'I told you that before today I hadn't seen a Pommy for fifty years. That was the truth, Mr. Craig.'

Royce stepped back out of Craig's line of vision, but the barrel of Joanna Benson's gun was aimed steadily at his heart.

'Why did you do it?' Miriam asked. 'I thought you liked us?'

'I do like you,' said Omar, and his voice was indignant, 'but I like money more.'

Royce struck then, using the edge of his hand with a careful economy of strength. Craig fell across the foot of the bed.

'You're right,' Royce said. 'Pascoe will be proud of us.'

He came back to consciousness in a stone shed that smelled of animals. He was lying on straw, and the straw stank. The shed was lit by an oil lamp hung high on the wall. His hands were tied behind him, and his neck ached vilely where Royce had hit him. His wrists, too, ached to the construction of the wire that was cutting into him, but he lay still, not moving, eyes closed, letting his mind and body regain strength.

Joanna Benson's voice said, 'I think he's conscious.'

The toe of a shoe crashed into his ribs, and he gasped with the pain. Pain he could see coming he could control, but pain from nowhere made the body's reaction inevitable.

Royce said, 'He's conscious.'

Hard hands grabbed him, propped him against the wall of the shed. His head lolled forward. He needed time to recruit his strength.

'We brought your girl, too,' said Joanna Benson, and his head came up then. Royce chuckled. Miriam sat in the straw a few feet from him, and before them Royce and Benson stood. Royce's gun wasn't showing, but Benson still held her .32. They looked relaxed, strong in the arrogant beauty of youth. The weight of Craig's years had never been so heavy.

'You're an innocent American,' Royce said. 'I'm a wise European.'

'And decadent too?' Joanna Benson asked.

'You tell me,' said Royce.

'Would a wise European help an innocent American to take her bra off?' Joanna Benson said. She even got the accent right. Miriam stood up, screaming.

'Stop it,' she yelled. 'Stop it. Stop it. *Stop it.*'

'Sit down, darling,' said Benson. 'You're not being dignified.'

'You have no right to do this,' Miriam sobbed. 'No *right.*'

'Tell me, Craig,' said Benson. 'Treat her like a child again.'

No, Craig thought. Not even a child. Any

168

kid over there could follow the logic of their situation.

'Sit down, Miriam,' he said wearily. 'Sit down and be quiet. She's got the gun.'

Miriam slid down into the straw, pressed her hands to her face. Benson looked at her. The look was that of one fighter appraising another before the bell went for the first round.

'You must do something very special, darling,' she said. 'I got absolutely nowhere.'

Royce said, 'I think we'd better get on with it,' and Benson shrugged.

'Loomis is very angry with you,' Royce said. 'He told us to kill you.'

'In certain circumstances,' said Benson, and Royce nodded agreement.

'In certain circumstances. Those circumstances are almost fulfilled.'

'But you can't,' said Miriam. 'He's on our side.'

'No, darling,' Benson said, 'he's on your side. *We*,' – the .32 flicked to Royce and herself – '*we* are on our side.'

Miriam's body tensed in the straw and Craig snarled at her, 'For God's sake sit still.'

Benson laughed, a husky, very feminine laugh.

'You really picked an innocent, Craig,' she said. 'I don't believe she's worked it out yet.'

Royce said to him, 'Perhaps you'd better

169

tell her. She'd take it better from you.'

Craig turned to her then, and for the first time Miriam could read emotion in his eyes, a vast and weary compassion.

'If they kill me,' Craig said, 'they won't leave any witnesses... I'm sorry.'

The girl swerved round, staring at him.

'I don't believe it,' she said. 'I simply don't believe it.'

'But you will,' Benson said. 'When it happens – you'll believe it all right. Won't she, Craig?'

He made no answer. Whether she was enjoying herself or simply softening him up, there was no need to help her. Royce took a quick step forward, his foot moved, finding the place he'd hit before. But this time Craig saw it coming. He made no sound.

'Answer the lady,' said Royce. Craig shrugged.

'She'll know nothing,' he said. 'She'll be dead. Like me. Like both of you, in all probability.'

'Loomis said you never gave up,' said Joanna Benson. 'Let's go on about your death.' She waited a moment. 'It's the best offer we can give you, you know ... death. Once you've told us where Kaplan is.'

'But you know where he is,' said Craig.

'Kutsk,' said Royce. 'That's all we've got. We reckon you have more.'

'Why should I?' Craig asked.

170

'Because you went to see Marcus Kaplan,' Joanna Benson said. 'Because she's here with you. There has to be more, Craig.'

Craig said, 'That's all I got.' Royce's shoe came back. 'I came here looking for you.'

The leather cracked again on his rib cage. Once more, and the ribs would break.

'Wait,' Benson said. 'We'll have time for all that.' She came closer to Craig. 'Look, darling,' she said, 'if this place was all you had, why did you bother coming? You knew we'd be ahead of you.'

'At Volukari you were behind me.'

'We were looking for you,' Royce said. 'We got a tip-off you were coming. You weren't all that hard to find.'

'You switched cars, didn't you? Followed us in a Fiat van?'

'Yes,' Benson said. 'Don't waste time, Craig. If all you knew was the town, why did you come?'

'To hijack him from you,' said Craig.

Royce drew back his foot again, but Benson spoke quickly, stopping him.

'It makes sense,' she said. 'You know what he's like – the middle-aged wonderboy.'

'But Loomis said–' Royce began.

'Loomis said somebody knew where Kaplan is, and somebody does.' She turned to Miriam. 'Right, Miss Loman?'

Craig said, 'You're completely wrong. She doesn't know a thing. I made her come here.'

'How?' Joanna Benson asked. 'By stealing her bra? Come on, darling. We know you're not that stupid.' She moved closer to Miriam. 'Force Three sent you, didn't they? They told you to let Craig pick you up. They told you to let him take you to Turkey. Help him get Kaplan out. Let him kill us, or the Russians if they were handy, and then let their boys take over.' Her dark eyes burned into Craig. 'You knew that all the time, didn't you, darling? But once you'd got Kaplan – you thought you could bargain.'

Miriam said, 'It isn't true. He did force me–'

'The innocent American,' Joanna Benson said.

'That was later. It just happened. I was scared. I–'

'No True Confessions,' said Benson. 'Just tell me where Kaplan is.'

'But I don't know. I honestly don't *know*.'

Benson said, 'Let me tell you about this place – and him.' She nodded at Royce. 'It's a barn. Part of a farm. The farmer and his family are away. There isn't another human being in five miles. You can scream pretty loud I should think, darling – you've got the build for it – but you can't scream five miles' worth. Now, our friend here. Where we trained, he did the interrogators' course. I gather he has a talent for it – and with talent there usually goes a certain amount of enthusiasm. He'll hurt you, darling. Later on you'll be amazed how very much he did hurt you. You wouldn't believe your body could stand so much pain. You'll hate him, of course, but you'll hate yourself more. Because you'll have told him, you see. All that pain will have been for nothing.' She looked down at Miriam. 'Now tell me. darling. Honestly, you'll do it anyway. Won't she, Craig?'

'Yes,' said Craig. 'She'll tell you.' He began to curse them both, a measured stream of the filthiest invective his mind remembered. Benson and Royce ignored him. Their whole concentration was on the girl.

'But I don't know,' Miriam said. 'Honestly I don't.'

Royce hit her, a hard right that left her sprawling in the straw. His hands went to his pockets and came out with a noose of wire. Quickly he twisted her hands behind her back, drew the noose around them till the girl screamed in pain as he twisted the wire to a spike in the wall.

'Shh, darling,' said Benson. 'He hasn't started yet.'

Royce sat on her legs, pulled the golden zipper of the dress, let it split open down her body. His hands moved again, and Craig turned away, tasting the horror of it, knowing what was to come. Suddenly Miriam screamed again, but not as she had screamed before. A blow hurts and you yell, but the pain is not so strong, and diminishes all the time: but this, this is appalling, degrading, unbearable, and its rhythm intensifies, this terrible, scalding thing he's doing: it never stops, it goes on, gets worse. Her screams ceased to be human, became an animal bellow of agony, continuing even after he'd stopped, he'd hurt her so much, so that in the end he had to strike her across the face, a savage left and right to bring her back to the awareness of the room, the man's weight on her legs, the woman looking down at her. The screams choked to sobs: the terror stayed in her eyes.

'Tell us where Kaplan is, Miss Loman,' Benson said.

'Please,' Miriam begged, 'please believe me. I don't know.' The man's hand moved and she screamed out, 'I want to tell you. Honestly I do. But I just don't know.'

Then the hand moved, the noises began again; the pain grew worse and worse, settled at a high peak of unbearable intensity, then again the blows on her face brought her back to reality.

'Three minutes,' said Miss Benson. 'He's only done it for three minutes... We've got all day, Miss Loman. How long have you got?'

'Don't know,' Miriam said, over and over. 'Don't know... Please.'

Craig said, 'Can I suggest something?' Benson nodded. 'Give me ten minutes with her. Alone... She'll tell you.'

'Royce is the expert,' Benson said.

'I don't need to hurt her,' said Craig.

'What then?'

'Talk to her.' The disbelief in her face was clear. 'What does it matter what I do, if I give you what you want? Ten minutes,' he went on. 'Suppose I fail. You said yourself – you've got all day.'

'Why bother, Craig?'

'I don't want her to be hurt any more.'

'You'll recall that once she tells us you'll die?'

'I recall that very well. I still don't want her to be hurt.'

Again the dark eyes looked into his. She examined him as if he were a member of an alien species; one she'd been briefed on.

'Ten minutes,' she said.

'And my hands free?'

Royce wanted to protest at that, but she moved behind Craig and her hands found the slip-knot, eased him free. The release was agony: the renewed insulation of blood so painful he had to exert all his strength not to yell. He looked at Royce.

'You did this,' he said.

'My pleasure,' said Royce, and got up from Miriam, looked down at Craig, eager for the word that could unleash the power to hurt. Craig looked at him empty-eyed.

'I don't like this,' Royce said. 'It's better to use the girl. With his hands free–'

'If he tries anything I'll kill him,' said Benson. 'He knows that.'

'I don't trust him,' Royce said.

'You like hurting people,' said Benson. 'Miss Loman just warmed you up. But we didn't come here to get you your kicks, Andrew.'

'We came here for Kaplan,' Royce said. 'There's only one way to get him.'

Benson looked down at the gun in her hand. It pointed between Craig and Royce, an impersonal menace.

'You can have ten minutes' rest,' she said. 'You go first.' Royce hesitated for a moment, then left. Benson looked down at Craig.

'There's a bucket and towel over there,' she said. 'Clean her up if you want to, darling. Andrew can always do it again.'

She left then, and Craig unhooked the wire round Miriam's wrists, soaked the towel in water, placed it on her. Even the touch of the towel made her cry out. He held it against her, and gradually the agony on her face faded.

'Oh, my God, that's good,' she whispered. Then the fear came back. 'But he'll do it again, won't he?' She began to cry, dry, racking sobs, and he took her in his arms, drew the dress around her.

'You really don't know where Kaplan is?'

She shook her head. 'If I did – I'd try to hold out against him. But I don't think I could. Not much longer. As it is – I guess it's all for nothing. What he did to me.'

'The postcard,' Craig said. 'Marcus didn't lose it, did he? He left it with you. What was on the postcard? Can you remember?'

'What's the use, John?' she said. 'I don't know where he is.'

He held her more tightly.

'Ten minutes isn't long,' he said. 'Just answer my questions.'

'It had a picture on it,' she said. 'A flock of sheep and a shepherd leading them.'

'What sort of shepherd?'

'Just an old man with a walking-stick.'

'Traditional sort of clothes?' She shook her head. 'What was the message?'

'He'd written it in Hebrew. It meant something like– This is a lovely place. The old man reminds me of old Rabbi Eleazar. Do you remember how he used to read the psalms to us? He was a good shepherd to us, wasn't he? I miss him very much, and you too, Marcus. Be happy. Aaron.' That was all.'

'Nothing else?' said Craig. 'You're sure?'

'Just the postmark, Kutsk. Marcus hired a private detective from Istanbul to come down. Nobody had ever even heard of him. But he must have been here, mustn't he?'

'You're sure there was nothing else?' She

was silent for a moment, examining the postcard in her mind.

'Just the date,' she said. 'That was funny too. He'd written it the Jewish way.'

'How is that?'

'We're in the year 5725. Aaron wrote 2.23.5725. Some lousy postal service.'

'Why?' asked Craig.

'Two must be February,' she said. 'The postmark on the card was April. Marcus got it in May.'

Craig said, 'When were you supposed to tell me all this?' He felt her body stiffen, and went on. 'You were, weren't you? Force Three set you up for me, didn't they? Just as Benson said.'

She nodded. 'They told me what to tell you – but when you made me come with you they said that was all right too. I phoned them, you know. When I went to the john.'

'Of course you did,' said Craig. 'Sometimes I thought you were never going to ask.'

'But when did you know?'

'Right from the start,' he said. 'It was all too easy. A girl in a fur coat – and almost out of it–'

'I hated that,' said Miriam,

'It's not a thing you forget,' said Craig. 'I was supposed to follow it up. Tell Loomis. Force Three knew he'd send somebody. It turned out to be me instead.'

'But you knew it was a trap.'

'There were nothing but traps,' Craig said. 'Yours was the prettiest. And it got me nearer Kaplan.' He looked at his watch. 'What did they tell you to tell me?'

'About the postcard,' she said. 'It seemed so stupid.'

'Not stupid at all,' said Craig. 'I'm surprised Marcus didn't see it.'

'See what?'

'Where his brother is.'

Cautious not to hurt her, he zipped up her dress. When Benson and Royce came back, they were sitting apart. This time, both the man and the woman carried guns.

Benson said, 'I hope you've got good news, darling.'

'Me, too,' said Craig. 'But at least I can tell you where he's been.'

'Get on with it, then,' said Royce.

'Marcus Kaplan got a postcard. There was a picture of a shepherd on it, leading his flock. The message was signed Aaron – his brother. The text had a reference to a rabbi they'd both known as children – that proved it came from Aaron. The rabbi had taught them the psalms. The whole thing was written in Hebrew – even the date: 2.23.5725.'

'So?' said Royce.

'2.23,' said Craig. 'It could be February twenty-third – except the card was postmarked April. On the other hand, if we remember the shepherd on the front of the

179

card, it could be the Twenty-third Psalm – second verse.'

'Go on,' said Benson.

'Do you happen to know what that is?'

'"He maketh me to lie down in green pastures; he leadeth me beside the still waters,"' Benson said, and added: 'I once had to write it all out ten times. So *useful*, being taught by nuns.'

'Then there was the date – 5725,' said Craig.

'That's a distance in yards, do you think?'

'No,' said Craig. 'Kaplan's a Russian. My guess is it means metres.'

'Green fields and a lake,' said Benson. 'About six thousand metres from here. Which direction?'

'You'll need a map,' Craig said. 'That's all she knows. She didn't even realize she knew that – till I got it out of her.'

'Maestro,' said Benson, and bowed. Royce raised his automatic.

'What a fool you are, maestro,' he said. 'You're going to die.'

'Well, actually, darling, not quite yet,' said Benson. 'We do have to be sure he's telling the truth.' She turned to Miss Loman. 'And that she told him the truth.'

'Do we leave them here?'

'They'll be safe for a little while,' Benson said. 'Get the car.'

'What about tying them up?'

'I'll do that,' Benson said. 'Give me the wire.' He handed it to her. 'On your tummies, darlings,' said Benson.

Royce watched as she drew the wire over Miriam's hands, heard the sharp gasp of pain, then went outside. Minutes later he came back, holding a large-scale map of the area. Craig and Miriam lay face down, wrists bound behind them, feet tied to staples in the wall. He grinned. 'Not even love could find a way,' he said.

'You've hardly made it worthwhile to try,' said Benson. 'Any luck?'

'Three possibles,' Royce said. 'It shouldn't take long.'

Benson crouched down by Craig. 'We'll do the whole thing in a couple of hours,' she said. 'Then we'll kill you, Craig. Sorry and all that, darling – but: you know what Loomis is like.' She got up then, and left them.

Miriam lay in the straw, biting her lip to stop herself from crying out. The pressure of her body was bringing back the pain. Beside her she could hear the movements of Craig's body as he fought against the wire that held him. The fool, she thought. The poor, brilliant, stupid fool. To stop me being tortured he gets himself killed, and now he's trying to burst his bonds like a comic strip hero. The movement of his hands must be agony, she thought. Even lying still was almost more than she could bear.

181

'Save it, John,' she said. 'We're going to die. Accept it.'

The writhing movements went on beside her.

'Look,' she said. 'You did it to stop me being hurt any more. All right. I couldn't take any more. I wanted to die. I really did. All right. I got what I wanted. I don't blame you for it. Only please will you stop fighting? It's just no use.'

The writhing stopped at last, and then he was bending over her, untwisting the wire at her ankles and wrists. She sat up cautiously, and he rubbed her wrists and ankles, chafing back the circulation.

'I don't believe it,' she said. 'It isn't possible.'

'No,' he said. 'It's impossible. Unless the girl who tied you up did it wrong.'

'You mean that man-eating debutante made a mistake?' Miriam asked. 'Oh, I like that very much. I love it.'

'No,' said Craig. 'Benson doesn't make mistakes. She meant it.'

'But why?'

'We'll find out later. She also meant it when she said we had just two hours to get out of here. Otherwise Royce will kill us.'

'She didn't say that.'

'She meant it. She handled Royce as well as anyone could handle him, but there are limits with his kind. Believe me, I know.'

He looked round the shed as he talked. The door was four great slabs of wood, hard and old, and bolted on the outside. The windows were too tiny even for Miriam to squeeze through. Patiently, he sought the straw for some kind of tool, but there was nothing. He went to the door again, tested its heavy strength. It could have stood up against a charging bull.

'She was only teasing us,' said Miriam. 'Making it worse.'

'There's a way,' said Craig. 'There has to be.'

He grubbed in the straw again and found a couple of horse blankets, heavy, ancient things that stank to heaven. Quickly he began to pile the straw up round the door, working with care, clearing the rest of the dirt floor, then threw a blanket to her, took one himself, and moved the bucket of water back to the window.

'Get over here,' he said.

She obeyed him, and he lifted the oil lamp from its hook, hefted it in his hand, then moved back to join her. 'Benson doesn't make mistakes,' he said. 'But Royce does. He left the lamp burning – and it's daylight.' He soaked the blankets with the water, then flicked his wrist. The lamp spun through the air, then burst like a bomb against the door. She had never believed that a fire could take place so quickly. There was a bang, as the lamp burst, and the blazing oil streamed down into the straw, tongues of flame reared up like waves, searing the side of the door, and the blast of heat made her throw up her hands to cover her face. Even pressed against the farthest wall, the temperature was almost unbearable. Pieces of burning straw spiralled up in the warm air, then drifted down on them. Craig pushed closer to the window as the room filled with stifling smoke. She stood there, whimpering softly, convinced that he'd gone crazy, that they'd burn to death.

Streaming-eyed, coughing, he watched the fire take hold of the door, reduce its weathered hardness to flame. At last, before the smoke made him unconscious, he went to the door, hands wrapped in the towel, holding the blanket in front of him like a shield, but even so the heat seared him through the heavy cloth. He drew up his knee, then kicked flat-footed at the burning door, aiming for the bolt, using every ounce of the karate skill. The flames bit into his leg, and he drew back his foot and kicked again, feeling the door yield slightly but not enough. Another kick was needed, delivering it a task almost beyond his powers. Sobbing, he went closer, bent his knee, kicked, and the bolt gave, the door swung open. He turned to Miriam.

'Put the blanket round yourself,' he yelled. 'Come on.'

But she stared at the flames and stayed, motionless. Her nerve had gone. Craig went back to her, wrapped one blanket round her, swathed the other over them both. When she realized what he was going to do she struggled, till he swore at her, threatening, and she was still. He took a last gasp of air at the window, then charged at the half-open door. Again flame leaped round him, then his shoulder hit the door, it opened wider, and he was through, running into the coolness of the morning, stopping at last, releasing her from the blanket as if she were a parcel.

'Gift-wrapped,' he said. 'That's nice.' He slapped at his trousers, charred from the flames, then sat down wearily, pulled up the trouser-legs, looked for the mark of the flames. Scorched, no more. He'd been lucky.

'I thought we hadn't a chance,' she said.

'We had the chance Benson gave us.' He looked at his watch. 'There's an hour and three quarters before they get back. We'd better use them.'

He turned and looked back. The fire was dying now, the straw spent, only the wood still smouldering. Behind their prison was a derelict farmhouse and a corrugated-iron shed. He got up and went towards the shed. Somehow Miriam got to her feet and staggered after him.

Inside the shed was the Fiat van. He went over it carefully, wary of booby traps. There were none. He opened the door, got into the van. The keys were in the lock. He drove it out, and Miriam got in beside him, picked up something lying at her feet, something heavy and metallic, wrapped in cloth. She handed it to Craig, and he uncovered his Smith and Wesson .38. He broke it, examined the magazine. It was loaded, but even so he took out each cartridge, checking that the shell was there intact, before he snapped it together, stuck it into his waistband. He turned to her and smiled.

'Nice, kind Miss Benson. Let's go and see Omar and give him a big surprise,' he said.

She shook her head.

'Look, darling,' he said. 'He likes money. remember? I bet he's liking mine right this minute.'

Miriam said, 'He's got a lot coming all right. But we can't give it to him. Not yet, anyway.'

'Why the hell not?' asked Craig. 'I've got to get you out of here, and that'll take money.'

'There was something else on the card. Something I didn't tell you. The picture.'

'An old shepherd with a flock of sheep.'

'It was sunset, John, and he was walking toward it.'

'So the place is west of Kutsk,' said Craig.

'That's right. And there's a chance they'll leave it till the last. We could still be there first.'

'Look,' he said, 'you're scared. You know you are. You've been knocked stupid, tortured, hauled through a fire. A very efficient sadist wants to kill you. If we stay here, he probably will – when he's finished playing.'

'I know it,' she said, 'but we've got to do this. It's what we came for.'

Craig's shoulders began to shake, weird sounds came from his throat. He was laughing.

'You innocent Americans,' he said. 'When will I ever understand you?'

A jolting track led from the farm to the road, and from there they moved on to Kutsk. There was no way of skirting the place, and Craig drove through it fast, hoping that if Omar saw them he would think they were Benson and Royce. The west road was smooth and easy till they reached a crossroads, and there Craig stopped. There were three roads to choose from. Two of them were at least metalled; the third was a pot-holed disaster. The girl chose it instinctively.

'That old shepherd looked as if he'd never even seen a highway,' she said.

Gingerly he eased the van on to its pock-marked surface, and they bounced along for a couple of miles in second gear. At last they rounded a curve, and before them they could see a sheet of water, rolling green hills, dotted with the puff-ball shapes of sheep. Craig drew to a halt and the girl rolled down the window, absorbing the scene.

'I think so, John,' she said. 'I think this is it.'

He moved on again, hurrying now, feeling the holes in the road menace his axle, till at last they reached the lake shore and a clump of olive trees. A mile beyond them was a hut, and from its chimney soft feathers of smoke drifted up in the still air.

Craig drove past the trees, then backed the van in behind them. If anything, the ground seemed easier than the road. He got out, walked back to the road, and stared intently. The van was perfectly hidden. As the girl climbed stiffly out of the cab, he went back into cover, opened his coat and drew the gun, replaced it, drew it again, over and over, till hand and fingers felt right and the gun's movement was smooth, inevitable. Next, the terrain. The hills were small, un-dulating, deficient in cover, but a man could hide there if he had to. And if a man were hidden there, and had a rifle, he could pick the two of them off with no trouble at all. On the other hand, it was early yet, even for a shepherd, and there was smoke coming from the cottage. He looked at the ground that separated them from it, working out a line of approach. When he'd got it he said:

'We can get there – but it won't be easy. If he's out there on the hill, he can kill us as soon as we're in range. Maybe I'd better go in first by myself.'

'No,' she said. 'This is what I came for, too.'

'You always do what Force Three tells you?'

'I do what Marcus asks me,' she said.

'All right,' said Craig. 'But take your time. Do exactly what I do – and nothing else. Understand?'

She nodded and he moved at a running crouch to the shelter of some bushes, then began a slow and agonizing crawl toward the cottage. Again the sleeping pain awoke inside her, but she gritted her teeth and crept on after him. Despite the blows he had taken, the exhaustion, the frantic escape from the shed, he moved easily, deftly, with the tiniest whisper of sound. When at last her strength gave out, he led her to the shelter of a boulder and made her lie behind it, flat on her back, legs and arms outstretched, then did the same himself. No recrimination, no argument, only an acceptance of physical limitations, but those limitations were pushed as far as they could go.

After five minutes her legs had ceased to tremble, and he made her go on again, till at last they reached the end of grass, bush, and stone, and found themselves among rows of vines. Beyond the vines was a neat kitchen garden, with orderly lines of melons, pumpkins, and tomatoes, and beyond that, the blank wall of the cottage. Craig very cautiously rose to his feet, and motioned her to absolute silence. A dog lay sleeping under a vine. Carefully, a step at a time, Craig moved toward it. As he moved, she watched his hands. They were both held out straight, the little fingers rigid.

The dog awoke to complete alertness and changed at once from a cuddly chum to something very like a wolf, teeth bared, mouth opened to snarl, as Craig flung himself forward, taking his weight on his left hand, the right hand thudding into its neck like an axe blade. The noise of breaking bone was the only sound she heard, and she knew at once that the dog was dead. His body pivoted on his left hand, and when he came up he was holding the gun. He moved off at once, not looking back, and she saw for the first time the Craig who had existed before he was tortured, a man who reminded her very much of Royce. Poor Marcus, she thought. Poor Miriam. What chance do we have?

She followed him round the blank wall of the cottage, waited at his signal as he moved round the corner, peered through a window, ducked down, and moved to the door. He never looked back at her, offered her comfort. He was an automaton now, programmed and set in motion, and it would be stupid on her part to regret it. She had done the programming. He reached the door, and contemplated its problem. It was flimsy enough, and its simple latch was rusted. He breathed deeply and evenly, then his foot came back once more, his body exploded into activity. The sole of his foot crashed against the latch, then his shoulder hit the opening door, he was inside the cottage in a dive that took him to the hard earth floor, looking up over the sights of the Smith and Wesson at a man trying to lift a rifle mounted on pegs in the wall.

'Shalom,' said Craig, and the man was still. Craig got up and moved to him, his left hand moved over the other's body, came away with a knife. He stepped back, the left hand flicked, and the knife spun away, stuck high in the wall. The man's eyes ignored everything but the gun.

'Miriam,' Craig shouted, and the girl came running, then stared at the man who faced her. He was taller than Marcus, and that was right. Thinner too, bone-thin, but then Marcus had said that Aaron favoured his father's side of the family, who were beanpoles. It was Marcus and his mother who'd had weight problems. The face was okay too, in a way. In it there were echoes of things she knew and loved in Marcus: the boldness of a splendidly Semitic nose, a sensitivity about the mouth, a chin she had always wished were a little more determined, especially when Marcus tried to persuade Ida it would be nice to have another cocktail before dinner. He was a Kaplan. She was sure of it; and yet he couldn't be. Aaron was supposed to be fifty-three years old; five years younger than Marcus. The man in front of her looked seventy at least. A tough seventy: the stringy body looked durable enough – but the deeply etched lines on his face, the wrinkled, work-worn hands – seemed to belong to Marcus's father, not his brother. 'Well?' said Craig.

'He looks right,' Miriam said. 'But he's too old.'

'Should he speak English?' Craig asked. She nodded.

'How old are you?' asked Craig.

The man stayed silent.

'Try him in Hebrew,' Craig said.

She spoke to him, first in Hebrew, then in Yiddish. The old man gave no sign of comprehension.

Craig waited, immobile, till she'd finished, then moved, suddenly, appallingly, so that the girl cried out. One stride took him to the old man, then the gun barrel swung, smashed into his neck, slapping him to the floor, and Craig's voice bellowed orders in a language she did not understand. At once, agonizedly, the old man scrambled to his feet, lurched to the wall, and put his hands against it in the classic pose of the prisoner waiting to be searched.

'We'll take him,' said Craig. He walked to the wall of the cottage, tucked the revolver in the waistband of his trousers and took down the rifle, slung it over his shoulder, then again orders streamed from him in that language she did not know, yet which seemed familiar. The man moved forward at once, and out of the cottage, Craig behind him. There was a weariness in the old man's movements, an acceptance of ultimate defeat that sickened the girl. No human being deserved to be so crushed by another.

Outside, Craig looked at his watch then walked the old man and the girl ahead of him, up into the hills, in a line parallel to the path. They found a dip in the hills near the olive trees, and he pushed them into its cover, then settled down to wait. The old man gave no least sign of resistance.

His whole being was concentrated on Craig's hands, watching them test the rifle, examining its sights and magazine with care, before Craig lay sprawled on the ground, eyes on the road, sights set at a hundred metres. Again orders streamed from him, and the old man bowed his head in submission.

They waited thirty-five minutes before they heard the engine, then the Jaguar streamed effortlessly round the bend in the road, the engine whispering its contempt at the speed it was held to. The girl was driving. Royce sat beside her, looking angry.

Craig waited till the car came past them, then the rifle came up, his finger squeezed on the trigger. The rear off-side tyre blew like an echo of the shot, and the girl fought the car to a standstill. As she did so, Royce was already moving, gauging his leap from the car, rolling out of it to the roadside before it had stopped.

'Good boy,' said Craig, and fired again. Royce went down as if his legs had been swept from under him. Benson stopped the car and left it, using it for cover as she too made for the protection of the road. Craig fired a third time, into the gas tank, and the car exploded in a roaring whoosh of flame that sent Royce scuttling like a wounded snake from the shelter of the ditch. Craig got to his feet then, and led them down to the Fiat, ordered the old man into the back of the van and got in after him, then handed the keys to Miriam.

'You drive,' he said. 'Back toward the village. Stop when I tell you.'

They found a place a mile out of Kutsk – a track that led to a deserted quarry. Craig told her to stop, and she got out. The rifle still in his hands, he ordered the old man out, then followed. The hard words of that elusive language were still in her ears when he switched to English.

'This woman does not speak Russian,' he said.

Russian, thought Miriam. Of course.

'We will talk English. First, your name.'

'Imares,' said the man. 'Mohammed Imares.'

'Profession?'

'Shepherd ... I used to be a business man, but I made a little money, you understand ... I thought it was best to get away from the wickedness of life in Istanbul.'

'Of course,' said Craig. 'Your age?'

'Sixty. Perhaps I should explain that I have been very ill. I know I look older.'

'You talk too much,' said Craig. The man was instantly silent.

Craig transferred the rifle to his left hand then, almost casually, knocked the man down with a back-handed blow. He fell, heavily, but scrambled at once to his feet as Craig yelled at him in Russian. Miriam ran between them.

'Stop it,' she said. 'For God's sake, stop it.'

'Get out of the way,' said Craig. 'There isn't time for all that.'

'No,' she said.

His hand moved again, pushing her to one side, and he moved up to Imares, who stood swaying on his feet.

'I'm in a hurry,' said Craig. 'Don't waste my time.'

'I told you the truth,' said Imares.

'I thought Volochanka had better teachers,' said Craig.

Imares's face seemed to disintegrate. Sud-

195

denly and silently, he began to cry.

'Kaplan,' said Craig. 'Tell me your full name.'

'Aaron Israel Kaplan.'

'Age?'

'Fifty-three.'

'Profession?'

'Agronomist.' Kaplan sobbed out the word, and covered his face with his hands. Craig let him weep for a moment, then turned to the girl.

'You see,' he said. 'There was only one way to handle it. It didn't take long.'

'But how could you be so sure?' she asked.

'You spotted him straight off,' Craig said, 'apart from his age. And you've never seen anybody who's been in Siberia. I have. If they age only twenty years – they're lucky. So I tried him with Russian. Talked like a KGB executive–'

'And acted like one.'

'No,' said Craig. 'For a KGB executive I treated him soft. But he's broken already. And scared out of his mind. Two blows and a few Russian curses and I had him back in Siberia. After that, he couldn't help telling the truth.'

'What happens now?' she asked.

'I'm going to see Omar. Get my money back.'

'And go back to the States?'

'Eventually,' said Craig. 'First of all I want

to get away from Benson and Royce. I bet they don't love us at all.'

'You didn't kill them,' she said. 'You could have.'

'Disappointed?' he asked.

'No. Surprised.'

'I haven't finished with them yet,' said Craig. 'It isn't their time to die.'

They drove back to the road, and on toward Kutsk. When they reached the outskirts of the village Craig made her stop and, climbed a nearby hill, stared down into the village. There were only a handful of boats bobbing in the harbour; the quayside was deserted, apart from three old men mending nets. It was a good time to call on Omar.

Chapter Nine

Miriam drove the Fiat up to the coffee shop door. Inside the van Kaplan lay trussed like an oven-ready bird with handkerchiefs and ties. Craig had done it himself; the knots would hold. As the van stopped, Craig stepped out soundlessly, moved from the morning heat to the coolness inside. In the gloom he could discern one man sitting at a table, his head on his arms. An old man, having a good rest, conscious of a night's work well done. Soundlessly Craig moved up to him, his hand moved, the Smith and Wesson appeared. On Omar's table was an empty cup of coffee and a glass of water half-full. Craig picked up the water glass, emptied it over the sleeping man, and Omar shot up at once, shocked into awareness. The gun was the first thing he saw.

'How are you, digger?' said Craig.

Omar stared into the gun's barrel.

'Looks like I made a mistake,' he said.

'Looks like it.'

'The other girl – that tall sheila – and that young bloke–'

'They had an accident,' said Craig, and Omar sighed. 'Come to that, sport, you might have one too.'

'You don't have to get violent,' Omar said.

'Maybe I do,' said Craig. 'They were going to kill me, Omar. I don't like that. And you had a gun on my girl. You took my money and my luggage. I think you deserve an accident.'

'I'll give you your money back – and your luggage.'

'Of course,' said Craig.

'Look, mister,' Omar said, speaking more loudly. 'I know I done you no good, but–'

'Omar,' Craig interrupted, 'your family are all asleep, aren't they? And you're trying to wake them. But ask yourself one question first: Is it wise?'

'I don't understand,' said Omar.

'Then put it this way,' said Craig. 'If anybody else comes in, I'll blow your head off.'

Omar looked again into the Smith and Wesson's barrel.

'Do you believe me?'

'Yes,' said Omar. 'Jesus, yes.'

'Let's take care of your family,' said Craig.

Omar's son and his wife snored happily on top of a bed. Craig locked them in their room. Two old women snored happily in the kitchen. He locked them in too. In the guest bedroom he picked up the valise, his and Miriam's clothes. That left the money. Back in the coffeeshop, Omar disgorged it, reluctantly, from his person. It smelled a little more than it had done, but it was all there.

'You see?' Omar said. 'You got it all back. You don't have to shoot me, mister.'

'Maybe,' said Craig. 'How many boats have you got?'

'Three,' said Omar, then stopped, angry. 'I'm not all that rich, mister.'

'I don't want your money,' said Craig. 'I'm not even going to touch the money you got from the other two for helping them. I'm going to be nice to you, Omar.'

The old man looked wary.

'You take me for a cruise and I'll let you live. Isn't that nice of me?'

'Where d'you want to go, mister?'

'Cyprus,' said Craig. 'Now.' He raised the gun, tapped the old man's forehead with the barrel. 'Think about it,' he said. The old man sighed.

'You're the boss, mister,' he said.

'Remember that,' said Craig.

Before they left he drained the gas tank of the Fiat, tore out its wires, unscrewed its steering wheel. Royce and Benson needed the exercise, he thought, and Craig needed time. They walked down to the quay then, and Craig's luck held. The three old men had finished mending their nets. The place was deserted. They walked in pairs, Omar and Kaplan leading. Kaplan, still groggy from the beating and tying up, seemed the older of the two. Behind them Craig and Miriam, he with a hand in his coat pocket, she limping along, carrying the rifle wrapped in sacking.

Two of Omar's boats were out on charter, fishing, but the third, the pride of his fleet, lay tied up at the quayside. It was a big and beamy craft with a diesel engine and a lateen sail, very like the *caiques* Craig remembered from twenty years ago. He helped Omar cast off and made him go out under sail, moving easily before a following wind until they were out of the harbour. Only then would he let him fire the engine, and then they moved off at a steady, pop-popping six knots, watching the land diminish behind them from a toy village to a picture postcard to a grey smudge against the intense blue of the sea. At last, even the smudge disappeared, and Craig lay back, content. Omar heard the sigh, and risked speech.

'It's not good for a Turk in Cyprus, mister,' he said.

'It's not good for a Turk in Kutsk. Not when he robs me and nearly gets me killed,' said Craig.

He turned to Miriam and Kaplan, motioned them to the prow of the boat. From there Omar was clearly visible, but he couldn't hear them.

'Why Cyprus?' Miriam asked.

Craig said, 'I know a man there who'll help me.'

'All we have to do is find Force Three,' said Miriam.

'And how do you propose to do that?'

'They told me how.'

He saw the obstinate set of her mouth, and smiled.

'And you promised you wouldn't tell, is that it? All right. I don't want to know. To tell you the truth, I don't want to go near them.'

'But they'll help you,' she said.

'No,' said Craig. 'They'll help you, love. They'll give me back to a man called Loomis.'

'The one Royce said had condemned you to death?'

'That's right,' said Craig. 'But he can't, now that I've got him.' He looked at Kaplan appraisingly.

'You'd be amazed how popular you are,' he said. 'Everybody wants you – and I've got you.'

'That's not strictly true,' Miriam said. '*We've* got him.'

'You forget so easily,' said Craig. 'Don't you remember when you told Royce and Benson we were all on the same side?'

'But you wouldn't hand him back to the Russians?'

'He's up for auction,' said Craig. 'Let's see what I'm bid.'

'But you've got no right to do this.'

Craig said, 'Force Three told you to use

me. Right?' She nodded. 'And that's exactly what you did. But there's something you don't realize. When you use somebody – you get what that person has to offer, and nothing else. I can only do this my way, love. If I did it your way, I'd lose.'

'You used me too,' said the girl.

'We used each other. It was the only good thing in the whole business.'

'And now it's over?'

Craig shrugged. 'We can't make decisions any more. We're lumbered.' He nodded at Kaplan. 'With him. The solid-gold leg iron.'

Kaplan felt Craig's eyes on him and looked away. Craig spoke in Russian again, and he nodded.

'I've told him you're going to interrogate him,' said Craig. 'Come here.'

He led her to the side of the boat, away from Kaplan. Utterly weary, she went with him.

'Don't try to explain who you are,' he said. 'Just ask questions. He's the one who has to answer. Talk in English – and if you think he's lying, switch languages on him. Try him in Hebrew – or Yiddish. If you still think he's lying, send for me.'

'Can't I even tell him about Marcus?' she asked, and he shook his head.

'Why not?'

'Because that would make him a person – give him an identity. At the moment he's nothing. So long as he stays nothing, we'll get the truth.' She wanted to argue, and he went on, 'Look. All he understands is fear. It's the only emotion that makes him react. Why do you think I speak Russian to him? For him, Russian's the language of fear.'

Suddenly Kaplan moved, scrambling toward the far side of the ship. Craig leaped from her and his hands grabbed for Kaplan as he went over the side, one gripping his shirt, the other holding his thick, white hair. Craig stood straddle-legged, and lifted Kaplan back aboard the boat as Kaplan screamed with pain. He released his grip on the shirt and tugged on the hair, lifting Kaplan to his toes, then the hand moved down, forcing him to his knees, and all the time he spoke to him in Russian. The fingers twisted, and Kaplan screamed again.

'You pig,' Craig said. 'You stupid, lying pig. Don't you ever learn? Don't you know you can't even die till we say so? You're still in Volochanka, Kaplan. You'll always be there.'

He pushed him sprawling, then picked up an end of rope, knotted his hands behind his back and tied the other end of the rope to the mast, then turned to Miriam.

'Ask your questions,' he said. 'He's ready.'

He went aft then, took the tiller, and sent Omar into the cabin to prepare a meal. Omar scuttled away and Craig lazed back against the strakes, giving his body ease and rest. He could hear the sound of Miriam's voice and Kaplan's responses, but not the words. It didn't matter. Miriam's interrogation was only a warm-up, anyway; the truth would come when he had Kaplan on shore, alone, when Royce and Benson were out of the way. He supposed that eventually he'd have to kill Royce. Maybe Benson too. But she'd let him escape; that made it harder to kill her. Why did she do it? Craig wondered. What was she trying to gain? He leaned forward and looked down into the cabin. Omar was old, but he was determined, and money acted on him as fear did on Kaplan. Omar had sliced bread and cheese and peeled fruit. The knife he had used was long and sharp, and he held it in his hand, looked at it with love.

'No,' said Craig.

Omar sighed and put down the knife, then fetched up the food and four bottles of water, gave some to Kaplan and Miriam, then came back to Craig, sat cross-legged beside him as they ate, and took the tiller.

'Effendi,' said Omar, 'you must be very rich.'

'Sometimes,' said Craig.

'One day you might need a partner.'

'Why?'

'A very small partner. One who could keep his eyes and ears open. Tell you things.'

'What things?'

'What the Americans and the Russians are doing. For money I could find out.'

'Why should I want to do that?'

'You are a spy,' Omar said. 'Just as Royce and Miss Benson are spies.' There was neither shock nor surprise in Omar's voice. He might have said: 'You're a grocer.'

'Who do you think I spy for?'

'Not the Russians or Americans. Not the British, either. You spy for yourself. For money. I could help you. Truly, I could.'

'You're still afraid I'll kill you,' said Craig.

'I'll always be afraid of that,' Omar said. 'But I want to show you I'll be more useful if you let me live.'

Craig ate bread and cheese left-handed. The bread was dry, the cheese old and tough, but he chewed on it stolidly. It was fuel.

'Always the left hand,' said Omar. 'You take care of yourself.'

'That's right,' said Craig. 'Show me how you can be useful.'

'That shepherd there. He was in hiding.'

'I found him,' said Craig. 'There's nothing for you in that.' He ate some grapes. 'Did you know Royce and Benson were looking for him?'

'No,' said Omar. 'The bastards didn't trust me.' Craig chuckled. 'But I guessed it.'

'How?'

'The Russians were looking for him too.' Somehow Craig went on chuckling.

'I know that,' he said. Omar's face fell.

'You know who they are?' he asked.

'No,' said Craig. 'I don't know that.'

'I do,' Omar said. 'How much is it worth?'

'A thousand dollars,' Craig said.

'It should be worth much more,' said Omar. 'This is big news.'

'A thousand dollars,' Craig said again. 'You're lucky I feel lazy today. I could get it for nothing.'

'That isn't very nice,' said Omar.

'We're not in a nice business.'

'They call themselves Israelis,' Omar said. 'They came to Kutsk three weeks ago. They are Jews, I think, and they had Jewish names – Lindemann, Stein – but really they were Russians. I heard them speak.'

'You speak Russian?'

'I know how it sounds,' said Omar. 'All Turks do if they've got any sense.'

'Go on.'

'First they tried to find the shepherd themselves. He was too well hidden. Then they asked me. I said there wasn't any such man. I should explain,' he continued, 'that the shepherd paid us money to say he wasn't there.'

'You'd have sold him out to me – or Royce and Benson.'

'You would have offered more money than the shepherd. The Russians wanted him for nothing.'

'Describe them,' said Craig.

'Lindemann is tall – about your height – heavy-shouldered, brown eyes, black hair. He is the younger. Stein is a head shorter than you, but a big body. Like a bear. A very strong man. His eyes are almost black. His hair was once black, now it is grey.'

'Their age?'

'Hard to say. They look older than they are, I think. The way you do, effendi.' He hesitated. 'What I mean is they look good at their job. Like you.'

'Where did they go after Kutsk? Back to Israel?'

'That's what they said in the village. They lied. They came in a boat, and my sister's husband's nephew saw it two days later. It was headed for Famagusta, in Cyprus.'

'Many Israelis go to Cyprus.'

'Perhaps they were Israelis who couldn't go to Israel.' His eyes searched Craig's face. 'Is it worth a thousand dollars?'

'Yes,' said Craig. 'You'll get it when you go.'

'I believe you,' Omar said. 'You're the biggest bastard I ever met, but I don't think you tell lies if you can help it.'

'Try to be like me,' Craig said. 'Tell me about Royce and Benson.'

'They came to Kutsk about three or four days ago. They said they were – those people who are interested in old things.'

'Archaeologists?' Craig suggested.

'Some Greek word. They drove all over the place. They were looking for the shepherd. At first they weren't in too much of a bloody hurry. Then one day Royce got a telegram.'

'What did it say?'

'You think I could get hold of somebody else's telegram?

'I'm sure of it,' said Craig.

'It was all numbers,' said Omar. 'A code. I couldn't read it. But I think it told them you were coming. They were worried after that. They came to me before you did.'

'Why should they do that?'

'I've got a reputation,' Omar said.

'You mean a police record?'

'No, no.' Omar sounded more surprised than offended. 'I'm not stupid, you know. But a lot of people know about me. I'll help in most things if the price is right.'

He squinted up at the sun, altered course a point, and continued: 'They wanted me to help them if you turned up. I said I would – and you know the rest. For such young people, I thought they did a pretty good job. The sheila–'

'Yes?' said Craig.

'She is very beautiful,' said Omar, 'and very dangerous. Even more dangerous than the man. I think they'll try to kill you. I don't want to be there when they try – not for just a thousand dollars.'

'You won't be,' said Craig.

He lay back again, relaxed and comfortable. Miriam and Kaplan talked on as they ate, and in the distance a long bight of land grew slowly visible.

'Cape Andreas,' said Omar. 'You want to make for there?'

'No,' said Craig. 'Famagusta.'

'For just a thousand dollars I don't want to see the Russians either.'

'You won't.'

'Famagusta's full of bleeding Greeks,' Omar said. 'Greeks don't like me, effendi.'

'What an old worry guts you are,' said Craig. 'Just do as you're told. You'll be fine. I'll even pay you.'

'You promise that?'

'I promise,' said Craig.

Omar sighed again, and obeyed. The big Englishman's strength was frightening, but there was comfort in it too – if you thought he was going to use it to protect you. There was also the money.

Craig dozed in the sun and watched the land slip by, white sand and scattered rocks, and beyond it a lush green vegetation, sloping back into the island's gentle mountains. Omar stayed well away from land, and to any casual watcher they would be just one more unhurrying boat in a sea full of boats that never hurried. He would be safe in Cyprus, and so would Kaplan, until his purchase price came through.

Craig thought of slaves and auction blocks, of men and women examined as if they were animals. He'd come down to that. And now he was a slave trader. The thought disgusted him, but he made his mind accept it. Once weaken, once relent, and Craig would be dead. And if he died, Miriam would probably die too, and Omar. Only Kaplan would have a chance to survive, a chance he might not want. Craig thought of the things he had done for Department K, cruel, terrible things. He thought of the smashed bones, the pistol beatings, the neat holes that a Smith and Wesson Airweight makes if you use it right. He thought of the things that had been done to him. He'd been shot, stabbed, knifed, clubbed, and tortured in a way that almost cost him his manhood. All for Department K. For the department and its chief, Loomis. He supposed that Loomis connected to other people, other places. To M-I6 and the government, ultimately to the people and the country. To Loomis's own highly personal view of Great Britain. But Craig hadn't felt like that. His loyalty had gone as far as Loomis and the department, and there it had stopped. (Mostly his enemies had been Russians and Chinese, because that was the way the world functioned nowadays – in a duality of terror and detestation that sometimes got very close to love.

Look at the bright kids. The ones in the West all wanted to be leftists; the ones in Russia all wanted to be Beatles.) But he hadn't ever had that depth of patriotism that rendered Loomis immune from pity or self-disgust whatever disgusting trick he'd played.

He'd gone into this thing because he was good at it. The fulfilment of each assignment had been the most complete satisfaction he could hope to know. And the enemy hadn't always been Russian or Chinese. There'd been Spaniards, Italians, Germans, Frenchmen, and more than one Englishman. He'd handled them all, just as efficiently. And now he was putting a middle-aged Jew on the auction block and forcing a young Jewess to keep him there. He wondered if Miriam would ever know just how terrible a price she was paying. I must want to live pretty desperately, he thought. When I get out of this I'll take a course in ethics and kill myself.

The girl came aft to sit beside him, moving clumsily against the movement of the ship.

'His arms are hurting him,' Miriam said.

'Has he answered all your questions yet?'

'Yes,' she said. 'But I think he's lying sometimes.'

'Go back and tell him I'll let him loose when he tells you the truth.'

Beside him, Omar cackled respectfully. The girl got up and went back to Kaplan. Despite her clumsy movements, her body was beautiful again.

'Not like the Benson sheila,' said Omar. 'A tigress and a deer, eh, effendi?'

Craig grinned at him. 'The world's big enough for both kinds,' he said.

The darkness came in quickly, and Omar was worried about the lights. Craig took the tiller as he lit them. Slowly they slipped closer to the shore, and then, in the last rays of the sunlight, Craig could see the white line of foam that marked the sunken ruins of Salamis, the speckled gleam of Famagusta in the distance. Craig got to his feet, picked the rifle up from the deck, slipped out the magazine and put it in his pocket. Omar watched without speaking. Next Craig took out his money, counted it, put it back in his pocket, except for ten one-hundred-dollar bills. Still silent, Omar licked his lips, then cried out aloud as Craig tore the ten beautiful pieces of paper in half, dropped one half into his lap.

'Half in advance. I'm going ashore soon,' said Craig. 'You'll get the rest when I come back. If you behave.'

'Yes, effendi,' said Omar.

'Are you a good Muslim?' said Craig.

'Pretty good.'

'If I were you I would pray a lot while I'm gone. Pray that nobody comes here looking for the shepherd. If they do, they'll kill you. If you try to contact anybody and do a deal, I'll kill you. Staying alone is your only chance of staying alive. Believe that, Omar.'

'I do believe it,' Omar said.

Craig went forward to the girl then, where she stood beside Kaplan.

'Well?' he asked.

'I think he's telling the truth now.'

Craig untied the man's hands, but lashed his ankles together. In Russian he said, 'You're too fond of swimming,' then to Miriam in English, 'I'm going ashore. I shouldn't be long. When I come back I'll have help.'

'For him?' She nodded at Kaplan who sat on the deck, head on hands.

'It's possible,' said Craig, 'but don't count on it.'

He told Omar to heave to, and together they manhandled over the side the stone that served as an anchor, then he disappeared into the cabin. When he came back he was naked, his clothes and shoes wrapped in a piece of waterproof and strapped to his head like a turban. The others turned away as he lowered himself into the water, swam in a steady breaststroke toward the lights of the town. The sea was calm and warm, tangy with salt, as placid as a bath, but the feel of it round him was refreshing, shook off his drowsiness. Too soon he reached shallow water and waded ashore to dry himself on a scrap of sailcloth, the only towel on the boat, and dress quickly, in the darkness. He walked along the beach, staying out of reach of the villas' lights, the sight of holiday-makers having one last outdoor drink before dinner, then reached a path that led up to a road, and walked along the road till he found a cafe with one car parked beside it.

He went into the cafe and ordered ouzo. The language he spoke was Greek, but with a Cretan accent, very different from Cypriot. The barman who served him showed a flicker of surprise.

'I thought you Greeks were supposed to wear uniform,' he said.

'I'm not in the army,' said Craig, and looked round the bar. Its only occupants were three men playing *xeri* under a portrait of Archbishop Makarios. The barman watched him nervously.

'Things are quiet in Cyprus now,' he said. 'Most people like them like that.'

'I like it,' said Craig. 'I haven't come for trouble. Just visiting friends.'

He put an English pound note on the counter, and the barman gave him his change in Cypriot mils.

'Which is the taxi driver?' Craig asked.

The barman called out 'Stephanou,' and a fat man put down his cards and gathered up his winnings, then walked out to the cab, the inevitable Mercedes.

Craig finished his ouzo.

'There are lots of UNO patrols now,' the barman said. 'The civil war is over,'

'I won't start it again,' said Craig. 'I promise.'

He went out to the cab, and in his mind he cursed himself, thoroughly and obscenely. It had been a mistake to speak Greek; a bad one. English was a far more natural tongue for Cyprus than the Cretan dialect that was the only Greek he knew. But Greek to him was the language of friendship: when first he'd been a fighting man, most of his comrades were Greeks. He'd lived with them and learned their skills. In the islands still there were men and women who regarded Craig as their brother. So out of his loneliness he'd spoken Greek, and like a damned fool forgotten that Cypriots regarded Greeks from Greece sometimes as heroes, more often as a dangerous nuisance, who took to the mountains and slaughtered in the name of Enosis.

And at one time Cypriots also had gone into the mountains, killed British troops and been killed by them. That had been a bad time for Craig. But the British had gone now, and UNO troops had replaced them: Irish, Canadians, unlikely Swedes, and highly improbable Finns on the island of Venus, drinking brandy at five shillings a bottle and persuading Cypriot Greeks and Cypriot Turks to stop killing each other. Enosis – union with Greece – was somehow forgotten;

the island was prosperous, not least because UNO paid its bills so promptly. The Greek and Turkish troops billeted on the island to protect their own nationals were already resented as a threat of war, a threat to prosperity. And Greek civilians were resented even more. They hinted that the days of terror might still come back.

Craig told the driver to head toward the port, which was the Turkish quarter.

'Greeks can't go there,' the driver said.

'I'm not a Greek,' said Craig. 'I'm an American. My father came from Heraklion.'

'Oh, an *American.*' The driver was delighted, and all at once relaxed. 'Why do you want to go to the port? Whisky – girls? We got plenty in our own bars.'

'I want to look at it,' said Craig. The driver shrugged, a comprehensive movement involving his whole torso, completely Hellene, that said more clearly than words that Americans made their own rules as they went along. Craig watched as they drove through the new town, Varosha, past the smart bars, tavernas, souvenir shops, then into the older town of cheap bars and night clubs, to the oldest Famagusta of all.

'This'll do,' he said, and remembering he was an American, gave the driver too much money. When he got out the driver roared off at once – to his favourite cafe, Craig hoped, to tell a worried barman to stop worrying.

He looked at the dark bastion in front of him. The Venetians had built that, more than four hundred years before: a staggering achievement in military architecture, massive yet shapely towers and walls built to keep the Turks out of Cyprus. For Cyprus was rich, and Venice had needed the money: but the Turks had got in even so, and flayed the Venetian commander alive. Craig thought that Omar would have been proud of his ancestors. Their descendants, huddled and restricted inside the walls, he would have had no time for. Every single one of them was poor.

Craig turned his back on history, and walked toward the bars and night clubs. The place he wanted was small and intimate, and famous for its bouzouki music. Angelos, the man who owned it, had been a waiter in London when the Second World War began, and had joined the navy. In 1945 he and Craig had been part of a Special Boat Service Group that had landed on the island of Cos. It was Craig's eighteenth birthday, and he had saved Angelos's life.

Craig walked in and spoke English to the waiter who led him to a table. It was early, but already the place was filling up, the air conditioning inadequate to counteract the heat of too many bodies. The waiter led him to a table near the back of the room, and Craig was quite happy about it. He refused the local champagne, and ordered a bottle of Arsinoe, a dry, delicate wine, and a plateful of the delicious Cyprus sausages called seftalies, and the chipped potatoes that are different from the chipped potatoes anywhere else in the world. The waiter brought the wine at once, and Craig sipped and smiled, and asked to speak to Angelos.

As he waited, the show began, and Craig found that the days of originality were not yet over. A girl came on and started to strip to bouzouki music, while Canadians, Swedes, Irishmen, and Finns looked on and cheered. He watched, intrigued. Two cultures met and ignored each other completely. The girl was preparing for love, or at any rate, sex – in a brisk, mid-Atlantic sort of way: the bouzouki was telling of death and sacrifice in a mountain battle a hundred and fifty years ago. But nobody else seemed to find it displeasing, except the bouzouki player. He became aware of a man moving toward him, a tubby man, sleek with success, in a black sharkskin suit and a Hardy Amies tie; a man who carried a plateful of seftalies and chipped potatoes because he chose to, to oblige a friend. He put the food down in front of Craig.

'Hallo, John,' he said, and sat at the table, snapped his fingers. A waiter seemed to grow out of the ground like a speeded-up flower.

'Bring another glass,' said Craig.

'And another bottle,' Angelos added, and Craig remembered that Cypriots always drink as if all the alcohol in the world is due to disappear next day.

'You recognized me, then?' he asked.

'Of course,' said Angelos, and poured wine, motioning to Craig to eat his food. 'You haven't changed, John. Not like me. See how fat I'm getting.'

'Prosperity,' said Craig.

'I have money, yes. If you need any–'

'No,' said Craig. 'I've got money too.'

'What, then?' Angelos asked.

'Does it have to be anything?'

Angelos emptied his glass, poured more wine, and smiled at Craig.

'Yes, John. With you it has to be something.'

'You're right,' said Craig. 'But do me a favour first. Tell me how you knew.'

'That day in Cos,' Angelos said. 'In a way, it was the most important day of my life – the day I should have died – and didn't. You were the reason I didn't die. I have thought about it many times. On bad nights I still dream about it. Mostly I dream about the fat German – the one you got with the knife.'

'I thought I shot him,' said Craig.

'No. You shot the young one, the one who had hit me with the gun butt. The fat one you knifed – in the throat. He bled all over me.'

'I'd forgotten that,' said Craig.

'That's the kind of man you are,' Angelos said. 'I'm not like that. I can't forget.'

'Maybe you're the lucky one,' Craig said. 'Go on about why you know I want something.'

'You are a very loyal person,' Angelos said, 'but you have no talent for friendship.'

'Now, wait a minute,' Craig said. 'If you don't want to help me, say so.'

'Of course I want to help you,' Angelos said. 'I *have* to help you.'

Craig looked at him across the table, expressionless grey eyes telling nothing. Angelos shook like a man in terror, but that was stupid. What was there to fear?

'I came back for you,' said Craig. 'I killed those two Jerries for you.'

'You killed them for the group,' Angelos said. 'That was where your loyalty was. For me – Angelos – you did nothing. You cared nothing. What did you do after that fat German died, John?'

Craig thought back hard. It had been in an olive grove, he remembered. One of so many running fights, scrambling, terrifying, ecstatic. They'd got back to the *caique,* and the pursuing Germans had run into a blast of Bren gun fire. But the details had gone.

'I can't remember,' he said.

'I'll tell you. You wiped your knife on the German, put it back in its sheath, then carried me back to the *caique*. The young German had hit me and broken my ribs. I couldn't walk. You carried me for half a mile, and you never said a word.'

'I was busy.'

'Not then, or afterwards. I was in hospital for a month, then I came back to the group. You never even mentioned what had happened. You have no talent for friendship, John.'

Craig said, 'Are you saying you hate me?'

'No.'

'What, then?'

'You'll never understand. You *can't* understand,' Angelos shouted, then lowered his voice as customers turned to stare. 'Almost everyone needs the friendship of others. They need it as they need food and drink. You – don't. All you need is a group to belong to – but for you the group is an abstraction, not people. Never people. Shall I tell you something. We've been talking for some while–'

'You've done most of it,' said Craig.

'–And you've never even spoken my name. After twenty-three years.'

'And yet you say you'll help me.'

'Of course I'll help you. I must. I've been waiting to do so ever since that night.'

'Do you mind telling me why?'

'I want to be free of you,' said Angelos.

Craig said, 'What I want – it isn't a small thing.'

'I'm glad of that,' Angelos said.

'There's risk.' He looked at the fat man. He was smiling. 'That makes you happy?'

'Very happy.'

'I want you to help pick up three people from a boat, then hide them, and me. Then I want you to act as messenger boy.'

'Who are these people?'

'An American girl, a Russian man, and a Turk.'

'A Turk,' said Angelos. 'That's all it needed. All right. I'll do it.'

'There's a risk in all of it,' said Craig. 'Being messenger boy is the worst.'

'It's a kidnapping?' Craig nodded.

'Yes,' Angelos said. 'It would be. Crime was inevitable for you, just as this' – he gestured to the club – 'is inevitable for me.' He finished his wine. 'Shall we go now?'

'Two more questions,' said Craig. 'And one request – I want all the British and American papers you can get here. Next – are you married?'

'No,' said Angelos. 'There are plenty of girls available. I shan't marry for another few years. And the other question?'

'There are two men in Famagusta – supposed to be Israelis. One's called Lindemann. About my height. Big shoulders. Brown eyes. Black hair. The other one's called Stein.

Stocky. Built like a barrel. Black eyes. Black hair going grey. Do you know them?'

'Very well,' said Angelos. 'They're sitting five tables away. Behind you.'

Craig's hands moved on the table, and Angelos watched them. They were weapons still, he thought. In twenty-three years Craig had only become more himself.

'They come in here very often,' he continued. 'They have what seems to be an inexhaustible passion for cabaret girls who don't cost too much. The girls usually find it flattering. I take it they are – business rivals?' Craig nodded. 'Do they know you?'

'I hope not,' said Craig. 'Otherwise the risk would be so big you'd be ecstatic. Can we go now?'

'Yes,' said Angelos. 'My car is outside. I have a boat, too. That will be useful.'

'Very,' said Craig. 'Where can you hide us?'

'In the mountains. I have a little place where I take a girl sometimes. It's very quiet. But I don't suppose you'll mind that.'

'Not a bit,' said Craig. 'Do you have only one car?'

'Two,' said Angelos.

'I want to borrow one of them,' said Craig. 'You won't refuse me?'

Angelos sighed. 'I forgot how clever you are,' he said. 'That was a mistake. I told you too much, didn't I? You aren't the kind of man to refuse an advantage just because it's unfair.'

He got up then and led the way to the door. When he'd reached it, Craig looked back. Lindemann and Stein looked just as Omar had described them. They were talking hard to the bouzouki stripper and another girl off the same assembly line. There were two bottles of brandy and four glasses on the table. They didn't look like men who were in a hurry to move.

Angelos's two cars were a Volkswagen and an MGB. Craig chose the Volkswagen. It hadn't the sports car's speed, but it was built for the mountains. They parked the cars near the beach and boarded Angelos's boat, a neat little outboard job that would just about hold five. Craig steered it toward Omar's sailing boat, another problem.

'Can you put that somewhere inconspicuous?' he asked.

Angelos thought. 'I could take it to Melos,' he said at last. 'My brother has a boat-building business there. I could say it's due for overhaul.'

'How far is Melos?'

'Just a few miles. Or better still I could get my brother to come and collect it. Now if you like.'

'That would be fine,' said Craig, 'if your brother keeps his mouth shut.'

'He will,' said Angelos. 'He owes me

money.' He hesitated, then said, 'Craig, do I have to hide a Turk?'

'Either that or kill him,' said Craig. Angelos said no more.

Chapter Ten

The house in the mountains was the best accommodation Miriam had seen since her night in Ankara. It had comfortable beds, a bathroom, and a workmanlike kitchen well stocked with food. It was the man who owned it who puzzled her. He behaved to Craig as if he detested him, yet obeyed his every word, and accepted all that Craig had done without question. When Craig had cut Kaplan loose for instance the fat man had accepted it without a blink; as if he expected violence from Craig, and cruelty, and a complete disregard for the comfort and dignity of others. The fat man wasn't like that, Miriam knew, yet he found it fascinating in Craig, as well as hateful. For his part, Craig simply issued orders, certain that the fat man would obey, and he did.

When the fat man had gone, Craig led her to the kitchen and made her cook a meal for Omar. Kaplan, and herself. They ate it in silence. When they had finished Craig took Kaplan to the bathroom, then to his bed. He looked at him in silence, then spoke in Russian.

'You've told the girl the truth?' he asked.

'Yes. I swear it,' said Kaplan.

'I hope so. Tomorrow you will tell the truth to me. Let's hope it's the same truth.' He turned away.

'Please,' said Kaplan. Craig turned back to him.

'Please. What are you doing to me? Why am I here? I thought I was going to be left in peace.'

'Tomorrow,' said Craig. He went out and locked the door.

In the kitchen, Omar was washing dishes, Miriam drying. Omar, Craig was pleased to see, looked very worried. 'Effendi,' he said, 'how long do I have to stay here?'

'A thousand dollars' worth,' said Craig. 'And maybe a bonus.' He sniffed. 'Take a bath, Omar, then go to bed.'

Omar left them. He still looked worried.

'Aren't you going to lock him in?' the girl asked. Craig shook his head. 'You trust him?'

'Nobody trusts Omar,' said Craig. 'But he's in Cyprus. The toughest part. The Greek part. A Turk out here alone wouldn't have a chance, and Omar knows it. He won't leave us.'

The girl slumped forward in her chair. She looked exhausted.

'It's just as well I've got you and your friends to arrange things,' she said. He said nothing. 'Are you sure you can trust your friend?'

228

'Yes,' said Craig. 'I can trust him. He's all alone. No woman to find out his secrets.'

She sat up then. 'Why do you have to hurt people all the time?' she asked.

'Do I? That wasn't supposed to be hurtful. I just said what I meant to say. Maybe that's what hurts.' He hesitated. 'I'm not cruel like Royce, you know.'

'But you are,' Miriam said. 'The way you treated Kaplan.'

'Cruelty's the key to Kaplan,' Craig said. 'All I did was use it. I didn't enjoy it.'

'The fact that you used it at all–'

'It's what we all use,' he said. 'Force Three, the KGB. Department K. We use it because it works.' He looked at her again, saw how tired she was. 'I wanted to hear what Kaplan told you,' he said, 'but it'll keep till tomorrow. Go to bed.'

'Are you coming with me?' she asked, and the question whipped the blood into her face.

'Suppose you get pregnant?'

'Would you care?'

He didn't answer. She would never believe that she was the only one he would look out for in the whole sorry mess. Better for them both that she wouldn't. He went with her to the bedroom and she came into his arms fierce and demanding, the body's needs drowning the questions her mind feared. But their bodies at least made a dialogue, a question and answer that at last achieved solution. When they had done, she fell asleep at once, and he kissed her as she slept, then fell asleep beside her, as relaxed as a cat, and as wary.

In the morning, as she put on her clothes, she put on her doubts, her fears, her wariness. It was early, but Omar was already in the kitchen, making omelettes. He looked cleaned and rested, and his omelettes were delicious. Craig took the girl onto a veranda that looked straight across the valley to the mountains of Troodos, rich, sweet mountains, green with vine and olive and pine tree, swift tumbling snow streams, houses perched like birds wherever a ridge made it possible.

'It's beautiful here,' Miriam said.

'And safe,' said Craig. 'What did Kaplan tell you?'

'Weren't you happy last night?' she said. 'Wasn't your body happy? Because if it was – that was thanks to me, wasn't it?'

'I was happy.'

'Then shouldn't you be grateful to me? Be nice to me? Or is it you just don't know *how* to be nice to people?'

Ask Angelos, Craig thought. He's the expert on my talent for friendship. He waited.

'Oh hell,' the girl said at last. 'Hell! *Hell!*'

She sat down opposite Craig, and her voice became cold, impersonal.

'First of all, I'm sure that Kaplan is Kaplan. I ran all the checks Marcus told me about, and he didn't fluff one. He told me about his work in Russia–'

'What about it?'

'How he was a successful scientist. Then he fell out with the Politburo and finished up in Volochanka. Craig, he escaped from there!'

'We know that,' said Craig.

'But you don't know how. There were ten of them – all Jews. It was like a miracle.'

She told him about the minyan, and the slow evolution of their plan to escape. ('Angelos should hear this too,' said Craig. 'He'd tell you all about my loyalty to groups as abstract concepts.') She told him of the break-out and how he got separated from the others; the long, agonized trek alone to freedom. How he'd wandered alone until he'd almost died, would have died if some Lapps hadn't found him and smuggled him over the border into Sweden, hundreds of miles away. Sweden was lucky for him. He had money in Stockholm. He'd got to the bank and taken out the money, but the Swedes were too interested in him. They wanted him to ask for political asylum, but he was afraid the publicity would betray him to the KGB. He'd had to get away. The money had bought him forged papers and a passage on a ship for Hamburg. From Hamburg he'd flown to Rome, from Rome to Ankara, and from there he'd drifted south, to settle finally at Kutsk.

'Why choose Turkey?' Craig said.

'Because the Turks hated the Russians,' she told him. 'They'd give him asylum if ever he needed it. And it was remote. The kind of place nobody ever went to. When he bought the flock of sheep he'd learned something else too. He was happy there, a hermit, alone. He hadn't been happy for as long as he could remember.'

'Isn't it wonderful?' said Miriam.

'Fantastic,' he said. 'What else is there?'

'He's afraid,' she said, 'of you and others like you.'

'Did you tell him about going to America?'

'You told me not to.'

'Did he say anything about our knowing his real name?'

'Yes,' she said. 'I don't understand that. He said Kaplan was supposed to be dead and buried. He said your people promised. I guess he meant the Russians.'

'I'm sure he did.'

Craig got up then and walked round the garden that encircled Angelos's house. He'd done it before, when they arrived the preceding night, but it was better to do it by daylight. The house was set in a fold in the hills, encircled by pine trees. A stream supplied its water, a turbine generator its power. A mud track was the only approach to it, and the nearest neighbour was seven miles away. He went back into the house and called Omar and Miriam, led them into the living room, where a big picture window looked out on the track that led to the house. For the last four hundred feet there was no cover at all.

'I want you to watch this place,' said Craig. 'If anybody comes up that road, call me at once.'

'You want both of us to watch?' Omar asked.

'Both of you. All the time, Omar.' The Turk looked up at him. 'It's possible the lady may want to leave this room. See that she doesn't.'

'Too right,' said Omar.

'What are you going to do?' the girl asked.

'Find out the truth,' said Craig. 'I'm sick of fairy stories.'

He left them, and she sat watching the path. After a few minutes she heard Kaplan cry out, and jumped to her feet. At once Omar also rose, standing between her and the door. He was an old man, but he was strong, she knew. She'd be helpless against him. Then Kaplan cried out again, and she ran at Omar, trying to get past him. But he picked her up, held her in his gaunt, work-worn hands, and looked at her with eyes that were curiously gentle, almost compassionate.

'It's no use, miss,' he said. 'We've got to do what the boss says. Now you sit down and watch the road. It's what we're here for.'

But she went on struggling until there was neither fight nor breath left in her, even when Kaplan yelled a third time. After that she sat down as Omar bade her, and there was no more noise.

Craig came back into the room forty minutes later, and Kaplan followed him. There was a bruise over his left eye and he was limping. Miriam got up at once and led him to a chair. Craig fetched water and gave it to Kaplan, who drank it eagerly.

'The shepherd's got a new statement to make,' said Craig.

'Looks like a pretty important shepherd,' Omar said.

'He is,' said Craig. 'A man could get killed just knowing what his real name is. Do you want to know it?'

'No, thank you,' said Omar. 'I think I'd sooner cook lunch.'

Craig watched him go, then said, 'I roughed him up a bit.'

'I heard you,' Miriam said.

'It was nothing like you got,' said Craig. 'That's work for experts. But this poor bastard's scared silly. He's got nothing left.' He turned to Kaplan, and this time he spoke in English.

'Now tell this woman what you told me,'

said Craig. 'Unless you want to change your story again.'

'I told you the truth,' said Kaplan.

'Now tell it to her.'

Kaplan looked at her, but his whole body was concentrated on Craig, standing beside him.

'I'm sorry,' he said, 'but most of what I told you yesterday was lies. There were no friendly Lapps, no smuggling across the border to Sweden.'

'You didn't escape?' Miriam asked.

'No. The other nine did – that is true. But I did not.'

'Tell her what you did, Kaplan,' said Craig. The agony on his face was unbearable.

'I betrayed them,' he said, 'to the commandant of the camp. The price of my betrayal was a pardon.'

'Get on with it,' said Craig.

'I told the commandant the night we – we were ready to go. You have to be in Volochanka to know how it was. Slow death in the camp, quick death outside. The commandant was drunk all the time. He was drunk when I came to warn him. He beat me. Threw me out. Went back to his vodka. Then it happened. We made our break. Only I didn't go. I went to the deputy commandant instead, told them where to pick up the others. He got seven of them. All the time I had to hide in his hut. If I'd come out, the other prisoners would have killed me. Then the commandant was shot, and the deputy took over. He put in a word for me, got my pardon. I was allowed to live. They gave me new papers, sent me to work in the Crimea. On a collective. I was happy there.' He paused till Craig raised his head, then went on immediately. 'Then a man came to see me from the Central Scientific Bureau. They'd opened up my dossier again, run some tests on my theory. He said I was to be pardoned.'

'But what had you *done?*' the girl asked.

'Slept with a man's wife and been found out,' he said. 'The man was a close friend of Lavrenti Beria. The charge was moral degeneracy.' He looked at Miriam. 'It wasn't that. I swear it. I loved the woman very much. It was the second time in all my life I had known what love was and—'

'Tell us about your theory,' said Craig.

'It's a way to bring water to desert places. It's part engineering – using atomic plant to make sea water into fresh water – and part agriculture – the growth of certain crops intermingled to help each other – catching the dew and so on. The Central Scientific Bureau said it ought to be tried out in a limited experiment. They were going to rehabilitate me. I couldn't stand it. I ran away.'

'You couldn't stand what?' Craig asked.

'Coming back to life. Beria was dead by that time, but his friend – the man whose wife I loved – he's still alive. Doing well. His wife is still with him. I'd have had to meet them again, go to receptions, parties – as if nothing had ever happened. And he knows I betrayed my friends. I couldn't face them – not with that. I ran away, stole money, crossed the Turkish border. It wasn't easy, but I'd been trained how to do it in Volochanka. In Turkey, I robbed again – it seems I have a talent for that, too, and bought papers. When I had enough money, I settled down, paid those peasants to keep their mouths shut. I had a life of my own then. It was a good life, but the peasants betrayed me. I should have expected it. It's what I did myself.'

'You felt safe?' Miriam asked.

'I'll never be safe. But the ones I feared were all Russian. If they knew I was alive, they'd kill me. The knowledge I have is too important to be taken out of Russia.'

'They know you're alive,' said Craig. 'They're looking for you now.'

'You won't give me to them?'

'Not if we can get a better offer,' Craig said. 'I'm pretty sure we can. The Americans want you, Kaplan.'

'They don't need my skills.'

'A gift to underdeveloped countries. A nice gesture from Uncle Sam.'

'Well, it is,' said Miriam.

'Of course it is,' said Craig. 'If they can keep him alive.'

Chapter Eleven

Late that afternoon, Angelos came back. Omar was watching the window and called out to Craig, who brought the rifle, held the MGB in its sights until Angelos stopped the car and walked up the path, a wad of newspapers under his arm. Craig left Omar on duty by the window, and let Angelos in. The rifle made him smile.

'I expected a Bren gun at least,' he said.

'I could use it,' said Craig, and led him to the kitchen. 'What's happening?' he asked.

'Nothing. The two Israelis got very drunk, but they made love to my girls first.'

'Nobody followed you here?'

'Nobody as far as I know. I haven't your skill in these matters. I brought you your papers. And came for my instructions.'

'I'll have to read the papers first,' said Craig.

He began to read through the small ad columns of the *Herald Tribune*, the *Christian Science Monitor*, the continental *Daily Mail*, the *London Times*, and the *London Daily Telegraph*. It was a long and boring process, but in the end he found what he wanted.

'Tell the girl to come here,' he asked.

Angelos stiffened to attention, the parody of a soldier.

'Jawohl, Herr Oberst,' he said.

He went out, and Miriam came in.

'There are a lot of messages for you. I've marked them,' said Craig. 'Look.'

He handed her the European edition of the *Herald Tribune*. An advertisement read, 'Darling, Won't you listen to Stardust just once more? Marcus misses you.' A box number in Paris followed.

'It's in every paper,' Craig said. 'Crude – but they're in a hurry – and worried about you. So they make you worry about Marcus.'

'They shouldn't have mentioned him,' she said. 'That gave it away.'

'Only to me,' said Craig. 'And they know you're with me anyway. So they mention Marcus – and tell it to me too. Stardust was your code name, I suppose?'

'Yes,' she said.

'How many times did they reach you?'

'Only once. In Istanbul. Our people aren't too strong in Turkey. They were blown – that's the word isn't it? – six months ago.'

'That's why they hired Loomis,' said Craig.

'What do we do now?'

'Write to the box number. Tell them our terms.'

'*Our* terms?'

'Mine, then. They can have him for me – if they'll get Department K off my back.

Otherwise he goes to the Russians.'

'Can *they* get Department K off your back?'

'If they want Kaplan badly enough, yes. But with the Yanks it's easier.'

'You can trust us, you mean?'

'Of course not,' said Craig. 'But you spend more money.'

He found a piece of paper and an envelope, wrote an answer to the box number in the *Herald Tribune*, and gave it to Angelos to post, watched the MGB back down the path to the road, then went to bed and slept for four hours.

That night, he and Omar took it in turns to watch the road, patrol the grounds. He trusted Angelos – all his instincts told him that he was right to do so, but he had no faith in his competence. For this kind of operation he needed a Royce and a Benson; what he'd got was a moralist, a female idealist, and an old man.

Next day, Angelos came back at dusk. Again Craig followed the drill in admitting him, and again Angelos grinned at the sight of the rifle, this time in Omar's hands.

'I have some news you should know,' he said. 'There are two English people in Famagusta asking for you. Or at least for someone who could be you. They are asking for a tall, well-built Englishman and his American wife, believed to be travelling with the girl's uncle and an elderly Turkish servant. The

Turk is causing a great deal of excitement.'

'I believe you,' said Craig.

'They are saying the Englishman has come into a great deal of money, that is why he must be found.'

'Who are they?'

'A solicitor and his secretary. The secretary is very beautiful. The solicitor has a limp.'

'Benson and Royce,' Craig said.

'They say the senior partner is flying out today.'

'Who are they saying it to?'

'Anyone who'll listen. They want the word to get around, it seems.' Craig thought hard for a minute.

'Where are they staying?'

'The Esperia Tower.'

'I want you to sit here for a while,' Craig said. 'Keep an eye on my guests.'

'Very well.'

Craig hesitated, then took out the Smith and Wesson, offered it to the other. 'Are they such reluctant guests?' Angelos asked.

'They have enemies,' said Craig.

'And so have you, no doubt. I have a gun, John. It's in the car.'

'I won't be gone long,' Craig said. 'You shouldn't have any trouble.'

He called for Omar then and gave him precise instructions. When the old man agreed, Craig took out ten more hundred-dollar bills, tore them in half and gave one half to him. That left Miriam. He called her into the kitchen.

'Department K's caught up with us,' he said.

'But how could they?'

'By knowing their job,' said Craig. 'I told you they're good. They're offering a deal.'

'What kind of a deal?'

'That's what I've got to go and find out.'

'Go to them? That's crazy.'

'No,' he said. 'It's sane enough. I've got Kaplan. They won't hurt me if I can hurt him.' She winced. 'This could be the end of it,' he said. 'You should be glad.'

'I want my people to have him,' Miriam said. 'They're the ones who'll help him do what he should be doing.'

'We'll listen to their offer too,' said Craig.

Angelos walked back with him to his MGB, and took from the trunk an old Webley .45 revolver.

'Who are you going to shoot?' Craig asked. 'Elephants?'

'I hope nothing,' said Angelos. 'But if I use this, I make sure the man I hit stays down.'

'If you hit anything at all. That damn thing kicks like a mule.'

'How much you forget,' said Angelos. 'In the old days I always used one of these. I didn't miss very often.'

Craig drove the MGB back that night. It

was fast, and he didn't have to use the mountain tracks. The new road from Troodos to Nicosia was finished now, a well-paved highway that seemed especially designed for testing out an MGB. It was an eager, thrusting little car, and Craig enjoyed it as he swung into the road's wide, planing curves, easing down at last as he came into Nicosia. The town was noisy with people promenading in the wisp of a breeze that sometimes stirred at evening. There were taxis and buses with vast overhangs and donkeys pulling carts, and pedestrians who walked as if the internal-combustion engine had yet to be invented. He was glad to thread his way through the town and get on to the highway to Famagusta.

This is a curious road. Once it had been a railway line, and when the railway was abandoned the track was pulled up, the road put in its place. It ran arrow-straight for almost all of its fifty miles, and the MGB liked this one too: rev-counter and speedometer climbed up and over in steady power. He kept going at speed till the last possible moment. If the senior partner of Royce's firm had arrived he would try anything, and the best way to combat him on a lonely highway was to keep moving fast. At last the lights of Famagusta grew bigger and brighter, and Craig eased off his speed and drove with finicking care through the old town to Varosha suburb. He drove past the hotel and found space to park. This seemed to be one of the few places left in the world where you could still find space to park, Craig thought.

He went into the lobby and asked for Mr. Royce. He was in the bar, the desk clerk said, with his secretary and another gentleman.

'A fat man?' Craig asked. 'Red face and white hair?'

The desk clerk said austerely, 'Mr. Royce's friend is rather fat.' Craig moved to the lift.

'Is your name Craig, sir?' the desk clerk asked. Craig said it was. 'You're to go straight up. Mr. Royce and the others are expecting you. They've ordered dinner at nine, sir.'

Whatever you did to Loomis he always bounced right back up, Craig thought. Dinner at nine, for instance. That was for his own benefit, not Craig's, designed to show Craig that he wasn't important enough to make Loomis miss his dinner.

He went into the bar. It was long and dark and cool, the air conditioning muted to a murmur. At the bar itself, a group of wealthy Cypriots drank Keo beer, deplored the price of oranges, and tried not to be caught looking at Joanna Benson's legs. She, Royce, and Loomis were sitting on low chairs round a table. A fourth chair waited for Craig. Loomis didn't look as if he were enjoying it much. He never did enjoy sitting on chairs that weren't specially made for him. Craig moved toward them. The girl's face was impassive. Royce's glance told him that Royce hated him. Loomis raised his massive head and gave him a two-inch nod.

'Ah, Craig,' he said. 'Good of you to look us up. What'll you have?'

'Same as you,' said Craig.

'Ouzo,' Loomis said, and they sat in silence till the barman brought it.

'Nice here?' Craig said at last.

'Too nice for you,' said Loomis. 'Where the hell d'you get your clothes these days?'

'Savile Row,' said Craig.

'Have your suit cleaned, then. It's disgusting.'

'One of the nice things about being retired is you don't have to worry about looking smart all the time,' Craig said. As he spoke, he watched Royce's hands. The left one clasped his drink, the right one fiddled nervously with the lapel of his jacket. Craig turned to him. 'Why bother?' he said. 'You can't start anything here.'

Loomis glowered at him. 'Sit still,' he snarled, then turned back to Craig. 'He could start something if I told him to. And so could this Benson person.'

'You're not that daft,' said Craig.

'I want you, son,' Loomis said. 'I want your hide in strips.'

'That's just self-indulgence,' said Craig. 'I've wanted to put you on a diet for years, but I know I'm never going to get the chance. Anyway, I heard I'd come into money. That's why I'm here.'

'A bloke called John Adams has come into money,' Loomis said.

'You didn't give my name?' Craig asked.

'No,' said Loomis, and his voice was wistful. 'Not yet.'

'How much?'

'A hundred thousand pounds,' said Loomis. 'Any currency you want.'

Craig said, 'You're taking a risk, aren't you? Talking of sums like that in front of these impressionable young people?'

'No,' said Loomis.

'You aren't afraid that one day they may follow my example?'

'No, cock, I'm not. They got more sense.'

'And I've got a hundred thousand pounds. It's not enough, Loomis.'

'How much, then?'

'Oh, the money'll do,' Craig said, 'but I want something else as well. Security.'

Loomis laughed aloud, a roaring boom that seemed to bounce against the walls of the room.

'Oh, son,' he said. 'The things you say.'

Craig waited as he wiped his eyes.

'You want our friend, don't you?' he asked. 'That's the price. A hundred thousand quid

I can enjoy in peace. Guaranteed.'

'And how could I guarantee a thing like that? Dammit, man, can't you see it's impossible?'

'You could give me a statement of what you did – and what these two did. What your orders were, how they carried them out. You could sign it and they could witness it. I'd call that a guarantee.'

'I'd call it bloody madness,' said Loomis.

'That's the price,' Craig said. He stood up.

'Wait,' Loomis said. 'Let's have dinner first.'

They went into the dining room, Royce limping badly, and Craig enjoyed the food and wine; enjoyed even more Loomis's struggle to be polite. It had been so many years since Loomis had had to be polite to anyone. He spoke of Craig's abilities, and praised in particular the skill with which he'd outwitted Force Three.

'Good chaps,' he said. 'Very good chaps. But they have the American weakness – and you used it.'

'What do you mean, sir?' Benson asked.

'They tend to think that patriotism compensates for skill,' said Loomis, 'so they used the Loman girl. Once Craig knew who she was, she had no chance.'

'How did you know Force Three was involved?'

'Those ads in the papers. "Marcus is

worried." They must have been desperate to take a chance like that.'

Craig said, 'It's not that bad. They knew I'd see the papers – and it's me they want to talk to.'

For a moment, Loomis looked up from his plate; his angry eyes burned into Craig's.

'That's right,' said Craig.

'What about the Russians?' Joanna Benson asked. 'Are you open to offers from them, too?'

'I'm open to offers from Martians – if they've got the money and guarantees,' said Craig.

Loomis went on eating.

'There's something interests me,' Craig said. 'I wonder if I might ask about it.'

'We'll see.' Loomis's words were a growl.

Craig turned to Royce and smiled politely.

'What happened after I shot you?' he asked. There was a silence, then Joanna Benson giggled.

'What a bastard you are,' said Loomis. 'All right, Benson. You tell him.'

She pushed away her plate and sat back. Royce continued to eat, his eyes looking downwards. It was impossible to look at Craig: to see the mockery in his eyes. At least, Loomis hadn't made him answer. He was grateful for that.

'You were really rather kind to us,' Joanna Benson said. 'I can't think why. Blowing up the Jag was a bit strong, though, wasn't it? Such a lovely car.'

'Sorry about that,' Craig said. 'But I had to set you on foot.'

'Poor Andrew was hardly even that,' said the girl. 'It was hands and knees most of the time. You got him in the leg, you know. Nothing serious, but he bled quite a bit. I had to use tourniquets and things.' Royce went on eating. His tournedos Rossini absorbed him utterly. The girl went on: 'It was all a bit of a problem. I couldn't carry Andrew and he needed a doctor. I walked back up the road and found a farm with a telephone and called the police. They produced an old boy who spoke a bit of German and I said we'd been attacked by bandits. You've never seen such excitement. Then I scurried back to Andrew and told him what to say, and the gendarmes arrived with an ambulance and took him off to hospital. After that it was all questions and statements and a big hunt for that mad shepherd. They patched Andrew up quite well, I think, and I said we had friends in Cyprus and we'd recuperate there, so they found us a boat and told us they'd let us know as soon as the found the mad shepherd. They thought he was running amok or something. His dog was dead, you see. They think he killed it.'

'No. I did that,' said Craig. He looked at Loomis. 'Why Cyprus?'

'Benson's a sensible young person,' said Loomis. It was as much praise as he ever offered a woman. 'She was in a spot of bother and she handled it well, then she reported back to me. When she phoned I had a look in your file. Sending them here was my idea.'

'What made you do it?' asked Craig.

'Where else in this part of the world have you got friends? But Angelos Kouprassi's your friend. He has to be. When you were a boy wonder in the SBS you saved his life.'

Loomis's passion had always been for detail, mountains of it. But he had an un-erring ability to pick out the one fact that was significant, and use it.

'So I sent the two of them here,' he said, 'and damn if you're not here too. How's Angelos?'

'Well,' said Craig.

'Up in that little place of his in the moun-tains?' asked Loomis. He chuckled. 'Nice people these Greek Cypriots, but the biggest bloody chatterboxes I ever came across. Still, it's useful. Benson here's a good listener. She's sensible, Craig. Wouldn't you say?'

'She is.'

'Then how the hell did she come to let you get away once she'd tied you up?'

'I'm afraid that's my secret,' Craig said.

Joanna Benson gave no sign of relief.

'But I did it the way Pascoe showed me,'

she said. 'It's impossible to– No, that's ridiculous, isn't it? You're here, after all.'

'You'll have to show Pascoe that one,' said Loomis.

Craig shook his head. 'That's over,' he said.

Loomis turned to the other two. 'Go and take your coffee on the roof garden,' he said.

Royce left, still not looking at Craig, and limping heavily. The girl made no move to help him.

'He'd kill you for nothing,' said Loomis. 'You've beaten him twice. He hates you for it.'

'He hates too much. And he enjoys hurting people too much.'

'Yes. So I gather. And Benson?'

'She watched. I don't think she enjoyed it.'

'Tell me,' said Loomis. 'How d'you come to beat an upstanding young feller like Royce?'

'You made me angry. It was the best thing you could have done, Loomis. It gave me my skill back.'

'How on earth did I make you angry?'

'You used me for bait. All that stuff about how I had one more chance to prove myself. I had no chance at all. From the minute I got to New York I was the decoy, wasn't I? Money but no gun, no proper contacts – just a twit from the FO – and Royce and Benson ahead of me all the time. When I was picked up in New York I didn't have a chance.'

The fat man sat, impassive.

'Tell me about that,' he said.

'What do you care?' asked Craig. 'I got away and came back to London and you were too busy to see me. You weren't too busy to see Royce and Benson.'

'Ah,' said Loomis.

He struggled and wrestled with his own body to get a hand to an inside pocket. It came out holding a cigar. Loomis looked at it, sighed, and handed it to Craig, then wrestled himself again for another.

'Go on, son,' he said.

'You saw them that day. You didn't see me. And I knew why. Craig was out. Finished. If the KGB didn't get me, you would. So I got out of the country–'

'Your friend Candlish is a very resourceful feller.'

'–went back to the States and got hold of Miriam Loman.'

'Royce and Benson should have got on to her,' said Loomis. 'Youth has its drawbacks.'

'They're not mine. The Loman girl took me right to Kaplan and I've got him.'

'In your friend's house in the mountains. Suppose we take him from you?'

'You can't,' said Craig.

Loomis clipped his cigar, lit it as if he were cauterizing a wound.

'We're chums with the Cypriots now,' he said. 'We could tell them some yarn. They'd let us use force. There's a unit of the RAF Regiment not far from here.'

'Kaplan's no good to you dead. Or have you started subcontracting to the KGB?'

'I see,' said Loomis. 'You'd go that far, would you? But suppose I'd sent some of the boys along now – to pick him up while you and I were chatting?'

'He'd still be dead.' said Craig.

'Your friend Angelos? No, I don't think so. And not the Loman person. She's hardly appropriate for the role. Omar the terrible Turk, eh, Craig?'

'Never mind,' said Craig. 'Just believe what I told you. You only get Kaplan alive if you pay for him.'

'A hundred thousand,' said Loomis.

'And a written guarantee.'

'Even I can't give you that without authority.'

'Then get it. I have other offers, you know.'

For the first time since Craig had known him, Loomis became angry in silence. No purple face, no outraged bull frog swellings of the chest, no pounded tables.

He said softly, 'I think you'd be very unwise.'

'The other offers have guarantees, too,' said Craig.

'You'd still be unwise.'

Craig got up then and looked down at Loomis. The fat man was as still as a statue, and just about as hard.

'You know what we businessmen say,' said Craig. 'Buy now and avoid disappointment. Let me know when you've got your guarantee.'

He went down to the foyer and spoke to the desk clerk.

'Could you ring Miss Benson and Mr. Royce?' he said. 'They're up in the roof garden. Tell them that Mr. Loomis wants to see them in the restaurant.'

The clerk lifted a phone, spoke briefly, first in Greek, then in English, and turned to Craig.

'They're on their way, sir,' he said.

'Thanks,' said Craig.

At least now they wouldn't try to stop him reaching his car – and Loomis would have lots to say to them.

Chapter Twelve

He drove back to the mountains fast, alert for following cars. There were none. When he turned off on to the track to Angelos's house, he was quite alone. Up to Loomis now, he thought, unless the Yanks come up with a better offer. He sounded his horn as he drew to a halt, then deliberately stood in the glare of the headlights, making himself visible before he switched them off and walked up the path. The door opened as he approached it, and Angelos stood in the light, the Webley massive in his fist.

'You forget things, too,' said Craig. 'Don't you know better than to make yourself a target?'

They moved toward the living room. From the kitchen there came a tinkle of glass, as Craig opened the living-room door. In the living room Miriam, Omar, and Kaplan sat waiting. Craig raced into the room, tipped up the heavy chair Kaplan sat in, pushed him behind it.

'Angelos,' he yelled. 'The lights. Get the lights.'

Angelos reached for the switch and a shot boomed out behind him. His body jerked to its impact, and he reeled into the room, took two stiff-legged strides and crashed down on to the floor. Craig fired into the hallway, and risked a look into the room. Omar had disappeared behind an upturned sofa, Miriam beside him. From the darkness behind the living room, a voice spoke.

'Mr. Craig,' it said, 'all we want is Kaplan.'

Beside him a rifle went off, an appalling explosion of noise in the confined space of the room, then Omar said softly, 'If I have to kill people – that's extra, effendi.'

The voice spoke again.

'It's no use, Mr. Craig. We've got all the advantages. Just send Kaplan out. That's all we want.'

Craig looked at Kaplan, who was whimpering with terror, then crouched lower behind the chair. The Russian was right. He had no chance at all, pinned down in the light. The chair and sofa they crouched behind were solid enough, but not solid enough to stop a heavy-calibre bullet. There was no chance of shooting out the lights, either: there were lamps all over the room, and he had no extra ammo... Something stirred by the door, and he looked at Angelos. The fat man, unseen in the angle of the door, had stirred. Blood soaked from a hole in his side on to the floor, but he was still alive.

Craig said softly in Greek, 'Angelos, turn

the lights off.'

The fat man stirred again, and moaned.

Craig spoke more urgently. 'Angelos, you can hear me. Turn the lights off.'

The voice outside spoke again. 'I shall count to ten. After that, we'll start firing into you. It will be your own fault, Craig. We only want Kaplan.' There was a silence, then– 'One– Two– Three–'

Craig said, 'Turn the lights off, Angelos – and then we'll be even. You won't owe me a damn thing.'

The voice had reached eight when Angelos rose with the shambling uncertainty of a drunk, lurched to the wall, and staggered into the doorway, his hand on the light switch. A second shot smashed into him, and it was the weight of his body falling that plunged the room into darkness.

Craig yelled to Omar not to fire, and swerved over the chair, wriggled on his belly to the door angle, waiting for a gun flash. When it came, he snapped off an answering shot and rolled behind the door. Another gun banged, and Craig noted its direction. In the darkness of the corridor a man was cursing – perhaps he'd hurt one of them, and he waited, tense, his hand stretched out in front of him, till he felt the softness of Angelos's body. He followed the outline of shoulder and arm, till at last he found the massive shape of the Webley, hefted it in his hands.

'All right, Omar,' he whispered. 'Give him three rounds, then cease fire.'

'Three rounds,' said Omar. 'A hundred dollars a round.'

The sound of the rifle was like blows from a giant hammer smashing the room, and after the third Craig leaped crouching into the doorway, sensed movement to his right and dropped flat. A gun banged, a shot cut the air where he'd been, and behind him, he could hear Miriam screaming. He fired the Webley, and the kick from it brought up the barrel until it pointed at the ceiling. The noise it made was scarcely less than the rifle's. He fired again, rolled to a new position. There was a sound of scuffling feet, the heavy thud of a falling body, then silence. Craig lay still in the darkness. One man was certainly out of it, and his guess was that there had only been two, and that the second one was hurt. But even so, there was no point in taking chances: if he miscalculated now they would all be dead. He waited a minute, two minutes. In the living room behind him he could hear Omar fidgeting restlessly with the rifle. At last, the voice spoke again. It sounded weak.

'There were only two of us, Mr. Craig,' it said, 'and you have killed my partner and wounded me. I should like to surrender.' Craig willed himself to stay silent. 'I'm going to put my gun down,' the voice said. There was a scraping sound and a heavy object scraped along the corridor. Noiselessly, an inch at a time, he stretched out his left hand until he touched it: a gun all right, an automatic; 9-millimetre by the feel of it. Three-gun Craig.

'I'm now going to stand up,' said the voice, and Craig became aware of a dark shape in the darkness before him. In the living room Omar's rifle clicked.

'Don't shoot yet, Omar,' Craig shouted.

'Thank you, Mr. Craig,' said the voice.

Craig rose to a crouch and moved to the light switch in the hall, pushed it up with the barrel of the automatic while the Webley covered the corridor. A tall, heavy-shouldered man stood swaying in front of him. Further back, in the kitchen doorway, an older man, squat, barrel chested, built like a bear, lay flat on his back. He was dead.

'Come forward slowly,' said Craig. 'Let's have a look at you, Mr. Lindemann.'

The young man's eyes flickered up at him as he lurched into the living room, one hand pressed to his shoulder. In front of him Miriam, Kaplan, and Omar faced him. Miriam had both hands pressed to her face, stifling the screams that had muted now to sobs, Omar's hands were clawlike on the rifle, his face alight with excitement. Kaplan looked once at Lindemann, then away, his face ageing even more as Craig watched.

Lindemann spoke in Russian.

'All that can wait,' said Craig, and led Lindemann to a chair, opened his coat, and looked at the wound.

'Get me some hot water,' he said. Omar moved, still holding the rifle. 'Not you,' said Craig. 'You stay here. Miriam.'

The girl's hands fell from her face and she moved slowly to the door. Angelos's body was in the way. 'Move him, Omar,' said Craig.

The old man slung the rifle over his shoulder and dragged Angelos out. Craig looked at the wound, a clean puncture through the right shoulder, a neat, purple-ringed hole back and front.

'You were lucky,' he said.

'In a sense,' said Lindemann.

Miriam brought hot water, and linen cloth torn into strips, then watched as Craig bandaged the wounded man, his hands deft and sure. Once he hurt Lindemann, making him cry out, but Craig went on as if nothing had happened, as if there were no blood on the carpet, no reek of cordite in the room, no ache in the ears from the crash of the rifle; as if Lindemann were a perfectly ordinary young man who'd had minor injuries in a car crash. When he'd finished he gave him a cigarette and a drink.

'So all you wanted was Kaplan,' Craig said. Lindemann was silent. 'Only you didn't get him,' said Craig. 'You got a mate of mine instead.' Again silence. 'Nice chap. Quiet. Ran a nice little business. You and your friend used to go there, didn't you? Chat up the girls. Is that why you killed him? So he couldn't identify you?'

'Stein killed him.'

'You didn't work all that hard to stop him. And now we can identify you. The girl, the old man, and me. Are you going to kill us if you get the chance?'

'The question is academic,' Lindemann said.

'Not to me... Maybe not to you, either.'

'All we wanted was Kaplan. Angelos – it was an accident. I am sorry for it.'

'Me too,' said Craig. 'He didn't have to die at all. You could have bought Kaplan. He's for sale.'

'Bought him?'

'A million roubles COD.'

'We are Israelis,' Lindemann said.

Craig looked over to Kaplan. 'Is that right?' he asked. Kaplan said, 'I don't know. I've never seen them before.'

'But you spoke in Russian.' Miriam said. 'They're Russian, aren't they? KGB?'

'Russian, yes. KGB, no,' said Craig. 'They're in your file,' he told Kaplan. 'They're the ones who survived the break-out from Volochanka. Their names are Daniel and Asimov. Daniel's the dead one. Right?'

The young man looked away again. 'You wanted Kaplan because he betrayed you. Isn't that right, Kaplan?'

Kaplan said, 'I have never – have never–' Then his voice choked. He turned away.

'You've wanted him dead ever since you got out of Volochanka.'

'One year, three weeks, and four days,' said Asimov. 'It was the only thought in our minds.'

'Tell us about it,' said Craig.

'He's sick,' the girl said. 'He should be in a hospital.'

'No,' Asimov said. 'That isn't important. What Kaplan did – that is important. I want you to know.'

'We do know,' said Craig.

'Not all. I am sure Kaplan did not tell you all.'

Asimov looked at Kaplan, then, with a hunger of hate such as Craig had rarely seen, an almost sensual appraising of the older man's body, as if Asimov were calculating how much he could endure before he broke.

'Please. I want to get out of here,' Kaplan said.

'No,' said Craig, and at once Omar moved in on Kaplan, who sat down and turned his face from them. He was willing himself not to listen, Craig knew, but his will was not strong enough.

'He told you about the minyan, no doubt,'

said Asimov. Craig nodded. 'And about our plan to escape? It was a good plan. A beautiful plan. Daniel made it.' He looked up then, facing Craig. 'There is something you must realize. I worshipped Daniel.'

'Go on,' said Craig.

'The plan worked perfectly, as Daniel had promised it would. Only – when we got out, Kaplan was missing. I thought he had been unfortunate, but even then Daniel knew better. He knew that Kaplan had betrayed us – and because he knew it, I am still alive. When we split up, you see, we took a different route – not the one we had discussed when Kaplan was present – and so we got out alive. We learned later that the others did not. The guards caught them and killed them, every single one.'

'What happened to you?'

'We should have died then. I mean – there was no real possibility that we could survive. And yet somehow we did. Fishing. Trapping animals. Digging up roots. We lived like beasts, and like beasts we survived, and got away to the West. The filthy capitalist West. A place called Vardo, up in the north of Norway. By then it was winter, and we got a job on the railway. We told the boss we were Finns and we'd lost our passports. He didn't believe us, but he didn't do anything about it either. Labour's scarce up there in the winter. We worked through till spring, then took off. It was time for him to tell the police about it. We got to Oslo. That wasn't easy, but after Volochanka, nothing was too difficult.'

'You could have told the Norwegians who you were,' said Craig. 'They'd look after you.'

'On their terms,' said Asimov. 'We wanted our freedom – to find out about Kaplan.'

'What happened in Oslo?' Craig asked.

'Daniel knew of a man there who could forge papers for us if we paid him.'

'Where did you get the money?' asked Miriam.

'We stole it. Stealing isn't difficult – not if you're taught by experts. There were many thieves in Volochanka. We got the money and the man gave us our papers. We became Israelis. Lindemann and Stein. Then we flew to Cyprus.'

He stopped then, as if the recital were finished. Craig thought otherwise.

'You didn't stay here,' he said. Asimov looked at Miriam.

'I really am tired now,' he said. The girl moved closer to them, her eyes fixed on Asimov, glowing with admiration. Behind her Kaplan sat like a stone man, but he had heard every word.

'Can't he rest for a while?' Miriam asked.

'No,' said Craig. 'He has to finish it. Then we can decide what to do with him.'

'He's been through so much.'

'More than you realize,' said Craig, and turned to the Russian. 'Tell us about when the KGB found you.'

Asimov's good hand clenched on his lap. He said nothing.

'Was it the man who forged your papers?' Craig asked. 'Is that how they found out?' He waited a moment, looking at Asimov. He was white now, exhausted, the onset of shock catching up with him at last.

'I've got all night,' Craig said. 'I don't think you have. But the KGB found you, didn't they? They even offered to help you. Weapons – money – information. And you took them all.'

Kaplan said, 'That can't be true. You know that can't be true.'

Craig looked at him. His face trembling, Kaplan walked over to Asimov, looked down at him, and spoke, his voice a scream. 'Is it true?'

Asimov lay back and closed his eyes, and Kaplan grabbed for him, shook him.

'You must tell me now,' he screamed.

Miriam went to him, pulled his hands from Asimov and pushed him into a chair.

'Let him rest,' she said.

'You will never know how important this is,' he told her.

'I know,' said Craig. He bent closer to Asimov. 'All right you're tired, so I won't make you talk. All you have to do is listen. But you'd better do that Asimov, or I'll leave you with Kaplan.'

'Talk, then,' said Asimov. 'It's all foolishness anyway.'

'The KGB reached you,' said Craig, 'and they told you what you already knew – that Kaplan had betrayed you. They said they'd help you to find him, because they wanted him dead too. They gave you money, and sent you to New York.' The girl turned to him, wide-eyed. 'You had to get information from Marcus Kaplan, I should think, but when you got there you found the Americans were ahead of you. Marcus already had a bodyguard. So then you went to see the man who'd interrogated Kaplan, a man called Laurie S. Fisher – at an apartment building called the Graydon Arms.'

Asimov leaned back further in the chair.

'Don't go to sleep now,' said Craig. 'This is where it gets interesting. You found Fisher all right. The way you found him must have been perfect for you. He was in bed with a woman. You killed the woman, then tortured him until he told you all you needed to know. Then you killed him.' He hurried on, not looking at Miriam. 'Then your KGB contact found out I was in town and sent a couple of blokes to kill me. They tried, when I was with Marcus Kaplan – and they made a mess of it. But that wasn't too important, was it? Fisher had told you Kaplan was in Kutsk, and you went there looking for him. You made a mistake at Kutsk, Asimov. That place is full of Omar's relatives. The only language they understand is money. But your luck held anyway. You stayed on in Famagusta, waiting. It's nice and handy for Turkey, and your cover was good. A lot of Israelis stay here. Then damn me if I didn't walk right in on you at Angelos's night club. And the girl who takes them off while the bouzouki plays said: "I can't understand Angelos. He's never at the club these days." So you followed him, didn't you, mate? And you did a spot of mountaineering and climbed in through the kitchen window and brought your score up to three.'

'How can you know this is true?' Kaplan asked.

'I saw Fisher and his girl,' said Craig. 'I saw what was done to him. And that's the only way our intrepid hero could have found out how to reach you, Kaplan.' He turned to Miriam. 'You think I'm rough,' he said. 'You should see this fellow's work. Even Royce wouldn't be ashamed of it.'

Asimov said in a whisper, 'That was Daniel.'

'You should record that and save your voice,' said Craig.

'I don't mean to excuse myself. I was there and saw it happen and did nothing to prevent it. I did nothing to stop him <u>killing</u> your friend, either. And Angelos had been very kind to us.'

'And this is the man you worshipped?' Miriam said.

'He saved my life so many times I almost lost count. Even in the camp, he helped me. Looked after me. He showed me how to survive – and how to hit back. If it hadn't been for Daniel, I'd still be an animal in the cage of Volochanka. When we got out – in Norway, in Sweden, then here – he taught me how to be a man again, and not just an animal.' He looked at Kaplan. 'Also he taught me how to hate properly. In this world, existence is hopeless unless you can hate. And I hate you, Kaplan. I will hate you till Craig kills me.'

'Maybe I'll let him do it,' said Craig. 'Maybe I won't do it at all. You puzzle me, friend. You really do.'

'I did what had to be done to kill Kaplan,' said Asimov. 'Why is that puzzling?'

'Can you tell him, Omar?' Craig asked.

'You don't have to tell a Turk anything about hating,' Omar said. 'We've been doing it for years. Greeks mostly. And Arabs. Almost anybody who isn't a Turk – and quite a few that are. But when we hate – we hate a man and his family. Not strangers. We don't torture strangers or kill a woman making love because she's in the way, or a fat man who has been kind to us, even if he is a Greek.'

Asimov said, 'Killing Kaplan was our whole world. Nothing else mattered.'

'I hate your world,' said Miriam.

'I spit on it,' said Omar. 'I spit on you.'

'Hate it, spit on it, my world exists,' said Asimov, and looked at Kaplan.

'Let the old Jew kill the young one, effendi,' Omar said. 'It's the worst punishment you could think of for the young one, and the old one will enjoy it.'

'No,' said Kaplan. 'I don't want to kill him.'

'He wants you to live,' said Craig. 'To remind him there's somebody else as bad as he is. After all that wonderful talk in the camp, you wound up working for the KGB.'

'Are you going to kill me, then?'

'Why should I?'

'I let Angelos die.'

'And I killed Daniel – the one you worshipped. Just how good a hater are you? Suppose I let you live – do I go on your list too? And Omar and the girl? They stood by and let me do it.'

'Please,' Asimov said. 'Please, I really am tired.' His lips curled up for a moment. 'Dead tired.'

His body slumped forward. Craig caught him and carried him into a bedroom, then came out and looked at the body of Daniel. Omar came up beside him.

'It's hot here, boss. Even up in the mountains. This one and the Greek – they won't keep long.'

Craig looked down at the dead face. It was strong and hard as a weapon, the face of a man with an overwhelming drive to the achievement of one objective at a time, a man who would feel neither pity nor remorse for what had to be done to achieve that objective. Asimov didn't look like that. Not yet.

'Put them in the garage,' Craig said. 'Take the air-conditioning unit out of your bedroom and plug it in.'

'Air conditioning, boss?' Craig did it for him.

Chapter Thirteen

They lay together in the coolness of the room, and she could sense his relaxation in the tenderness of his hands as he embraced her, the sigh of content when he lit a cigarette after they had made love. In the darkness her fingers explored the scars on his body.

'There was a time when I thought you were the most hateful man in the world,' she said.

'You had a remarkable way of showing it.'

She dug an elbow into his stomach and he grunted with pain.

'It was partly cracks like that that made me think it,' she said. 'But now I know you're only Little League stuff – compared with Kaplan, Daniel, Asimov. You're just an amateur.'

'I was never in Volochanka,' he said.

'You've had things done to you–'

'And I've hit back.'

'Sure – at your enemies. Not people who haven't harmed you. And you didn't betray – like Kaplan.' She put an arm round his chest. 'I hate that man,' she said. 'Liar. Betrayer. And now he's happy – just as you said – because somebody else is as bad as he is. What a credit to my people. He's like a cartoon Jew in a Nazi comic strip.'

'He's what other people made him,' said Craig.

'He could have done so much.'

'He will.'

Suddenly the girl's body moved away from his. He put out his hand, felt the tender weight of a breast, then his fingers moved up her throat to her face. She was crying.

'I say, look here. Dash it, old girl. What?' he said.

She giggled for a moment, but her tears continued. He gathered her into his arms and held her gently, whispering to her as the tears spilled on to his shoulder. She was weeping for a world of illusions wrecked, of values destroyed, and for Kaplan too. Soon and late, Miriam would shed a lot of tears for Kaplan. Craig got up and dressed. It was his turn to keep watch.

As he entered the living room he knew at once that something was wrong. Omar sat in the chair, as he should – but he was too still, too relaxed. Craig went to him. The old man lay back in his chair, breathing in great snoring gasps. A bruise darkened the side of his head. The rifle was gone. Craig raced to Kaplan's bedroom, took the key from his pocket, unlocked the heavy door, and went in. Kaplan lay sleeping, and Craig raced back to Asimov's room. It was empty.

He roused Miriam and sent her to look after Omar, then went back to Kaplan, grateful for the solid doors in Angelos's house, and for the fact that he'd locked Kaplan in every night. He'd locked in Asimov too, even though he'd looked so weak, and so defeated. But he'd found a way past the door. And now he was up in the mountains with a rifle. Craig woke up Kaplan and told him what had happened. The fear that was a part of his life came back to his face.

By the morning, Omar had recovered consciousness. His face looked grey, and very old, but his strength was astonishing. Craig marvelled at the hardness of the old man's head, and the stamina that had brought him round.

'I was a fool, effendi. A bloody fool – and at my age too,' he said. 'He asked me if he could go to the toilet.' He put a hand to his head. 'My oath, he can hit.'

'It wasn't your fault.' Craig said.

'He'll be up in the mountains.' Craig nodded. 'With a rifle. But he won't use it, boss. Not with that shoulder the way it is.'

'Why not?'

'It'll kill him.'

'I don't suppose he cares,' said Craig, and made for the door.

Omar called out to him. 'Did he take my money, boss?'

'No,' Craig said. 'It's here.' He rummaged in a dressing-table drawer and produced the half bills, put them in Omar's hands.

'Thanks,' said Omar, and went to sleep holding his money.

Later that day a Land-Rover appeared on the path. Miriam was watching, and she called Craig at once. Joanna Benson was driving, and beside her Loomis sat, enormous, liquescent, and very angry.

Craig told Omar to stay out of sight, and left Miriam on watch, then he went into the kitchen, collected Kaplan, who was preparing lunch, and locked him in his room, warning him to stay away from the window. As Loomis waddled angrily to the open front door, Joanna following, Craig stood inside it, the Smith and Wesson in his hand. Loomis puffed past him without a word, and Craig let Joanna go by and took them into the kitchen. The smell of food made Loomis angrier than ever.

'All right,' he said. 'I accept your offer.'

Craig raised the Smith and Wesson.

'What the devil are you looking so coy about?' asked Loomis. 'And put that thing down.'

'I hardly know how to say this,' Craig said. 'Face the wall, please.'

'You really have gone potty,' Loomis yelled.

'Face the wall.' The gun, that had pointed between them, now concentrated on Loomis, and he obeyed.

'Handbag on the table, Miss Benson,' Craig said. She put it down. 'Now, turn around. Put your hands on the wall. Lean forward.'

In silence, they did as they were told. Joanna Benson's handbag yielded the .32 she had carried before; neither of them had weapons concealed on them.

'All right,' said Craig. 'You can turn around.'

'I bet you enjoyed that,' Joanna Benson said, and Loomis said only, 'There are limits, Craig. You've reached them.'

'It's a compliment, really,' said Craig. 'There's nothing you wouldn't try to do me down, and we both know it.'

'Balls,' said Loomis. 'I told you. I accept your offer.'

'Let's see the guarantee,' said Craig.

Loomis reached into his pocket and handed over a sheet of paper. It contained all that he had asked. 'The money,' said Craig.

'Ah,' Loomis said. 'We got conditions about the money. Kaplan goes to New York – the Yanks insist on delivery – and you take him. When you get there you get a hundred thousand quid in dollars – less fifty thousand dollars you pinched from the emergency fund.'

'Why doesn't the department take him?'

'I want my hundred thousand quid's worth,' said Loomis.

'I may need a bit of help.'

'Why?'

'The KGB want Kaplan too. Let me have Royce and Benson here.'

'All right.'

'She can take you back in the Land-Rover, then come back to pick us up. Royce too.'

'His foot's still bad,' said Loomis.

'He doesn't shoot with his foot. She can also get a man's white wig, a man's yellow wig, a Cyprus stamp on Miriam Loman's passport – and mine. And air tickets to New York.'

Loomis glowered at him once more.

'You like your pound of flesh, don't you?'

'That brings us to Omar,' Craig said. 'You'll have to smuggle him out, or it's no deal. Well?'

'I'll find a feller to do it,' said Loomis.

'That's it, then,' Craig said. He stuck the gun in his waistband. 'You're a pleasure to do business with, Mr. Loomis.'

Loomis used three words. Craig had heard them all before. He put the .32 back in the handbag and gave it to Joanna Benson.

Miriam was delighted to be going home. Omar also was happy. He'd lost his boat – that was unfortunate – but instead he had a vast wad of hundred dollar bills. Craig found him a roll of transparent tape and Omar was happy. Kaplan alone made difficulties.

'I don't want to go to America,' he said. 'I was happy in Kutsk.'

'You can't go back there. Asimov will find you,' Miriam said. 'And anyway – what's wrong with going to America? Your brother's there.'

'I'd like to see Marcus. That's fine,' said Kaplan. 'But what will they make me do there?'

'Work,' said Craig. 'The kind of work you should be doing.'

'But the KGB will find out. They'll come after me again.'

'You'll be looked after,' Craig said.

'I was happy in Kutsk,' Kaplan said again.

'You had six months,' said Craig. 'You're lucky it lasted that long.'

The Land-Rover arrived, and in it were Royce, Benson, and a taciturn sailor whose business was to take Omar back to Turkey. Craig sent them both off at once in the Volkswagen. The old man turned to Craig, his fingers counted the money for the last time.

'You made me rich, effendi,' he said. 'The only rich man in Kutsk.' He sighed. 'Now I'll have to buy my wife a fur coat.'

'Don't tell her,' said Craig.

'Boss,' Omar's voice was reproachful. 'She's a woman. How can I help it?' He bowed to Craig. 'Have a good journey. And come and look me up some time. Maybe we can do some more business together.'

Craig watched him go, then turned to Royce. 'How's the limp?' he asked.

'Fair,' Royce said.

'Let's see you walk.'

Royce braced himself, then moved across the room. For a short distance, at least, the limp was hardly noticeable.

'That's fine,' said Craig. 'Now you and Kaplan change clothes.'

'What is this?' said Royce.

'Didn't Loomis tell you who was boss? Go in the bedroom if you're shy.'

When they'd gone, Joanna Benson looked from Miriam to Craig.

'Isn't there someone missing?' she asked.

'Who?'

'Your friend Angelos. I thought he was with you.'

'He is,' said Craig. 'But it's better if you and he don't meet.'

'Fair enough,' said Joanna. 'Then there's the Israeli pair. I had a look for them, Craig. They've disappeared.' She hesitated. 'Is that why Andrew's changing clothes with Kaplan?' Craig didn't answer. 'Loomis was right. You really do like your pound of flesh.' She turned to Miriam. 'Doesn't he, darling?'

Royce and Kaplan came back and Craig fitted on the wigs Joanna had brought.

'These wouldn't fool anybody,' said Royce.

They'd fool a man on a mountainside, watching a moving car, Craig thought.

Asimov would soon be ill. He'd taken another look at his wound, seen how inflamed it was. His temperature was rising too, and soon he'd have fever. But there was food enough to keep him going – last night he'd robbed the kitchen – and water in the mountain streams. And he didn't have to hold out for long. He was certain of it. The Land-Rover would be coming back soon, with Kaplan in it, and no matter what precautions Craig took, he, Asimov, would then kill Kaplan. The likelihood was that he would then die, of exposure and weakness, up here in the mountains, or by execution, if they hanged murderers in Cyprus. He didn't know. It was funny. He was going to commit a murder and he didn't know what the penalty was. Life imprisonment, perhaps. The British had abolished hanging, and maybe the Cypriots had too. Life imprisonment he could face, so long as the prison wasn't Volochanka, and he'd even escaped from there.

Asimov lay on his back, nursing his strength as Daniel had taught him. He was weary now, utterly weary, with a tiredness of the will that exhausted him as completely as the mine at Volochanka. He thought of the ten of them, the plot to escape, the lectures, the preparation, the training. They had all meant hope for the future, and with hope even Siberia is bearable. And when he and Daniel had escaped, they still had a reason to go on fighting life. Revenge, this time. An ignoble emotion, though the Elizabethans, he remembered, had made a whole literature out of it, with Hamlet as its finest flower. Love was better, the philosophers said, and he'd loved Daniel. He must have done, not to have stopped him that day in the Graydon. But revenge was better than nothing. It made you keep on living till you achieved what you set out to do. But it would be better if he could forget that day at the Graydon: the surprise on the girl's face just before she died: the man's agonized screams smothered by the gag. Daniel had been so skillful, and he'd stood by and watched.

Maybe he'd enjoyed– The thought was unbearable. If it were true, it made him everything that Turk had said. No better than the guards at Volochanka, no better than Kaplan.

He began to think of a poem he had written in prison. A pattern of ice on a birch tree, and the dull red disc of the sun. Since they'd got out, he hadn't written a line of poetry. Couldn't. He looked up into the darkness of the pine tree that sheltered him. Behind it were the mountains of Troodos, rich, fat mountains, alive with hares, birds, fruit. If it weren't for his shoulder, he could live here indefinitely. From the distance he could hear the growl of a heavy engine. Asimov rolled over on to his stomach. The rifle was by his side, the shoulder of his jacket stuffed with grass to take the impact of its recoil. He was as ready as he would ever be.

Craig had rehearsed the move to the Land-Rover carefully. First Joanna, going quickly into the driver's seat, backing it up to the door, then Miriam, then Kaplan, limping, wearing a blond wig, then Royce in a white wig, then Craig, Kaplan and Craig acting like bodyguards. Royce got into the Land-Rover next to Joanna, and Craig sat beside him. Miriam and Kaplan were in the back. Joanna let in the clutch and drove off at once, and the four-wheel drive tackled the mud track as if it were an autobahn. Mindful of his instructions, she hit a good pace and kept to it.

'Something's up,' Royce said at last. 'And you know what it is.'

Craig kept his eyes on the mountainside. Slopes and ridges, outcrops of rock; perfect sniper country.

'You've got no right to do this to me,' said Royce, then yelled at the silence: 'For God's sake, tell me what's happening.'

'It's possible there's a sniper out there,'

said Craig.

Royce hunched down in his seat, and as he did so a bullet starred the window by Craig, smacked into Royce as they heard the report of a rifle. Joanna accelerated, and reached a corner in a burst of speed as Craig yelled instructions. The car skidded round the corner and stopped. Craig leaped out of it and raced up the side of the hill, rolled into cover behind a rock. From where he lay he could see Kaplan bending over Royce; Joanna getting out of the driving seat, examining the engine with what looked like frantic haste. He could see, too, a ripple of movement in the long grass on the mountainside, the movement of a man who had been trained to move with caution and skill. Craig took out the 9-millimetre automatic. It had nothing like the range of the rifle, but if Asimov came close enough, it would do.

The ripple of the grass came closer, and at last he could see Asimov's body as he wriggled his way between Craig and the Land-Rover. The group on the road didn't see him until he raised himself to his feet, the rifle held at the hip. Craig could see that he was swaying, very slightly.

Joanna and Miriam froze, as he had told them to do, but Kaplan panicked, turned and dived out of the car seat, racing across the road. And as he moved, Asimov saw him. He raised the rifle, his body swaying more than ever, though the gun was steady. Behind him. Craig got to his feet, his arm raised in the classic pistol-shooting position.

'Asimov!' he yelled, and the Russian checked, then started to turn, far too late. Craig fired once, then again, and the impact of the heavy bullets knocked Asimov sprawling, set him rolling over and over down the long, lush grass until he came to rest at last by the Land-Rover's front wheel. Joanna Benson looked down at him. Two wounds: one through the side of the head, one through the heart, fired from fifty feet away as he turned. Asimov had had no chance at all, and that was exactly as it should be.

Craig came slowly down to them, his eyes on Kaplan as he walked back across the road. Miriam, for the first time, saw emotion in his eyes, a boiling rage it took all his strength to contain. He looked down at Royce, picked up a spent bullet embedded in the floorboard of the car.

'Is he dead?' he asked.

'No,' Kaplan said. 'The bullet hit him across the neck. Creased a nerve, I think.'

Craig pulled Royce upright. The bullet had furrowed a great gouge from his ear almost to his nape. He'd be marked for life, unless Loomis paid for plastic surgery, but he was alive. Joanna got a first-aid kit from the back of the Land-Rover, put lint on the wound and held it in place with tape.

'Poor Andrew,' she said. 'It's all I seem to do for him.'

Still looking at Kaplan, Craig said, 'Asimov wasn't so lucky. You damn fool, why couldn't you stay still and let me take him alive?'

'I was afraid,' Kaplan said. 'I can't help it, Craig. I'll always be afraid.'

'That's what makes you so dangerous,' Craig said. 'You get scared and somebody else gets killed.'

He bent, picked up the rifle, and dragged Asimov into a cleft behind a rock that hid him from the road. The face that looked up at him was suddenly ten years younger, smooth and untroubled. He'd lived through horror, and he'd seen and done terrible things, but he hadn't been irreclaimable, like Daniel. There had still been loyalty in him, and courage, and a zest for life. Something could have been done with Asimov, but not nearly as much as could be done with Kaplan. And so, thought Craig, he died. No. That was dishonest thinking. And so I killed him.

Royce recovered consciousness on the road to Nicosia. He looked up, and saw Craig beside him. 'You bastard,' he whispered.

'If it makes you any happier, the man who did it is dead,' said Craig.

'You set me up for this, didn't you? You wanted it to happen.'

'Rest,' said Craig. 'You're suffering from

shock, poor boy.'

Joanna had their air tickets and passports, luggage waited for them at Nicosia airport, and the fat man himself waited to see them off. The sight of Royce displeased him, and he said so. Royce closed his eyes as the great voice roared on. Craig took him to the bar.

'I had to do it that way,' he said. 'I knew Asimov was up in the hills with a rifle.'

'You get him?'

'Yes,' said Craig.

'That leaves Daniel.'

'No,' Craig said. 'He's dead too.'

'You *have* come back to life,' Loomis said.

'My swan song. Anyway, I muffed it. I let Asimov get away. And Daniel killed Angelos.'

Loomis looked at him and said carefully, 'Rule number one in our business. Never have any chums.'

'He wasn't my chum,' said Craig. 'He didn't like me at all.'

'What was he, then?'

'My debtor.'

'Not any more,' said Loomis. 'I reckon he's paid. Which reminds me – Royce is no good to you now either. D'you want me to send some people out from England?'

'We'll have to go to Athens to get to New York,' said Craig. 'Force Three could be waiting for us. I'll need a man there. A Greek if you've got one.'

Loomis downed a massive jolt of local

brandy, and wrapped on the counter for another.

'We got a bloke in Athens already,' he said.

'I'll need him too,' said Craig, and began to explain. When he'd finished, Loomis thought for a moment, then said, 'It might work, cock. If you're as good as you think you are. But are you sure two men's enough? You don't want any help after that?'

'Benson's all I need,' said Craig.

'At least she's on your side,' said Loomis. Craig turned to him, wearily going through the motions of calm, hand steady as he lifted his glass, knowing he didn't fool Loomis for a second.

'What the hell does that mean?' he asked.

'She helped you get away, and we both know it. That day they had you and the Loman person prisoner in the barn, she measured you against Royce and opted for you. Why?'

'Royce tortured Miriam,' said Craig.

'You're saying Benson's squeamish?'

'I'm saying she thinks ahead. Royce enjoyed his work – and it showed. And Benson saw it was a weakness. Look, Loomis – Benson talks like a deb and acts like an idiot with a daddy in the peerage, but she's as shrewd as you are. So she let me get away. It was her way of making a deal.'

'And very nice too,' said Loomis. 'Except I'm the one who pays the bill. I must have a word with her about that. Royce too.' He sighed. 'Pity about that. He was damn good at the school. Think I should send him to a psychiatrist?'

'You could try,' said Craig. 'Too bad Asimov missed him, isn't it?'

'Tut tut,' said Loomis. 'The things you say.'

'Like a couple of weeks ago. I said, "You can hardly just let me go, can you?" And you said, 'No. I can hardly do that.'''

Loomis said, 'One of these fine days I'll drop dead of overeating, and a nice little feller in a bowler hat and pinstriped underwear'll come and see you and offer you my job. What'll you do then, son?'

'Refuse.'

'That may not be easy.'

'I can always shoot myself,' said Craig.

The flight call came then, and they went out to the aircraft. For once Loomis had been generous, and they travelled first class. Craig sat beside Kaplan, and they made the journey in silence. Joanna and Miriam didn't talk much either.

Chapter Fourteen

They had four rooms in a hotel in Constitution Square. It was a pleasant hotel, big, shady, cool, with a fifty-year-old elegance that was already as valuable as an antique. The hotel was full of Americans just off to Delphi, Germans just back from Crete, Italians making a film, and Swedes absorbing sun and culture in such quantities that only the bar could save their sanity and their skins. Craig watched them as he waited for the lift. There were too many of them. Kaplan shouldn't stay here. And yet in America it could only be worse. When the lift doors opened, Craig watched approvingly as Joanna pushed Kaplan in ahead of her, her tall body covering him. Then Miriam went, and Craig last, his right hand inside his coat, ready, waiting.

The rooms were on the fifth floor, and the clang of contemporary Athens was muted below them. Athenians have never been an inhibited people: noise as an art form they find as convenient as any other, and cheap to practice. Craig sent Kaplan to his room. locked him in, and turned to the others.

'What do you want to do?' he asked.

'I want to go out,' said Miriam. 'I'm sick of being cooped up.'

'All right,' said Craig. 'I'll go with you.'

'If you want to,' she said. 'Wouldn't you sooner take a rest?'

'I would. Yes,' Craig said. 'I'm just worried about you, that's all.'

'Oh, I'll be just fine,' she said. 'All I want to do is be a tourist for a while. Go to the Acropolis, maybe.'

Joanna Benson opened her mouth, saw the look in Craig's eye and shut it again.

'Off you go, then,' said Craig. 'But don't be late. I'm waiting for a cancellation on a flight. If we get it, we leave at dawn.'

Before she left, Miriam kissed him. Then the door closed and Joanna Benson said, 'Darling, I know she sleeps with you and all that, but aren't you being a teeny bit self-indulgent?'

'No,' said Craig. 'She'll be followed. I set it up with Loomis before I left.'

The tall girl sighed her relief. 'Do you think there's much danger in Athens?'

'Some,' said Craig. 'The CIA made a deal with Loomis – information for Kaplan. Then they subcontracted to Force Three. If Force Three picks up Kaplan here, Loomis doesn't get his information and I don't get my money.'

'So you let her take a walk,' said Joanna.

'I like to know who the opposition is,'

said Craig.

It was pleasant to be out alone, to walk across the square, to feel the press of an anonymous crowd about you. That reminded her of New York, and the thought made her smile. She had always hated the crowds in New York. She crossed the street to a cafe in the middle of the square, and Maskouri, who was following her, hoped she would sit down and drink coffee. It was much too hot to walk very far. She chose a table in the shady part, and Maskouri was relieved. Too many Americans liked to sit in the sun. He found a table nearby and ordered beer, sipped first at the glass of cold water that came with it. The Loman girl ordered a large, and, to Maskouri's eyes, disgusting ice cream, and spooned it up with enthusiasm. Then suddenly she hesitated. A tall American was approaching her. He was carrying a transistor radio, and it was playing a tune Maskouri recognized vaguely, and somehow associated with a sad-faced little man who played the piano. The American looked down at the girl, then said:

'Why, Miriam Loman! Well, for heaven's sakes. I was talking to Marcus just two days ago.'

The girl smiled at him, and said 'Hello,' and asked him to sit down. Maskouri doubted that she had seen the tall American before, and this might be important. And once he'd sat down, he wasn't talking loud enough for Maskouri to hear. He wondered whether he should report back or not, when the American rose, took the girl's hand and said, 'Great to see you, Miriam. Just great. Be sure to give my love to Marcus when you see him.'

'Oh, I certainly will,' said Miriam.

The tall American went off, and Miriam paid her bill, changing dollars with the waiter, then walked to the taxi rank. Maskouri got up to follow, and was promptly knocked flat by a couple of Americans, who apologized profusely for not looking where they were going. They picked him up and the grip they had on him seemed friendly enough, but Maskouri was sensible. He knew enough not to struggle. When the taxi had gone, one of the Americans said, 'Sorry, feller,' and offered him a cigar. Maskouri, being Athenian, was a philosopher. He accepted it.

'She's taking her time,' Joanna Benson said.

'So's the man Loomis sent to Athens,' said Craig. He looked at his watch. 'He should have rung in an hour ago. I think we'd better make arrangements.'

'Such as?'

'They'll come for Kaplan – alive. And to

make sure of that, they'll immobilize us first.'

'Immobilize? Do you by any chance think they'll kill us?'

'Not if they can avoid it,' said Craig. 'But the bloke Maskouri saw talking to her will do it if he has to. He'd prefer to use knock-out drops or a bang on the head.'

'Neither's terribly pleasant.'

Craig grinned. 'Neither's going to happen,' he said. 'Listen.'

He began to talk; and first Joanna smiled, then laughed aloud.

'But darling, it's positively kinky,' she said.

'Get the silencer.'

She produced it from her handbag and Craig screwed it on to the end of the Smith and Wesson, then broke the gun, looked into the magazine. Three shots left. But the silencer wouldn't last more than three shots anyway. After that he would have to fall back on the Webley, and an utter lack of privacy.

'You'd really use that thing on our allies?' the girl asked.

'I have no allies. I'm a freelance,' said Craig.

'Yes, but even so—'

'Listen,' said Craig. 'These aren't nice, gentlemanly Ivy Leaguers from the CIA. These are professionals. The way you think you are.'

'You'll find out,' Joanna said.

'I always knew. Forgive the sarcasm,' said Craig. 'Just take my word for it. These are blokes the KGB would be proud of.'

The phone rang. Craig picked it up and listened, then turned to her.

'That was Loomis's man,' he said. 'Miriam met two more Americans at the Acropolis. He couldn't get close enough to hear.'

When Miriam returned, she found the others in Craig's room, having a meal of coffee and sandwiches.

'Aren't we dining downstairs?' she asked.

'No,' said Craig. 'Too risky. Have a sandwich. Joanna, pour Miriam some coffee.'

'Risky?'

'Yes,' said Craig. 'I've had a premonition. Do you ever have premonitions, Miriam?'

Joanna handed her a sandwich. The whole thing was as English as a thirties farce: sandwiches and tinkling spoons, and the distinguished elderly foreigner who was about to upset his cup any minute. And there was farce in the way they were overplaying it, too. Farce or its nearest neighbour, violence.

'John,' Miriam said. 'What *is* all this?'

'An hour and a half ago I heard from a dark stranger,' said Craig. 'At least I expect he's dark. Most Greeks are. Chap called Maskouri. You didn't see him, by any chance?'

'I didn't see anybody – except a man who used to know Marcus. But I got rid of him.

Then I had some ice cream and went to the Acropolis.'

Craig turned to Joanna. 'Why would she lie to me? A nice girl like that.'

'*Do* have another sandwich,' Joanna said to Miriam, then to Craig, 'Patriotism, perhaps?'

'You mean the American she met told her it was in her country's best interests not to tell a soul that they had met?'

'He probably showed her a picture of Lyndon Johnson or Bugs Bunny or somebody.'

'More likely music. Music to remind her of happy days. Junior Proms and old films on TV and travelling in the elevator at the Hilton. I bet he played her "Stardust."'

Joanna's eyes had never left Miriam's face.

'Do you know,' she said, 'I believe he did.'

'You followed me,' said Miriam. 'But you got it wrong. He was a friend of Marcus.'

'Good heavens, we British chappies don't have to follow people,' said Craig. 'We get ruddy foreigners to do that. No, love. We deduced it.' He moved a step closer to her. 'I'm afraid you're going to have to tell us, you know.' She was silent. 'Ah,' he said. 'I know what you're thinking. Royce isn't here, you tell yourself, and a decent chap like Craig wouldn't do things like that, and Miss Benson's an English gentlewoman after all. Sews Union Jacks on her panties.

But that isn't the point, love. The point is we know they're in Athens.'

'How could they be?' Miriam asked.

'Loomis sent a wire to that box number in Paris,' said Joanna. 'Told them the deal with Craig is off. And there's only three ways out of Cyprus, darling – Turkey, Israel, and Greece. They'll be watching them all. But it's the ones in Greece who'll get hurt.'

Craig said, 'We won't hurt you, Miriam, and I don't want to hurt them. You tell us what they're up to and we won't hurt them. If you don't – it might get a bit messy.'

'You're angry with me – for what I've done,' she said.

'If I am, I have no right to be.'

'It's my country, John. My people.'

He nodded. 'And it's your people who'll get hurt – if you don't tell me.'

'Don't you ever fight fair?' she asked.

'How can I?' said Craig. 'Now, drink your coffee and tell me all about it.'

Suddenly the mockery had gone. She was aware that he wanted to be kind to her, kind and uncomplicated, and that he was finding it difficult.

It was early morning, the dead hour, the hour of the ultimate spy. The one who will kill if he must. There were three of them. One stayed in the corridor, watching the rooms of Kaplan and Joanna, the others entered the room that Craig had given to Miriam. Her bed, they knew, was to the right of the room, facing the bathroom, and Craig would be in it. That had been Miriam's assignment, to get Craig into her bed, and she'd resisted it furiously at first. She'd taken a lot of convincing, but in the end she'd agreed. And having got him there, the team leader reckoned, she'd keep him pretty busy. Craig was a tough one. Exhausted or not, their instructions were to keep out of range of his hands. Those hands of Craig's could batter like steel clubs.

The lock specialist took out his skeleton key and got on with it. Hotel locks, even the locks of good hotels, didn't keep him waiting long. He probed with the casual skill of a surgeon performing a routine operation. Two tiny clicks sounded, and the lock specialist withdrew the key, slipped it into an oil bottle and inserted it again. Next time he turned it, the door opened without a sound, and he and the team leader entered in a whisper, the door drifted to behind them as they stayed still for a count of ten, their eyes grew used to the blackness.

At last, the leader touched the lock man. In the imperfect dark they could see the two shapes of bodies lying on the bed, one hunched over the other. The lock man moved to the wall, switched on the lights, and as he did so his right hand made an abrupt gesture, ending up holding a short-nosed Colt .45 fitted with a silencer. The leader stood six feet away from him, holding a similar gun, and one of the figures on the bed stirred and shot up indignantly.

For a moment the leader thought they'd gone into the wrong room – a mistake so elementary he wanted to kill himself – for the figure in front of him was that of a beautiful and very naked woman. He hesitated just a split second too long, and was already starting to turn when Craig's voice spoke behind him.

'Be sensible,' said Craig. 'You can't win them all. Guns on the bed, please.'

The lock expert waited until the leader's hand moved, then he too threw his gun down. The gorgeous broad moved as if she was wearing clothes up to her chin, and tucked the guns under her pillow. The lock expert began to sweat, then sweated harder as she got out of bed and put on a negligee. She moved like a stripper and her body was perfect. The last thing the lock expert saw before Craig hit him behind the ear was the splendid curve of one deep, full breast. Craig caught him before he fell, lowered him to the floor. The leader turned then, fast, but the gun was already on him. When he looked up, the dark girl held a gun too, his own, and the leader had no illusions about its accuracy. In the bed, Miriam Loman slept. She, too, was naked. The dark girl pulled the covers over her.

'You got one outside?' asked Craig. The leader nodded, 'Tell him to come in. You'll need some help with your friend.'

The leader hesitated, and Joanna said, 'I'd do what he says. Honestly I would.'

'Come on in, Harry,' the leader called, and Harry came in to see the team leader covered by Craig, and a broad in the kind of negligee they used to wear at Minsky's pointing a gun at him.

'Tell Harry what to do with his gun,' said Craig.

'On the bed,' said the leader, and Harry obeyed, and his gun went on the pillow.

'Sit down over there,' said Craig, and nodded toward two chairs in the corner of the room. The leader moved first. 'Stay away from the bed,' said Craig. 'This isn't a party.'

Carefully, the two men sat.

'What is this? A dyke affair?' Harry asked.

'No, darling. The girls' dorm,' Joanna said.

'Miss Loman seems a good sleeper,' the leader said.

'I put a little something in her coffee,' said Joanna. 'Poor darling, she needs her rest. She's had too much excitement lately.'

The leader nodded. Even with two guns pointed at him, he managed to look elegant enough for a whisky ad.

'You're looking better, Craig,' he said.

'I'm feeling it,' said Craig.

'No hard feelings, I hope?'

'None,' said Craig, and spoke to Joanna. 'This gentleman took me on a drug party in New York. I wound up telling him the story of my life.' He turned back to the leader. 'Do you have a name?'

'Lederer will do. Where's our mutual friend?'

'Dickens,' said Joanna. 'I adore intellectual conversation.'

'In the bathroom,' said Craig. 'Go and take a look – but mind how you walk.'

Lederer looked round the bathroom door. Kaplan sat strapped to the toilet, fast asleep.

'That's some coffee you serve,' said Lederer. 'I'll give you half a million dollars for him.'

'I've got half a million dollars.'

'A million – tax free.'

'You shouldn't talk in such vast sums. It's what makes you Americans so unpopular,' Joanna said.

'And guaranteed protection,' said Lederer.

'I've already got a deal – with Loomis,' said Craig.

'So has the CIA. He wants information. I'd sooner spend money.'

'I'm sorry,' said Craig. 'I really am.'

It was at that moment that Harry found it necessary to prove his manhood. A broad halfway through a burlesque routine seemed to him an insult to his maleness, even if she did hold a Colt .45, And anyway, he reasoned, a Colt is too big a gun for a broad. And with Lederer watching he'd be doing himself a whole lot of good. He'd been watching her, and sure enough the gun barrel had sagged, her concentration was all on Lederer and Craig.

Harry swivelled slightly on his chair. She took no notice. Careful to show no evidence of tension on his face or body, Harry prepared himself the way they'd taught him and made his grab. What happened was like a nightmare in slow motion. She seemed to have all the time in the world to bring the gun up, to choose the spot where the bullet would go. There was no tension in her eyes, only a glittering excitement as she pulled the trigger, the gun popped, and Harry felt as if the room had fallen on his shoulder before he lost consciousness. And all the time, Craig's gun stayed on Lederer.

'He's a little over excitable,' Lederer said.

Joanna went to him, opened his coat.

'He's lucky he's not a little dead,' she said. 'He didn't give me much time to choose a spot.'

She went into the bathroom and came back with a towel.

'First they make one shoot them, then they expect one to patch them up. It's no fun being a woman,' she said.

'The information Loomis is asking for is a little expensive,' Lederer said to Craig. 'Why don't you and I just settle this privately? I could go up to a million five.'

'No deal,' said Craig. 'I'm sorry.'

'It's too bad we need that bastard,' said Lederer. 'He costs too much.'

Joanna looked up from Harry.

'What makes him so very expensive?' she asked.

'He can make the deserts blossom,' said Lederer. 'Put him down on sand and sea water and he'll turn it into an orange grove. It takes money and it takes technology, but he can do it. So we'll work out the technique, and sell it round the world.'

'Sell it?'

'Not for money. As you say – we Americans have enough. For cooperation. For commitment.'

'You should start with Israel,' Craig said.

'We intend to.'

'He's not exactly a willing worker,' said Craig.

'He will be. Who else has he got but us?' He looked into Craig's eyes. 'You don't like him much, do you?'

'I don't like him at all. But he's needed. A lot of better men died because of him, but the world hasn't any use for them. They couldn't do his trick.'

'Give him a few years and he'll be just as

friendly and lovable and integrated as any other millionaire,' said Lederer. The lock expert groaned and twitched feebly.

'I guess we better be going,' Lederer said. It sounded like a question.

'I think you had,' said Craig.

'Just one thing I want to ask. How on earth did you know we were coming?'

'We had her followed.'

'Sure. I know that. Your local guy. We blocked him off before he could get near.'

'We rather thought you would,' said Craig. 'You're very efficient. So we put another man on to her as well. Flew him in from England this morning.'

Lederer accepted it without regret. 'I guess we had it coming,' he said. 'One way or another, we gave you quite a runaround.' He looked at the sleeping figure on the bed. 'And Miss Loman.'

'If your own operators hadn't been blown, you'd have got him yourselves,' said Craig. 'You did all you could do – under the circumstances.'

'The circumstances were lousy,' Lederer said. 'But at least we've got Kaplan.'

'You will have, tomorrow,' said Craig.

'You're flying him back?'

'BOAC. It was funny how every American airline just happened to have four seats available.'

Lederer grinned. 'Can't blame us for trying, son,' he said. 'Next time, we'll block you off before the operation even gets started.'

'There won't be a next time,' said Craig.

The man on the floor groaned again. He should have been happy.

For the Americans, getting out of the hotel was easy. They used the same drunken-party technique they'd used with Craig, a hundred-drachma note to a night porter, and a waiting Buick. When they'd gone, Joanna put down the gun, stretched her arms and sighed. Translucent silk slid over her hips, stretched taut across her breasts.

'What a very exciting night,' she said.

'Stop being the middle pages of *Playboy*,' said Craig.

She moved toward him.

'I feel like the middle pages of *Playboy*,' she said. She stood very close to him, and kissed him. He made no response. 'Is it her?' she asked, and looked at the bed.

'No,' Craig said. 'That's over. In a way, it never even started. It was all loneliness and fear and' – he struggled for the word – 'compassion. It almost got her killed. She deserves better than anything I could give her.'

'I don't,' Joanna said. 'I don't expect it. I don't want it. You're what I want.'

'Is that why you let me go free?'

'Of course it was.'

Craig laughed. 'And I thought it was because you thought you had a better chance with me than with Royce.'

Suddenly, she was laughing too. It made her more beautiful, more exciting than ever. Still laughing, she pressed herself against him once more.

'You and I will get on beautifully, darling. You've so much to teach me,' she said. Her arms came around him. 'And vice-versa, of course.'

Chapter Fifteen

They flew to Rome, and then to New York. This time the movie was about sex in the Deep South. Craig's sympathies were with the South. He had always understood it had problems enough without that. Back in time they went, eating the same plastic meals, drinking the exactly measured drinks; bored, restless, embalmed in space. Craig sat beside Miriam, and tried to think of ways of saying good-bye. There were none.

'I'm taking a holiday,' she said. 'I reckon I deserve it.'

'Send the bill to Force Three,' he said. 'The least they can do is pay.'

'I thought maybe you'd like to come along.'

'You've had enough of me, and everybody like me.'

'Listen,' she said. 'Sometimes I hate you. Sometimes I could kill you for the way you can always get a rise out of me. The way you look at life – the things you do – it hurts me even when I think of them. The trouble is I love you.'

'The trouble is I make you unhappy.'

'I was happy for five nights,' Miriam said.

'Maybe I was lucky it lasted so long. You said something like that to Kaplan – that night in Troodos. Only he had six months.'

'Maybe he earned it,' Craig said.

'After what he did?'

'After what he suffered. You had it rough, Miriam, and most of it was my fault, and I'm sorry. But Kaplan – we can't even begin to guess the things they did to him.'

'What about the things he did to the Jews? His own people.'

'He's paid for some of them,' said Craig. 'He'll go on paying. Even more than he owes.'

'How?'

'The United States wants his knowledge – to help underdeveloped countries. They'll protect him, give him asylum, and in return he'll work on desert-reclamation problems.'

'What's wrong with that?'

'The first place they'll send him to is Israel.'

'Israel?'

'Can you imagine the propaganda the Russians will make out of that? The things they'll say about him? What he did to the friends who trusted him?'

'Israel won't accept him,' Miriam said.

'Israel must,' said Craig. 'They need the water. But he'll never be one of them, love. He's alone now till he dies. You should pity him.'

'He deserves it,' the girl said. 'He deserves much more. Even a Jew couldn't pity him, after what he'd done.'

Craig leaned back in his seat. Maybe the best thing was silence, after all.

He'd hoped for a glimpse of Marcus Kaplan when they reached Kennedy, but instead they were whisked into a VIP lounge and a smart matronly person like a successful beautician took Miriam away as soon as they'd said goodbye. Three men waited for Kaplan. Two of them were Lederer and the lock expert, the third a scientist whom Kaplan recognized at once. The scientist began asking questions, and Kaplan's replies at first were hesitant, dredged up deep from the well of memory.

'It's been so long,' he said.

'Wait till we get to Utah,' the scientist said. 'We have everything set up there under test conditions. You'll soon catch up.'

He went on talking, and as they watched, Kaplan came to life.

'How's Harry?' Joanna asked.

'Mending,' said Lederer. 'But you've really shaken his faith in Western woman. If he doesn't watch it, he'll wind up a fag.'

A chauffeur and two more men appeared, and Lederer tapped Kaplan on the shoulder. He started, and for a moment the fear returned, then he relaxed. *He* was important now, with a bodyguard of his own. Gravely he waited as the big men surrounded him, walked him to the door. Craig wondered if he'd lied to Miriam after all: if the Kaplans of the world ever paid back a cent.

He and Joanna were alone now, except for a short, stumpy figure who had waited for them patiently. Now he came forward: a chubby, benign man wearing hexagonal rimless glasses.

'Hi there,' he said.

'Hi,' said Craig. 'How's the Pentathol business?'

'That's what I came to see you about,' said the benign man. 'Oh, say. My name's Mankowitz. Excuse me, sugar.' He walked Craig away from Joanna. 'I came to ask if we could run some more tests on you.'

'Who's we?'

'Force Three. You know that,' Mankowitz said. 'Mind you, last time you thought I was KGB. That helped. They really scare you, don't they? Come and see me. If you pass, there's a chance we could use you.'

'Mr. Mankowitz, do you know how old I am?' asked Craig.

'Know everything about you. We really could use you, feller. If the tests work out. Tell you the truth, I could stand to know what happened to you during the last ten days. Last time I saw you, you were finished.'

'I still am,' said Craig. 'Sorry.'

'Suit yourself,' Mankowitz said. 'You ever

change your mind, I'm in the book. First name Joel. Psychologist, 419 East 59th Street. That's in Manhattan.'

'Isn't everything?'

'Cynicism suits your age group,' Mankowitz said. 'Work at it. And don't forget my address.' He clapped Craig on the shoulder and was gone.

Because he was rich Craig took a taxi to the hotel in the West Forties. He and Joanna had suites booked already, and letters awaited them both. Craig's was a statement from the First National Bank that two hundred and thirty-nine thousand dollars were at his disposal and they awaited his instructions. His very truly. Joanna's was a brisk but cordial request from Loomis to get back as soon as she could. She handed it to Craig.

'How long have I got?' she asked.

'He'll usually hang on for two days. After that, he gets mad.'

'That isn't what I meant,' she said.

'I know it wasn't. Look, I've got to go out for a while.'

'Must you?'

'Yes,' said Craig. 'Just to make sure this money's okay. Wait for me, will you?'

'I'm glad you said that, John.' She began to loosen her coat. 'It sounded as if you really wanted me to.'

As he went down in the elevator, Craig thought it might be the last time he'd ever see her.

He came back two hours later with the beginning of a black eye and two inches of skin missing from his left elbow.

'Darling, what on earth did you do at the bank? Rob it?' she asked.

'The bank? No. The money's fine. I just beat hell out a man called Thaddeus Cooke,' said Craig.

She was still shaking with laughter as they began to make love. Later they rose, dressed, drank in the murky twilight of the cocktail bar, ate at the Four Seasons. They were asleep when the knocking began, but she, like Craig, was awake at once. Quickly they put on dressing gowns, and Craig slipped the .38 into the pocket of his as she reached for her handbag.

'What is it?' asked Craig.

'Telegram for Mr. Craig.'

Craig moved into the lounge, unlatched the door.

'Bring it in,' he said. 'The door's not locked.'

He moved into the space behind the door. Suddenly it flew open, and Marcus Kaplan came into the room. In his hands was a skeet gun. He seemed almost crazy with rage, but the hands on the gun were steady. If I give him half a chance he'll blast me, Craig thought. The only sane thing to do is put a bullet in him now. But he couldn't. It was impossible. The realization flicked through his mind as Marcus started to turn. Craig tossed his life up in the air like a coin, and took a long stride toward him, put the muzzle of the gun on Kaplan's neck. 'Just drop it,' he said.

Kaplan tensed, willing himself to turn and blast, and Craig found he couldn't even hit him.

Joanna's voice spoke from the bedroom door. 'I shouldn't, Mr. Kaplan,' she said. 'You kill him and I'll kill you. You won't die quickly.'

Kaplan's hands opened; the skeet gun thudded on the carpet. Craig grabbed it up and pushed on the safety catch, then went to the door. The corridor was empty, except for a long, soft leather bag. He brought it inside, and steered the other man to a chair. Marcus was crying. Craig opened the drinks cupboard and poured whisky.

'I'll have one too,' said Joanna.

Craig offered one to Marcus, who pushed it away. He waited till the man's sobs died, and offered it again.

'Murder doesn't come all that easy to you,' Craig said. 'Take a drink, you need it.'

Reluctantly, Marcus Kaplan accepted it, and choked it down. Craig poured him another.

'D'you want to tell me why, Marcus?' he asked.

'I've just finished talking to Miriam,' Marcus said. 'She told me – she told me–'

'She'd been to bed with me?'

'I hate you, Craig. I want you dead.'

Craig waited once more, and Joanna came to the room and poured herself a drink.

Suddenly Marcus sprang from the chair and hurled himself at Craig, a pathetically unskilful attack; the onslaught of a civilized man who doesn't know how to hurt. Gently Craig took hold of the clumsy hands and forced him back into the chair.

'Don't try it,' said Craig. 'You don't know how to.'

He increased his pressure a little, and Marcus was still.

'Did she tell you how we became lovers?' Craig asked, and Marcus nodded. 'And you can't forgive her for it?'

'Her? Of course I can,' Marcus said. 'I could have understood you, too. But you kicked her out, didn't you? For this – this–' He turned on Joanna.

'I did right,' said Craig. 'You know I did.'

'You left her when she was helpless.'

'It won't be for long,' said Joanna. 'And Craig has no future in the millinery business.'

The words hit Kaplan like blows.

'Joanna, for God's sake,' said Craig.

'But he's jealous, darling. Surely you can see that.'

'I've never touched her,' said Kaplan.

'But you'd like to, wouldn't you, Marcus?'

'Lay off,' said Craig, and turned to Marcus once more. 'It happened. There's nothing anyone can do. Accept that.'

'No,' Kaplan said. 'One of these days I'll catch up with you. I swear it.'

'Marcus, you're no good at this. That telegram gag's archaic,' Craig said. 'You don't even know how to hate. Believe me. I've seen experts. Forget about me. She's the one you should be looking after–'

'It's easy for you,' said Kaplan. 'You do this to her and just walk away–'

'I did rather more than that,' said Craig. 'I got her father back.'

Joanna swirled round. The whisky slopped in her glass.

'She's your niece, isn't she?' Craig said. 'Aaron's daughter. You brought her out of Germany in 1946. You should have told her, Marcus.'

'I couldn't,' Kaplan said. 'By that time Russia was the enemy. I didn't want her to think her father was – one of them.'

'Before we set out to get him,' said Craig. 'She had a right to know then.'

'By that time she was virtually my daughter,' Kaplan said.

'What about your wife?' asked Joanna.

'Ida never knew,' said Kaplan. 'Aaron wrote to me just after the war – but it was to the office. He asked me to look out for a girl he'd met. He'd been ordered back to Russia, and the girl had moved out into the Western zone. I – I didn't like to tell Ida. I faked a business trip to Europe and went to see her. Brigitte, her name was. Brigitte Hahn. She was dying then – tuberculosis. Aaron hadn't even known she was pregnant. I adopted the baby – it was easy then. She didn't look like Aaron at all.'

'What did Ida say?' Joanna asked.

'I told her I'd found her in a Jewish orphanage. That I couldn't resist her. Ida loved her as soon as she saw her,' Kaplan said.

'Why Loman?' asked Craig.

'It was the name on her papers,' said Kaplan. 'Forged papers. They cost me seven hundred dollars. It was like investing in Paradise.' He sipped at his drink. 'How did you know, Craig?'

'I guessed it,' said Craig. 'It fitted so well it had to be true. Except – you still haven't told me why you kept quiet before we went to Turkey.'

'I wanted to find out if she loved him,' Kaplan said.

'And now you know. She hates him. What are you going to do, Marcus?'

'What can I do?'

'Keep quiet.'

'But she's his daughter.'

'He doesn't deserve a daughter like that – but you do,' said Craig.

'But I came here to kill you,' said Marcus.

'That's part of it. Go home, Marcus. Put your skeet gun in its nice leather bag and go home.'

He watched, empty-handed, as Marcus Kaplan picked up the gun and packed it into its container.

'You take some terrible chances, John,' Joanna said.

Marcus looked up, genuinely puzzled.

'Oh,' he said. 'The gun. Believe me, Miss Benson, I wouldn't – I mean, I'm very sorry, I–'

'Forget it,' Craig said. 'Just tell me how you knew I was here.'

'This was the thirty-fifth hotel I phoned,' said Kaplan. He picked up the bag. 'Well–' he said.

'Forgive me,' said Joanna, 'but didn't anybody ask you what was in your bag?'

'Why should they?' asked Kaplan. 'Some very important people shoot skeet.'

He left then, and Joanna snorted with laughter. This time Craig didn't join in.

'Darling,' she said. 'Wasn't he funny?'

'Hilarious,' said Craig. 'But he had to break his heart to do it.'

Next morning, Craig went through what he intended to be a ritual for the rest of his life. After bathing, shaving, and ordering breakfast, he looked first at his bank statement, then at the letter Loomis had signed. The bank statement was fine; the letter was a blank page. Craig held it to the light, ran a finger over its surface. It was a blank paper and nothing more. He went into the bedroom and woke Joanna, held the paper out in front of her.

'You knew, didn't you?' he asked.

She shrugged. There was no sense in denial.

'Yes, darling. That's why we made you wait a day. Loomis didn't need authority. He needed the ink. It had to be flown out from London.'

'The bastard,' said Craig. 'The great, fat, cunning bastard.'

'You've still got two hundred and thirty-nine thousand dollars,' she said, then. 'He gave me a message for you.'

'Well?'

'We can travel back together if we want to. Economy. If we go back first we pay the difference.'

Craig took off his coat, began to loosen his tie.

'What on earth are you doing?' she asked.

'I've got two days of freedom,' said Craig. 'I'm going to enjoy them.'

'But you said you'd show me New York.'

'You can begin with this ceiling,' said Craig.

The publishers hope that this book has given you enjoyable reading. Large Print Books are especially designed to be as easy to see and hold as possible. If you wish a complete list of our books please ask at your local library or write directly to:

Magna Large Print Books
Magna House, Long Preston,
Skipton, North Yorkshire.
BD23 4ND